If LOVE
CAN LAST

If Love Can Last

BY: JA'TEIA RUSHING

iUniverse, Inc.
Bloomington

If Love Can Last

iUniverse books may be ordered through booksellers or by contacting:

iUniverse
1663 Liberty Drive
Bloomington, IN 47403
www.iuniverse.com
1-800-Authors (1-800-288-4677)

ISBN: 978-1-4759-1779-6 (sc)
ISBN: 978-1-4759-1780-2 (hc)
ISBN: 978-1-4759-1781-9 (ebk)

Library of Congress Control Number: 2012908357

Printed in the United States of America

iUniverse rev. date: 02/18/2013

CONTENTS

Everyone Has Problems

Tavon

I sit in the office looking around at the all too familiar room. I remember the first time I got sent to this office. Three years ago in freshmen year of high school this boy named Angel in eleventh grade had, had me corner in the back stairwell of the school trying to rob me for my new Nike's. In ninth grade I was smaller than most ninth grade girls but I was brave.

"Take off your sneakers or I'll take them off for you." He said pushing me hard into the wall behind me.

"Hell no." I said getting my balance back. Then a loud thud echoed in my ear as Angel fell to his knees then to his stomach in front of me. I look at him confused and look up to notice Derek standing there with a world history textbook. Derek was my best friend from middle school.

"Thanks, I was beginning to think that I was done for." I say relieved.

"I went to get you out your class but you weren't there. So I had to look for you, you're such a lucky nigga." We chuckle.

"What's going on here? Who did this?" Mr. Barren said loudly startling us as he got our attention. I snatch the textbook from Derek and clear my throat as he rushed to Angel's side to check his vitals.

"Well?" He said looking up at me.

"It was me Mr. Barren. I hit Angel with this textbook because he was trying to rob me for my sneakers." I say stepping up to Mr. Barren.

"Derek bring Tavon to the principal's office at once and tell Principal Hale I will be there in a moment." He said. We leave the stairwell and walk toward the Principal's office.

"Tay, what are you doing?" Derek said confused.

"Let's just hope my luck didn't run out."

"Tavon Holmes, Principal Hale will see you now." Ms. Clomber said, without looking up at me, getting my attention. I stand up and sigh as I walk into his office.

"Ah yes, Mr. Holmes first day back from summer break and your already in my office. How unexpected this visit is." He said leaning back in his seat as the door closed. I sit across from him and slouch in the seat.

"I was really hoping I wouldn't have to see you this year, unless you're running for your touchdowns this season." He said laughing.

"Hale let me just say . . . . -"

"Save it Tavon I already spoke to Ms. Weinberg." He said shaking his head.

"She be lying on me Hale, don't believe her."

"Tavon why can't you and Mr. Kendrick get along for fifty-five minutes and go on about ya'll day."

"I can't Hale, David don't deserve the privilege to sit in my presence for five seconds." I say sitting up straight.

"And with an attitude like that you'll be sitting in my office again tomorrow." He said raising his voice.

"Do you want me to call your father Tavon? Because I will if I have to."

I suck my teeth and sit back. The thought of my Dad being called made me irritated.

"No." I sigh.

"It's just he always saying slick shit."

"Profanity is not allowed Mr. Holmes."

"Sorry, but he does."

"So you throw a desk at him?"

I chuckle.

"He dared me."

"Your already eight-teen Tavon, grow up. You need to start doing what you need to so you can get these recruiters to pay you any attention. You've been left back once so you need to do the extraordinary to get into a really good college." He said as his face turned red.

"Okay, okay sorry Hale it won't happen again." I say sincerely.

"Look, I'm going to let you slide because it's the beginning of your last year here but mainly because I want you to shine this year in your football games. You know many colleges want you Tavon and small things like this on your transcripts won't look good." I lean further back in the chair and sigh.

"I know you're tired of hearing me say this but your football career is on line so at least act like you care."

"Okay, is that it? Can I leave?" I ask nonchalantly.

"Yes you may, oh yeah Dean Smith was looking for you earlier so while you're heading to class make a pit stop at his office."

"Okay Hale." I stand up and head for the door.

"Let's start fresh this year and let's win this year. Go Wolves go kick some ass!" Principal yells as I step out.

"Profanity Principal Hale, profanity." I yell behind me as the door shuts. I continue out the main office down the hallway to the Dean's office. As I approached his door I could hear him arguing with someone. As I turned to leave the door swung opened. The twelfth grade science teacher Mrs. Smith, also the dean's wife, stood there. All the guys that had her class said she was on a twenty-four seven PMS mode. And the girls said Dean Smith dick is too small that's why she angry all the time. Even with all the comments they made about her they always included the fact that she was fine as hell. I always saw her from a distance but looking up close saying she was fine was an insult. She was beyond beautiful. No older women seem so appealing or attractive to me before but then again I never met her. She had to be about 5'5 but with her heels gave her the extra 2 inches in height. She was a beautiful brown color and her hair was jet black and shoulder length that brought her eyes out. She was more on the thick side and it fit her just well. I stared in awe stunned by her beauty. Even though her eyes were puffy, obviously from crying, she was still an eye sight. Finally she broke eye contact with me and looked down to the floor.

"Excuse me." She said in a faint whisper. I moved aside apologizing. She scurried pass me and swiftly walked down the hallway. I watched her hips sway side to side as her behind sat plump and round with her thick thighs. Feeling my temperature rise I looked away, hoping that I didn't catch a hard on in front of the Dean. I walked in and closed the door behind me.

"Yo, Hale said you were looking for me." I say walking into the office fully.

"Tavon?" He asked looking up from his computer.

"You know it." I answered grabbing a chair.

"Well Lehman NFL University contacted us the other day. Their looking for you, I gave them your number and address after speaking with your mom and I believe this could be your big break."

Knowing the bad news was heavy I spoke.

"So what's the problem?"

"Your science class, you have to pick up your grades this year or it can be the reason they choose someone else. So if you can just keep it up to at least B minus they may not pick you unless you stay on your A-game on the field. Even with that if you fail science you can kiss your scholarship to Lehman University goodbye."

"I thought you said if I pass everything with higher than a sixty-five I would get the scholarship?" I say sitting up.

"No, I told you'd get an advanced regents diploma but in order to get the scholarship you must pass everything with a seventy-five."

I suck my teeth and slouch back.

"Then fuck this man, I'll do something else."

"Tavon watch your mouth."

"Sorry."

"Secondly as long as you participate, do your homework, and classwork you'll pass with flying colors."

I sigh deeply.

"At least try Tavon, and if you fall behind in science I'm pretty sure you could make it up with extra credit or tutoring."

"Alright I'll try." I said irritated.

"And when you get a chance try to get in touch with the University."

"A'ight." I say standing and going to my class.

Carmen

I walk down the hallway quickly trying to hold in my tears, at least until I made it to my classroom. I would've ran but the dress skirt I was wearing stopped at my knees and prevented me from doing that. I couldn't believe Erin.

"You're the reason this marriage isn't working, it looks like you've gained twenty pounds." His voice echoed in my head. It kept replaying loudly making my ears ring. Damn, how could he even say that? I married him and all he could ever do is point out my flaws. Basically he said my weight is hurting our marriage, no his limp dick put a limp in our marriage. Thinking about it I start to laugh. I should've told him that, I bet that would've pissed him off for the day. I walk into my classroom with the urge to cry gone. I sit at my desk and look over my class lesson for the day to make sure I had everything I needed. As a kid I was always one of the prettiest girls but even that wasn't enough. Some people just didn't like me not to like me. As I became a teenager and my breast and behind grew, the hate people had for me grew also. The girls turned their noses up at me and the boys only wanted to touch and feel. So when Erin proposed I felt wanted, and cared for. I loved him for that but I guess my love wasn't enough either, he wanted more but I didn't know what else he wanted. After two years I regret saying "I do" at the altar which leaves me where I am today. Grading homework and still get called bitches and whores by students with they're stank looks. Maybe I wouldn't be such a bitch if I hadn't stayed up almost every night for six months straight waiting for a no-good-nigga that wasn't coming. Just maybe if I wasn't cold all night, every night I wouldn't have such an attitude with the world. I snap back to reality and notice my cheeks were wet from tears. I wipe my face with back of hand.

"I love myself. I love myself. I love myself." I say with a weak smile but the truth be told I hated myself just as much as everyone else does. I finish overlooking everything, then the bell rung for the next class. I stood up and start to write the lesson on the board as students' grabbed seats. I put the chalk down as the second bell rung. I looked up and a few smacked on their gum and rolled their eyes. Just then I spotted a boy in the back. He had his black long hair braided in cornrows with designs. The diamond studded earrings took up his ears, he had a caramel complexion, about 6'2, his lips was juicy but conservative and his biceps and abs was ripping through his "I Love NY" t-shirt. His muscular body wasn't too bulky but just enough to get your attention. He was surely made out of God's image. He was the boy staring at me as I left Erin's office earlier. I jump back to reality and pick up the attendance sheet off my desk and started class.

"I see a lot of new faces so, for those who don't know me my name is Mrs. Smith. It's a new year so let's start fresh." I said friendly.

I called a few names off and they replied "Here". Until I knew this unfamiliar name was his.

"Tavon Holmes." I say and look up towards his direction.

"Here." He said with his deep and sexy voice. He smiled at me showing his pearl white teeth. I looked down and marked him present. But the truth was I didn't want the class to see me blush. I called off the last few names and began my lesson.

HOME IS ANOTHER WORD FOR CELL

Tavon

I open my locker and throw some books inside and sigh deeply. I grab my math books out thanking God this was my last class for the day. Since I had passed most of my classes last year I only had four classes' and two make-up classes. As I closed my locker Monica leaned on the locker beside mine. Monica had been one of my friends since tenth grade.

"Hey, Tay." She said smiling and opening up her arms inviting me in for a hug. I embraced her lightly and kissed her cheek.

"Hey Mo, what's up?"

"Nothing, you feel like ditching with me, I'm about to go light it up?"

"You know I don't smoke, plus it's the first day of school."

"So what . . . you down to ride with me or not?"

"Maybe some other time." I say turning to leave. She grabbed my arm and followed.

"Come on Tay, please."

"I can't I got try outs and I got plans to go chill with my girl after class." She sighed.

"What?" I say looking at her.

"It's about Ariel." She said stopping me to get my full attention.

"Somebody gotta tell you so why not me."

"Tell me what?" I say hoping it had nothing to do with my girl and David.

"There's been rumors that David and Ariel are seeing each other again."

My anger built up so quickly. I tried to breathe and stay calm but it was too hard.

"Mo, I'm catch up with you later." I say walking away knowing I could find Ariel by her locker. As I walked there from down the hallway

I could see her standing by her locker laughing with the nigga. I step to them and Ariel's eyes widened and the smile on her face faded. David sighed and looked away knowing what was in store for him.

"Get the fuck outta here." I say to David.

"Whatever." He said as he walked away.

"We were only talking Tay." Ariel said rolling her eyes.

"Sure you were, after all the rumors going around you expect me to believe that. I'm more than tired of hearing he say she say about my girlfiriend and I don't think I can take it anymore."

"What are you talking about?" She asked putting her hand on her hip.

"What the fuck I look like, an idiot? You acting like the word wouldn't get back to me. I know there's something going on between you and David."

"No, Tay that's bullshit and you know it." She said reaching out to touch me. I took a step back so she missed me.

"Baby you gotta understa . . . -" I cut her off before she could finish.

"Yes I understand, I understand you ain't my girl no more." I say nonchalantly.

"Baby I love you and you know that. So how the hell you going to believe everybody else before you believe me?" She said in a shaky voice.

"Because I know you better than you know yourself." I said looking her in the eye. She whispered my name as I turned around and began to walked away from her shaking my head.

"What the hell do you want from me Tay?" She yelled.

"Nothing, maybe you should be asking David." I yell behind me as I continue to walk to class as I could hear her kick the locker. Me and her use to be really tight, nobody could come between us but things changed. I met her in tenth grade. She had just broken up with David and was half way begging for me to go out with her. So I did. A year later we were talking about our future promising each other the world. So I introduced her to my mom. My mom fell in love with her. Everything was great until last summer when she and David started hanging out again. She said they were just friends but everyone could see straight through that lie. And when you love someone you tend to look pass their wrong but I could tell she was having sex with him I didn't need proof because it was written all over her face. And if she really loved me she wouldn't continuously do me wrong. I'm just tired of being hurt. After a boring fifty-five minutes of tryouts I headed home. As I walk in the door I heard talking and sobbing. I rush into the living room assuming something was wrong with my mother and immediately regret walking into the apartment. Ariel sat there on my couch crying as my mom had her under her arm. Ariel wiped her nose saying "I know" repeatedly. I clear my throat loudly and fold my arms. My mother gave me a stern look and Ariel smiled weakly.

"Yo, what the fuck you doing here? Maybe you didn't understand when I said we ain't together."

"Tavon Wilson Holmes, don't you curse in my home." My mom said standing up. I dropped my book bag on the floor.

"Either she gonna leave or I am mom."

"Tay, you have to talk to her about this." She said raising her voice.

"Talk to her about what, I'm done with her. There's not one reason in the world you can give me to make me wanna stay with her." I say looking at her with disgust. My mother looked at Ariel.

"Did you tell him?" She asked. Ariel shook her head no. I stepped closer to them.

"She didn't tell me what?"

She wiped her nose and cleared her throat.

"Tay, I'm pregnant."

I lifted my eyebrow at her then burst into laughter. My mom looked lost but Ariel knew why I was laughing. I sigh.

"Don't you dare say that baby is mine, because we both know that's not true." I say in a serious tone. She stood and took a few steps closer to me.

"Can we talk about this privately?"

"Maybe you two should step into Tay's room and talk." My mom said walking into the kitchen. I roll my eyes and walk in my bedroom. My full size bed was by my window leaving little space for my night stand in the corner. Magazines and past due homework covered my night stand. The blue paint that covered my bedroom walls matched the sky. I tossed my book bag by my laptop that sat on the edge of my bed. I sat on my bed and sighed. Ariel closed the door and stood there staring at the floor silently.

"Well talk, shit." I say rudely just to annoy her.

"Tay you have to believe me, I'm not having sex with David."

I let out a loud chuckle.

"Seriously, just because I'm hanging out with him don't mean I'm giving it up."

"Yeah, okay."

I pick up a magazine and pretend to ignore her.

"Damn it Tay, you hang out Monica and all those other bitches but I ain't never accused you of sleeping around on me."

"First off let me say none of the girls I hang out with are my exes."

"So since he's my ex and we're hanging out we're automatically doing something."

"Well, what other reason would you have to hang out with him. You two broke up a year and a half ago. You hated him now everything is great between you guys."

"Exactly your just assuming. What if I just started to accuse you of cheating just because I heard some rumors?"

"Even if you did accuse me you would've been wrong." I say sternly dropping the magazine.

"What if I called you a liar and laughed at everything you said as you tried to convince me you didn't."

"I guess I would go harder than just saying it I would prove it. But then again I'd never hurt someone I claim to love."

"Well what do you want me to say, how do you want me to prove it to you?"

"You can start by telling me the truth." I say looking her in the eye. She stood there for a moment silently as her eyes shifted around the room. She leaned back against my bedroom door and closed her eyes. She sighed lightly.

"Alright." She said under breath.

"Yes I had sex with him but it was a while ago and it meant nothing."

"Then why would you lie about it if it was nothing?"

"I don't know."

"Wow, really? You don't know."

"I'm sorry Tay."

"Why did you do it?"

"I don't know."

"So you don't know why you cheated either. Hmm, so you just cheated to cheat?"

"No."

"Then why would you do it?"

"Because . . . everybody kept saying when you become a football player things will change, you'll change, your feelings will change. Where am I supposed to be in your life if your life is changing constantly? What if I'm rearranged in your life where I'm at the bottom of your list of important things? Or even worst, what if I'm removed from your life. So I talked to my sister about it and she said I would need a backup plan. You know, something to lean on just in case I fall."

"Why didn't you come to me about it?"

"Because I already knew what you would say "baby I ain't never gonna change I love you", but you don't know what may happen when you start your career."

"Neither do you. You put your guard up expecting me to hurt you when I've never done anything to make you doubt that I love you. Why can't you just trust me?"

"Have you took a look in the mirror lately? Like come on Tavon, your handsome, your built, smart, funny, sweet, and on top of that you'd be an athlete. Let's be realistic, what chance do I have against thousands of beautiful women that's going be on you?"

"So you can't trust me because your insecure about yourself?"

She rolled her eyes at me.

"I'm not insecure, I just know when I've been beaten."

I shook my head.

"So if you can't trust that I love you, then why you trying to hold on this, us?"

"Because . . . I found out I was pregnant and I was pretty sure this was going to put "us" on the right track. Yes, it will be difficult but it gives us a stronger bond, a stronger love so I'll know for sure we will always be together." I look at her and she was smiling. I stood up and walk over to her.

"How do you know the baby is mine?"

"Tay, trust me I know this baby is yours."

I pull her closer to me and embrace her. I wanted to forgive her but something just didn't sit right with me.

"If I see you hanging around that nigga I'm done." She nodded

"Now, let me go talk to my mom. I'll be back." I kiss her forehead and go to the kitchen. I walk into the kitchen and my mom was cooking. Every time she was stressed she would overcook and she was beginning to do just that. She had already pulled out her beef, rice, veggatables, and seasonings and had them spread out on the counter. Her light pink and yellow kitchen was smelling good from the seasonings she had sumerged her meat in. The oven was on and two pots of water was warming up on the stove. Mom had her back to me.

"Ma?" I say leaning on the counter behind me.

"I told you to wear condoms, you never listen to me. If you would've just kept ya little Johnson in your pants you wouldn't be standing here right now."

I try to hold in my laughter but it was unbearable. I burst into laughter.

"Your situation is not funny. How is it going to look when you're starting your football career and you got a baby? Both of you are only eighteen, your still young."

A smile remained on my face as my laughter simmered down. She pulled out a knife and begin cutting her peppers as her pot of water begin to boil. I just listened to her speak, sometimes she cools her own self down.

"This is looking like repeat of your father's life. She's going to ruin your career before it has even started."

Memories of my father in my childhood were very blurry. The ones I could remember were just distant. He didn't know how to be a father and no one could blame him he was too young. He was seventeen when I was born and he left me and my mother in the cold so he could live his dream as a NFL player. He got what he wanted. Money and fame but during his seventh year he broke his leg and dislocated his hip. He couldn't play like he could after that so he retired early. He tried to be a father then but his new young wife took his attention so I was put on the back burner again until I got to middle school and started to play football. Then he took interest in me but by then I didn't need a father my mother had done all the work. But that didn't stop him. He started coming to my schools for parent and teacher conferences, and PTA meetings. It got overwhelming but to my mom it was step in the right direction and it made her happy to see dad and son moments so I never complained. But now and days he spoke with my teachers, Dean, and Principals often and it was just irritating.

"I'm going to be nineteen in December. I can handle myself ma."

"I know that, I'm the one who had you."

I folded my arms. She put the knife down and took a deep breath. She looked up at me as she leaned on the counter.

"You're growing up so fast and leaving me behind. Who's going to be left to take care of me?" She said getting teary eyed.

"Mama, I'm always going to be here to help you."

"Baby all I'm really saying is, don't grow too fast because you'll miss out on life and you'll wish you can get it back, but you won't be able to."

I nod.

"Yes ma'am."

Carmen

I look at the clock and read eleven twenty-five. I sat in the dining room staring at my watch. The lit candles around the room glistened off the wooden floors and golden walls. The chandlier was dimly lit adding romance to dinner setting I provided for the night. I sigh and look up at the empty chair across from me. The food I cooked three hours prior was now cold and my appetite was gone. He said he'd be here by nine, I guess he got caught up being that he's the Dean of the school. I shake my head knowing he just lied like any other day. I thought my cooking for empty tables' days were gone. I really had my hopes up. I stare down at the steak, lo mien and peas on my plate that has been untouched and threw it at the wall. I pick up his plate and dumped it in the garbage, plate and all. I grab a piece of paper and began to write: If you're looking for your plate, check the garbage.

Then I taped it to the fridge door. I blew out the candles and turned off the lights as I left the room. Any other night I wouldn't care but today's our anniversary. Seven years ago today he made his vows to me, and never lived up to them. He promised this morning he was going to change. He gave me his word he'd be home early if not on time. And I believed him, like a fool I trusted him and the truth was I didn't even know why I did. Six months ago I was still putting up with his nonsense but I loved him. Now I just put up with his nonsense. I already heard rumors last year about him cheating on me with the tenth grade English teacher Ms. Drew. I just never fed into it because they were just rumors no one had real proof. I sit on the living room floor after grabbing the house phone. I dialed my mother's number and put the phone to my ear. It rung twice then she picked up.

"Hello?"

"Hey mama, how you doing?"

"I'm living, taking one step at a time."

"That's good, how's everybody doing?"

"Everyone's fine. Bella just started her new job at a nursing home, Melissa and Dennis are still doing the same, but how are you doing?"

I sigh.

"Mama, I'm making it."

"Good, but I doubt it."

"Why?"

"Because you've never called me this late before to talk about your sisters and brother. So what's really wrong dear?"

I inhaled deeply trying to hold back my tears.

"Oh mama, it's him again. He doesn't know how to treat me, please all he does is lie. This marriage is tearing me apart." The tears fell from my eyes like running water as my voice got shaky.

"Today I cooked his favorite meal for our anniversary, and he didn't even show up. I sat there for nearly three hours trying to lie to myself saying its traffic or something at the school is holding him up, but I know it's not traffic it's him. Why does he treat me like this, I do everything and more for him even though he never acknowledges it. Then the other day he called me fat. He thinks my weight is hurting our marriage. How could he even say something like that to me?" My voice started to fade in and out from me sobbing. I wipe my eyes and smear the wet mascara across my cheek.

"He treats me like shit. Sorry ma, please excuse my language but I'm just a dog in his eyes. He's so selfish all he thinks about is him, him, him. Mama he got me so broken up and hurt. I'm lost, I don't know what to do. Even though I'm almost twenty-five years old can you give me the answer? I'm all out of options. Can you help your little girl get back on the right track?" I say whining like a young girl in pre-school who wants her way. I wiped my face with the back of my hand trying to regain self-control.

"Carmen, you're a grown woman and you're strong but you let others make you weak. I can't run your life for you and I certainly can't be a woman for you. I have never told you life and marriage would be easy, because if I did it would've been a lie. Now I can't tell you how to deal with your husband, you'll just have to find out how to do that yourself . . . but I can tell you this, when you're fed up and have had enough you'll know just what to do."

"But what do I do in the meantime mama?"

"Carmie, all you can do is pray and ask God to be merciful. Now suck up them tears, keep your head up, and stop whining." She laughed lightly putting a smile on my face.

"Well I wasn't expecting that prep talk, but it was good mama." She laughed again. I knew mama been through a lot with dad so I knew she had the answer but no answer could've been better than the one she gave me. When I was nine mom was still with my dad but he use to beat on her. She acted like it never happened until he hit my little brother Dennis with a pot because he wet the bed. He was only five at the time. Mama beat dad with a bat and left with us to Harlem. I knew mama was strong, I just wished I was as strong as she was.

"Mama, if dad would've never hit Dennis would you have stayed?"

"Either way, I would've done what was best for my children. Plus I was about fed up with your father."

I nodded my head.

"Well ma, I'm going to jump in the shower, so I'll speak to you later."

"Alright Carmie be strong, bye now."

"Bye mom."

I hung up feeling so refreshed from letting all that baggage off my chest. I jumped in the shower until my skin became soft and fragile. I got out, lotion down my body, slipped into a pair of panties, and got into bed. I pulled out my favorite book, "Love Stories". I wished I was loved the way Brian loved Sylvia in the story. I guess that's why I loved the book the most. Then I heard Erin's car pulling into the driveway. I put my book on the nightstand, cut off the light, and got under the covers. He opened the front door and closed it softly. He walked around downstairs obviously looking for me then came upstairs. I snored lightly. I pretended to be asleep because I'd rather not hear the lie he put together before getting here.

Boys Will Be Boys

Tavon

I walk with my boys Brandon, Calvin, Caesar, and Derek through the hallway after lunch picking on some of our other friends on our way to class. I saw Albert, one of the big boys in our school that was overweight but he was my boy. He was wearing a Biggie Smalls shirt, Jordan's, and skinny jeans.

"Yo Al, what's up?" I say loudly getting his attention.

"Hey Tay, nothing I'm chilling what's up with you?"

"I'm good."

"I bet you are, looking like the feminine side of R. Kelly."

Everybody that heard him cracked up laughing. I smirked and nodded my head.

"I know you aint talking with those thirty cent knock off Jordan's nigga. Wearing those tight ass jeans cutting off your circulation, that's probably the reason why you breathing like you ran a mile. Nigga go take those tight ass jeans off."

The laughter echoed through the hallways as I kept walking knowing he had no comeback for that one. I doubt if anyone even heard the last of what I said because they were too busy laughing. As we continued down the hall the laughter died quickly as I gazed upon Ariel in David's face giggling. As we got closer Ariel noticed me and stepped in the way of my path.

"Tay it's not what you think." She said quickly trying to get my attention, but I couldn't look at her. How could I? She knew how I felt about her being around him and still she found herself with him.

"Tay believe me, I was trying to hook him up with Jennifer. I swear."

As I pushed past her David took off running down the hall with my boys hot on his heels. Ariel gripped onto my arm tightly. I spun around to face her.

"Trust me, you can even ask Jennifer."

"Fine, I guess I'll just have to pay David a little visit." I watched her expression trying to catch her feelings for him out there, but none showed. So I was going to test her, I pulled away from her.

"But if you don't want me to I won't." I say raising my eyebrows.

"Do what you have to do Tay." She said lowly. I took off following the direction they chased him in. As I got to the ending of the hallway I saw Calvin and company pulling David into the bathroom. I walk into the bathroom then stand by the door. David stood up and tried to catch his breath.

"Yo David, why every time I turn around I see you all on my girl?"

"Listen, if Ariel can't keep her hands off me then maybe you need a leash." He replied laughing lightly.

If he knew was best for him I would advise him to act mature because another joke like that in a closed in space would be bad for his health.

"Look, I'm only going to tell you this once . . . If I see you around her again . . . -"

"Don't be threatening me because ya girl's lips be on my dick." He said cutting me off. I smiled at him and nodded. That was the last straw for me. I lifted my fist to punch him but it was too late Derek swooped in punching him in the face. Before I knew it they all had jumped in and beat the hell out of him. After we stomped him out he laid on the bathroom floor. The bell rung letting us know to go to class. I bent down next to David grabbed his face and forced him to look at me.

"I know you probably ran up in her a few times but those days is over. There won't be a next time." I said roughly. Derek grabbed my arm.

"Let's go."he said pulling me. I stood up and left the bathroom and took off down the hallway. I ran to my locker to get my science books knowing being late was an automatic detention. I put in my combination and my door jammed. I hit it a few times and played with the lock and tried it again. The door swung open and I quickly got my belongings and slammed the locker door shut then made a quick dash for the science room. Just as I was in ten feet and closing the second bell rang. I opened the door and Mrs. Smith looked up at me.

"Hello Mr. Holmes, you have detention with me after class. Now sit down so I can start class."

I quickly walked to my seat sighing. After four pages of notes and reading chapters eight through ten in the science textbook my go home bell rang. I sighed. Mrs. Smith sat at her desk and begins to write.

"Mr. Holmes please move to the front row and get out a sheet of paper." She said sternly not once looking up to make eye contact. I pulled out my binder and sat at the desk in front of hers.

"Now write me two paragraphs on why you should be early to my class." I nodded.

I stared at her for a moment noticing how much she was like a flower. Her beautiful hair, curvaceous body, and long legs. As we all know flowers are beautiful but no one ever takes out the time to appreciate them. She ran her hand through her hair moved it to the left side of her face. Her skin looked so soft and moisturized. Her dark brown complexion was beautiful. She looked up at me and I shifted my eyes to my desk.

"Holmes, keep your eyes on your paper." She said looking back at her work. I smiled and continued to sneak glances at her.

Carmen

I tried to finish grading and ignore Tavon's constant staring but his eyes were so intense that I noticed them even when I didn't look. It was like he was looking into my soul and seeing how I was treated and it made me uneasy. No guy has ever looked at me for so long and so hard, it made me wonder what he could be thinking. The truth was, it distracted me from own work. I looked up at him and leaned onto my desk with my forearm. He looked me in the eye and smiled. His smile was incredibly handsome and it made me blush so I looked down to regain myself and then back up.

"Why are you staring at me so hard?" I ask trying to sound stern but how it came out was the total opposite.

"No reason." He said. He looked at his paper and began to write. His voice made him so much more attractive. I shook my head. No I didn't mean that, I take back those thoughts. I looked at my papers trying to get the thoughts of him out of my head and continued to grade papers. I'd look up every once in a while to catch him still looking at me. In between me fighting my thoughts I had begun to daydream. We were in bedroom and he was slowly unbuttoning my shirt and I was kissing on his chest. My room phone begins to ring snapping me back into reality. Tavon put his completed assignment on my desk.

"You're dismissed." I say. He wave goodbye and left. I cleared my throat and answered.

"Mrs. Smith, classroom 202."

"Carmen it's, Ms. Funnell. Go to the Dean's office right away." She said quickly.

"Why? Is there something wrong?" I say worried.

"You need to see what your husband is up to, go now! Hurry up!" She hung up. I jumped up and scurried down the hall to his office. I opened the door and my mouth dropped. Ms. Drew the English teacher sat on Erin's desk, with her skirt hiked up on her hips, panties on the floor, and her shirt unbuttoned revealing her breast. Erin had his shirt off, pants and briefs around his ankles, and his hands gripping Ms. Drew's thighs tightly as he thrust into her continuously. She moaned lightly with her head thrown back and he gasped for air. As I took all of it in everything was clear. No sex, no trust, and no us because he had her. The door slammed behind me scaring the hell out of both of them. She tried as hard as she could to cover herself and pull her skirt down and he went for his pants.

"Carmen, don't you fucking knock." He said breathing heavily. Tears slipped from my eyes.

"You're fucking Helen and the first thing that comes out of your mouth is 'do I knock'! What the fuck? I don't even know why I even married your simple ass!" I yelled.

Ms. Drew was buttoning up her shirt quickly.

"Shit don't let me stop you, please finish what you started!" I said I yelled before running out to my classroom. Tears were running down my face like a leaky faucet. I grab my work and put it in my bag. Grab my purse and jacket and left the school quickly. I drove home recklessly and left my stuff in the car, I wasn't planning on staying very long. I ran upstairs and threw all my clothes in duffel bags then put them in the trunk of my car. I went back inside and looked around at the prison I lived in for so long and screamed at the top of my lungs. I skimmed the room frantically and my eyes stopped at the closet door near the foyer. I opened the coat closet and pulled out my steel bat and went into the living room. I swung the bat as hard as I could into his 50inch flat screen television. It flew into the wall as glass flew everywhere and crumbled into many pieces. I broke the lamps, the 15 hundred dollar glass frame table, put holes in the walls, got a knife and ripped up his clothes, the bed, carved "Limp Dick Mutha Fucker" on the walls and "Cheater" on the front door. As I was walking to my car to leave he pulled up in front of the house in his silver Mercedes Benz. I dug my key into the side of his car leaving an uneven line. He yelled but my rage blocked out the sound. I picked up a brick and threw it through the front window and watched the glass shatter. Breaking his things helped me release my stress and anger but the damage was done. He grabbed my arm and forced me to face him and I swung wildly at him. He forced my arms to my sides as I beat on his chest. He pulled me close and tried to embrace me and I fought him off as hard as I could. He shook me yelled out my name, but there was nothing he could do or say to calm me down because I refused to give in and be the helpless little girl I was. He fought me down to the ground and pressed his knees into my arms to subdue me. Our neighbors stood in there yards and watched from their windows.

"Carmen just listen to me." He said holding my face so I would look at him. I stopped screaming and finally looked. I knew he wasn't the man I was married to, it couldn't be. The tears on my face and the pain in my soul confirmed that.

"How could you do this to me? We've been married for eight years, doesn't that mean anything? It kills me every time I look at you. The pain actually kills me, I hate this pain and I'm done with it. Just get off me and let me leave . . . because if I stay . . . I'll die of heartache." I said in between sobbing. He stared at me for a moment before he got off me. I laid in the grass for a second to catch my breath before I stood.

"Please, just here me out." He said reaching for me. I moved away from him with my hands in the air. I got into my car and drove off. I pulled up in my mom's drive-way then got my things and knocked on the door. She opened the door and smiled. She didn't have to ask she already knew why I was here.

"You know where your room is baby." She said and kissed my forehead. I brought my things up to my old room and shut the door. Diana Ross and Black Street posters covered the walls. I looked around and noticed my Barbie doll collection. My room looked exactly the same as I had left it years ago. I sat down on my twin size bed with pink flower like blankets and sighed. I felt like crying again so I pulled out my work and started grading papers. It was my way of ignoring problems life handed me. Soon I got to Tavon's paper he did in detention and there was a post-it note on the side of it.

It's beautiful petals that's soft to the touch.
With bright and radiant colors.
Such a near perfect creation.

Before I could realize there was a smile on my face and Erin wasn't on my mind. Flowers are beautiful and the way he put it was touching. I liked it a lot. The question was why did he leave it? Did he purposely want me to read this? And if yes, then why? I guess I'll ask him when I see him on Monday. No, I can't he's a student. I pop myself on the hand.

"You shouldn't be thinking about him like this." I say to myself. I shake my head trying to get thoughts of him out my head but he was stuck.

5 Minutes of Pleasure
A Lifetime of Trouble

Tavon

I was in the basketball court with my friends and after playing two games, we hit the benches with our water bottles. I wiped the sweat from my forehead with the back of my hand then gulped down my drink. After finally catching my breath I spoke.

"Ariel's pregnant." I say bluntly.

"Oh shit." Brandon said quickly choking on the water in his mouth.

"Damn, that's fucked up." Calvin said looking at the sky. Derek slouched back.

"Is it yours?" Derek asked.

"She says she's a million percent sure."

"Whoa." They say in union. I shake my head and laughed.

"Hold the fuck up. It's yours?"

"Yeah."

"Oh hell naw." Cesar and Derek said.

"All the women on Maury's say they a hundred percent sure then the results come back and Maury is like . . ."

"You are not the father." They say in union laughing.

"So what are you gonna do?" Calvin says finally looking at me.

"Abortion." Brandon said loudly. Derek and Calvin chuckled. I push Brandon playfully.

"No, I'm going to be a father to my child."

"What?" Cesar said with wide eyes.

"How do you even know it's yours?" Derek asks seriously.

"I don't, I'm going by her word."

21

"Naw, fuck that shit. To be sure you better get a DNA test nigga."
Brandon said,

"It's called paternity test dumb ass." Calvin said.

"Leave it to the smart ass nigga to tell you that shit. Nigga in my hood
its DNA test." Derek said making us chuckle.

"Naw, I don't even know if I wanna know if the baby is mine or not."
I say sighing.

"The hell you don't nigga. Trust me you don't want to be taking care
of a kid that ain't yours. So you better find out." Brandon said.

"You say it like you've been in that type of situation."

"I was." We all look at him in disbelief.

Yeah, a'ight nigga." Calvin said sitting back on the bench.

"You bullshitting." Derek said waving him away.

"For real, dead ass." Brandon said nodding.

"With who?"

"Remember Crystal."

"Yeah, she dropped out of school last year."

"I know, she was pregnant. She said it was mine."

"Get outta here."

"Anyway, I was going to be a father to my child. So I started hustling,
got her all this baby shit. It was all name brand too. She has the baby and
I'm still buying the baby some things, I'm not even gonna lie I was buying
her Victoria Secrets and her secrets were expensive. Two months later the
baby got sick we took it to the hospital. The baby needed blood so I was
going to donate mine. Come to find out the baby wasn't even mine."

"Damn." I say. I could tell he felt used but at least the child got new
name brand clothes.

"Nigga you acting like you didn't know she fucked the whole basketball
team." Cesar said laughing.

"Shut up nigga." Brandon said playfully pushing me into Cesar. We
laughed while Brandon shook his head at us.

"Yo, where were you the other day after school? We waited for like
ten minutes you were nowhere to be found." Brandon asked changing the
subject.

"I had detention with Mrs. Smith."

"Mrs. Smith is stuck up." Calvin says sucking his teeth.

"I know, last year in detention she made me write a five hundred word
essay on how to be early to class." Derek said chuckling.

"Naw, she did me dirty. She made me do a project on how not to cut class." Cesar said. We burst into laughter thinking of how that project may have looked.

"What she made you do?"

"Two paragraphs on why I should be early to class."

"Well she must like you because she never gave me an easy assignment like that."

"Even though she stuck up she looks sexy." Calvin said licking his lips wildly. We laughed.

"Damn right, she got a body of a fine ass stripper." Brandon said giving Calvin a pound.

"Once it was cold as hell in class and she had on a thin white shirt and it couldn't hide her nipples." Cesar said.

"I was in class that day. I could not stop staring at her tits." They laugh in union. Maybe if they were talking about someone else I would have laughed with them but as they spoke about her I got more serious.

"She's not stuck up and it's a shame you'd rather stare at her body then to do classwork." I say grimly. They stopped and looked at me then burst into laughter again.

"Wow, you say it like she's your girl dog." Cesar said pushing me slightly. I smiled weakly noticing how defensive I had gotten.

"Shit, I don't blame him. I'd rather be the one fucking her than old ass Dean Smith." Calvin said jokingly.

"Oh did you hear about what happened after school? Dean was fucking Ms. Drew the tenth grade English teacher in his office and Mrs. Smith walked in on it." Cesar said. As they continued to talk I zoned out. I could see their lips moving but my mind was somewhere else. I knew she was unhappy but I didn't think it was because of their marriage. She had to be feeling hurt because basically Ariel did the same thing to me and I felt empty, but she must feel worst. First she walked in on it and second because they're married. I wish I could hold her tightly in my arms and take away her pain but I knew that would never happen.

Carmen

My weekend has been so miserable. I walked around my mom's house depressed and sad. I cried the majority of the time lying in my bed staring my prom picture. I wore a red strapless dress that looked more like a wedding dress as Erin held onto my waist wearing a burgundy suit. The same night he purposed to me. Maybe if I had put the photo down I would've stopped sobbing and feeling sorry for myself but my heart wouldn't let me. Monday morning finally came and I found the strength and courage to get up and go to work. I drunk two cups of coffee mixed with vodka and a shot of Hennessey to get me pumped and ready to face the fucked up world I live in. I got to the school and walked swiftly trying to make it to my classroom without being seen. I saw the stares and heard the whispers but I walked with my head high. It wasn't like I should be a shamed of what Erin did to me, he was in the wrong not me. As I got to my classroom I saw Mrs. Funnell Standing in front of my classroom door. I walked up to her and put on a fake beautiful smile like every other day.

"Hello Mrs. Funnell, how are you this morning?" I say hiding my depression with my fake happiness.

"Hey Mrs. Smith, I'm fine. How are you doing?" She said looking at me searching for my true feelings.

"Couldn't be better. It's a beautiful day today." I say pushing pass her and entering my classroom with her on my heels. I knew she was here to get something to gossip about and I wasn't going to give it to her.

"Are you sure you're okay?" She asked arching her brow.

"Yes. Why do you keep asking me that?" I say unpacking my lessons for today, graded testes, and homework.

"Do you have short term memory loss? Just Friday you walked in on Erin fucking Helen."

I smile at her and then turned around to the black board and grabbed a chalk and started writing the lesson.

"Erin is the last person on my mind. I'm great, trust me. He cheated everyone knows, but I'm over it and I have to move on with my life. Now I have a class in less than ten minutes and I have to write the assignment on the board, make copies of these quizzes so I have a copy to show the parents on parent and teachers conference night. Do you care to help?" I say proudly to her over my shoulder. She nodded.

"Yes of course. I'll do the copies." She said picking up the testes and quizzes on my desk.

"Thank you."

"Don't mention it." She said walking out. I sigh in relief and continue to write on the board. Minutes later I finished and put the chalk down.

I sat in my chair and cut on my computer. As it loaded up Ms. Clomber came in and gave me my attendance sheets for my 5 classes.

"Thanks Ms. Clomber."

"You're welcome." She yelled back to me from the hallway. Then the bell rang. My classroom quickly got loud as students rushed in grabbing seats beside their friends. Within two minutes the last students were walking in and the second bell rung for class to begin.

"Students began writing down what's on the board quietly and pull out your homework. Listen up for your names and say present loud and clear."

Four classes later it was time for lunch. Half of the day was gone and went by like a breeze. Ms. Funnell walked in and handed me the copies.

"Thank you so much." I say as she walks out. I sigh as I stack my papers up on the side of my desk. I grab my purse with my jacket and leave my classroom. There was no use in waiting around for Erin to pop up. My days of waiting are over and I made my way for the exit. Just as I thought I was in the clear Erin walked out his office and begin to walk in my direction. There was no sense in going the opposite way because he already saw me. I roll my eyes as he stood in front of me blocking my way. I sighed and folded my arms. Anger built inside me as watched him. He smiled at me as if nothing happened just three days ago.

"Good morning Carmen, hope you had a good weekend. An also hope you've come to your senses and thought things through."

I glared at him and arched my eyebrow. I looked at him and saw how pathetic he was. I threw my head back and laughed at him. The more I looked at him the more amusing he appeared to me.

"What are you laughing at?" He asked looking uneasy. I calmed my laughter then took a deep breath. I shook my head at him. I put my happy face on with a matching beautiful smile and looked him in the eye.

"What am I laughing about? Shit, there's a lot. I'm laughing at the fact I put up with your no-good-trifling-limp-dick-bitch-ass for ten years, and eight of those years actually married to you and for what. No damn reason. I'm laughing about how when you was broke you came crawling up in my bed because you got evicted."

By now teachers and students were crowded around us.

"I'm laughing about how just Friday I walked in on you fucking slutty ass Helen and you stand in my face today asking how my weekend went. But then again I may be laughing about the brick I threw through your car window. Or I could be laughing about how I dismantled your house with a butcher knife and steel bat. No, no, no I'm laughing about how much money you'll be paying me when we get a divorce."

Embarrassment was written all over his face and a frown replaced the smile he had, had on.

"Now, excuse me I have places to go." I say pushing pass him and leaving out the exit. As the fall breeze hit me I took a deep breath. I felt so much better because finally he felt what I felt. If not then maybe the big hole in his pocket from buying furniture or fixing his car would do the trick. As I get down to the end of the street I saw a few teenagers on the corner all in each other's face. As I got closer I was ready to cross the street so whatever they were getting ready to do wouldn't involve me. As I cross the street Tavon caught my eye. He stood in the middle of the crowd angry. He was in another boy's face as though they were going to fight, but as I look closer the boy was a man. He had to be in his thirties. As the man stepped closer to Tavon I became defensive. I felt scared for him and my body acted before I could think. I swiftly made my way over to the crowd and pushed through the guys circling him.

"What the fuck you gonna do nigga?" Tavon asked the man as I pushed the boy to his right to the side. I stepped in between the man and Tavon then pushed them away from each other.

"Mrs. Smith?" I heard a few voices say out loud.

"What are you doing in this young boy's face? How old are you, like fucking forty!" I yell.

"Yo, who the fuck are you?" He said stepping closer. Maybe he didn't know but he was two inches away from having my 4 inch heels up his ass. Even though the man was larger than the females I fought back in my high school days, I'd beat his ass if I had to.

"Yo, don't step to fucking female like that! Nigga you better back the fuck up." Tavon said trying to get around me.

"Back up." I say pushing them away from one another again.

"If you don't leave I'll call the cops on your black ass." I say raising my voice to the highest pitch I could. The guy exhaled deeply taking a few steps back.

"I'll get yo ass later pretty boy." He said walking away with a few people that were crowded around.

"I'm counting on it." Tavon responded. I turn around to face him with a stern look recognizing the four boys beside him.

"Cesar, Calvin, Derek, and Brandon." I say looking them all in the face.

"I'd expect this from you four but Tavon . . ." I say looking him in the eyes. He shifted his eyes and put his head down.

"Tavon to my classroom I think it's time we had a talk." I say motioning him to walk.

"Mrs. Smith I really don't think . . ."

"Let's go." I say pointing towards the school's direction. He hesitated as he looked at me. I gripped him by the ear.

"Ouch, chill on the ear Mrs. Smith." He whined as I dragged him along. His friends laughed as we made our way to the school. He complained about the pain up until we got to my classroom. I let go of his ear and closed the classroom door. He took a seat in the first row in front of my desk. I walked over to my desk and leaned against it and looked at him.

"I don't know what you've been going through and I can only begin to imagine how messed up it maybe, but you got a good head on your shoulders. Your smart and athletic, those two things alone can bring you to great places in life. Why do you choose to fail and get into fights?" I say trying my best to stay serious, but thoughts of having him with whipped cream and cherries were overwhelming. He sighed deeply.

"I don't get into fights purposely and the only class I'm failing is yours."

"Do you know why you're failing my class?"

"I don't do homework."

"Yeah but you hardly ever show up. You've been coming to my class probably twice a week since October and here it is the middle of November, so you've missed the testes and quizzes I've given out."

"I don't even get science."

"I can help you or get you a tutor."

"Naw, I don't do tutors."

"Well, how come you never came to me?" I ask.

"I don't know." He said standing up.

"Do you have a plan on what you want to become?"

"A Football player."

"Well you have to go to college."

"I know."

"Then what are you waiting for?"

"Did you get the note I left for you?" He said completely discarding what I asked as he walked over to me.

"Umm, what note?" I ask nervously as he stood directly in front of me. His cool breath ran across my cheek like the winter's icy breeze.

Goosebumps popped out all over my body as he looked me up and down.

"Come on stop playing. I know you read the note . . . about the flower."

I swallowed hard as he twirled his fingers in my hair.

"Oh yeah, I read it. It was lovely." I say trying to remain calm.

"I was hoping you'd like it."

He rubbed his hand down my arm causing me to lose my breath. His soft, gentle, warm, big, strong hand made me shiver as my heart skipped a beat. If only he knew what he was putting me through. I removed his hand from my arm.

"Tavon that is inappropriate." I say trying to sound stern. I knew if a teacher walked in I would get into huge trouble.

"I am your teacher. You should never touch me like that."

"I can't help myself, you're so beautiful. It's so hard to resist you." He said seductively inching even closer to me. As the words escaped his lips my body began to tremble. He wrapped his strong arms around me pressing my breast against his abs. I push back from him. I didn't want to but my mind knew better than to listen to my body. I wanted him and probably needed him but my mind raced with all the consequences.

"No Tavon, I can't."

His arms dropped to his sides as I tried to gather myself.

"I could lose my job messing around with you or worst. It could even affect your growing career." I say trying to convince myself getting involved would be a bad idea. I knew better than to mix business with pleasure.

"But what if this could actually work out?" He asked taking my hand into his. The passion in his voice made me want to but I just couldn't.

"Trust me, it couldn't. Plus I'm so much older than you." I say trying to turn him off but it seem to have no effect. The spark in his eye was still there. He took my chin in his hand and leaned in to kiss me. I could imagine how his pink, juicy lips may feel and taste but it was best to leave it in my imagination. I turned my face and he kissed my cheek. I moved away and put my back to him so he wouldn't see the want in my eyes that burned through my soul.

"Tavon, I don't want to have to report you so I think its best you leave."

I could hear him begin to move slowly to the door. I closed my eyes, took a deep breath, and tried to stop myself from saying anything else that may lead him on. The door shut and he was gone. I just hope I didn't make the biggest mistake of my life by pushing him away and letting him walk out.

Moving On

Tavon

Days go by like minutes to me. Life moves quickly never stopping just like Mrs. Smith. I could tell she was avoiding me. Ducking in the hallway when she sees me and acting like I don't see her practically running from me. I tried to catch her after class but she could move pretty quickly in heels. After it happened a few times I begin to realize it was no coincidence every time I saw her, with a blink of an eye she was gone but today I was determined to talk to her. After pushing past students in the hall I raced outside and caught her in the parking lot approaching her car.

"Mrs. Smith wait up." I said walking up beside her.

"Hey Tavon. Is there a problem?" She asks smiling uncomfortably.

"Besides catching up to you, nothing."

She opens the back seat of her car door to put her bag in the back.

"What? I see you every day in science."

She closes the door and walks around to the driver's side. I follow behind her quickly then jump in front of her, blocking her way.

"Why have you been avoiding me?"

She walked around me and went for the door. I maneuvered myself in front of her again and leaned against it. She sighed as she clung onto her jacket trying her best to keep out the cold weather.

"What did I do so messed up that it got you running from me?"

She looked me in the eye and exhaled deeply before speaking.

"Nothing, I just . . . I gotta know what's best for me. And you distract me from my thoughts and I shouldn't let you."

"I ain't trying to distract you. I just want you to know how I'm feeling about you."

"You're my student Tavon, I can't be with you."

"Do you want to be?" I said staring at her intensively. She looked away from me.

"I could get into so much trouble." She said shaking her head.

"How?"

"If someone was to tell the board of education I can be arrested."

"Who would tell them?" I ask taking her hand into mine.

"Somebody, I don't know." She said taking her hand back.

"And how would they find out unless we tell them. I can keep a secret, so why can't we keep this between us?"

"Tavon, there are consequences to everything you do."

"But it's worth it to me."

She looked me and I knew she could tell I was serious. Her eyes shifted toward the ground.

"Is it worth it to you?" I ask standing up.

"I don't know."

She was unable to look me in the face. I step closer to her and lift her chin until her eyes met mine.

"Do you want to be with me?"

She hesitated to answer. I look through her eyes searching her soul for the truth. As her mouth her opened to speak I held my breath.

"Mrs. Smith, I've been looking all over for you. Happy I caught you before you left." Dean Smith said walking towards us. Mrs. Smith swiftly moved my hand from her chin. My heart sank in my chest as I thought of her loving him. How could she even speak to him after he did what did to her? Thinking about it made me angry, but his entrance was my cue to leave. Only seconds away from getting my answer and it's ruined by little dick dean.

"Well, I'm going to go. Catch up with you later Mrs. Smith." I say as I look her in the eyes, then walk away.

"Bye." She said softly.

After getting halfway down the block I heard Ariel calling me. Not really in the mood to talk I kept walking pretending not to hear her.

"Tay, I know you hear me." She said catching up to me. I slow down knowing there was no way to dodge her. She gripped my hand.

"How you been babe?" She asked kissing my cheek.

"I've been great."

"That's good. I got a doctor's appointment coming up soon. You gonna come right?"

"Yeah, I'll go. Are you going in for a checkup?"

"Yes and a sonogram."

"Okay." I say nodding.

"I was telling a few of my friends today I was pregnant and they were saying I should have a baby shower. So I decided we . . ."

As she spoke her voice faded in the distance. Something inside me was constantly saying that this child wasn't mine. Maybe it was just my gut, but something about this wasn't adding up. Too many rumors, too many questions unanswered. There were too many holes in this story of hers. Maybe I should ask David, I knew he would to tell me about it.

"What you think about that Tay?"

"Tay?" She yelled catching my attention.

"Huh?"

"Do you like that idea?"

"Yeah it's great."

Carmen

"What was that about?" Erin asked confused.

"Nothing." I say not really knowing what that was about.

"Carmen, I know what I did was wrong but can't we get pass this." He begged. I watch Tavon leave quickly down the street. I was waiting for him to leave fully so he wouldn't see me ditch Erin. Maybe I was hiding the fact we was having problems but more than likely he already knew.

"Carmen." He said stepping closer. I looked at him and rolled my eyes. I opened the car and got in. I closed and locked the door quickly.

"Carmen come on, you're behaving like a child. Open the door and let's talk about this." I cut on the engine and the radio to drown out his voice. Keyshia Cole's single "I changed my mind" bumped through the speakers. I mouthed to him "I can't hear you" and I could tell he was getting angry, by the vein popping out his neck. I waved bye as I pulled out the parking space and drove off. When I got home I made a pit stop in the dining room dropping my keys on the table and headed for the kitchen. I pulled down a bottle of Hennessy and reached for a cup. Before I could pour my glass my cell phone rang. I sighed knowing that was God himself telling me no. I picked up my phone and answered.

"Hello?"

"Hey Carmie, what's up babe?" Jasmine said jokingly.

"Hey girl, I'm doing fine. What you been up to?"

"Nothing much besides watching after these bad ass kids of mine."

We both laugh. Jazz and I had been friends for almost twenty years. We met at a park my mom brought me to when I was seven. I was playing on the monkey bars as she sat across the park on the benches. She had tears falling from her eyes and she wore a black lacy dress. She had been sitting there since the time I had gotten to the park. Something told me to go talk to her. I walk over to her then sat beside her.

"Hi, my name's Carmen. What's your name?" I said smiling wide at her. She wiped her eyes and looked up at me.

"Jasmine."

"That's a nice name."

"Thanks."

"You're welcome. Why are you crying?"

She pulled her knees up into her chest.

"My daddy's gone." She mumbled into her knees.

"Why is he gone?"

"Because he died."

"How did he die?"

"Mama told me I won't understand."

"Well I like your dress."

I touch the lace on her dress.

"My mom made me wear it but I know daddy would've let me wear my pink one."

"My daddy's gone too."

She looked at me.

"He died?"

"My ma says "he died a long time ago"."

She wiped her eyes again and hugged me. She cried harder as I hugged her back. We've been best friends ever since. I was with her when she had her first miscarriage. She was there when my mom left my dad. The nights when Erin didn't come home she would be there with me. Throughout my whole my marriage I was more married to her than Erin. Recently though, we haven't been able to hang out as often since she had her third child. And I knew her family needed her more than me.

"They can't be that bad."

"Mama told me "you reap what you sow" and she was right."

"You were a pain in your mom's behind so your children are giving you what you you're your mother."

"I know, that's why I be tearing they asses up." We laugh so more.

"I can't believe you."

"Shit its true. I beating they ass when they mess up."

"And Jacob has nothing to say?"

"Shit, I am beating his ass too. We haven't had sex in months I'm beating his head as we speak."

I laughed until tears formed at the rim of my eyes.

"At least your life you can laugh about. All mine make me do is cry."

"What's been going on?

"Marriage is what's going off."

"What has Erin done now?"

"First I caught him in his office with the English teacher and they wasn't studying."

"He cheated on you?"

"And lately I've been kind of stressed out, so I've been gaining weight. And prior to him cheating he called me fat."

"And what did you beat the hell out of him with?"

"I didn't hit him."

"So what did you do?"

"I prayed."

"You prayed?"

"Yes."

"I hoped you prayed about what weapon to use."

"And after that he cheated and I left him. I went home packed my things, dismantled his house, and car, then came to my mom's."

"That's what I'm talking about." She said clapping loudly.

"Now he's practically begging on all fours for me to come back to him. After work today he was half way crying, while I left his no good behind in the parking lot looking like he had a muscle spasm in his neck."

She laughed.

"So you're not going to give him a second chance?"

"What another chance to mess up?"

"You right girl, because ever since ya'll got married he been shacking up."

"An mama was telling when I had enough I'd know what to do, and she was right."

"Damn skippy. That's why God gave us mothers, even if they're the worst parent ever they still teach you the lessons of life."

"But then again, I'm risking my job divorcing him."

"Naw, you got him that job. He risked his job when he dropped his draws and stop thinking."

Then an awkward silence came between us.

"Do you still have feeling for him?" She asked.

"No, I'm done with him."

"Are you sure?"

"I'm more positive than I've ever been."

"Then when it comes down to it, you gotta do what you gotta do."

"I will."

"Then you gotta start by showing him you don't need him. And that you can do just fine by yourself."

"And how do I do that?"

"Easy, get back on your own two feet. Get your own place, a new job, and if you have to get a new man."

I laughed.

"What did I say?" She asked.

"And how do I do that?"

"Get yourself a condo catalog and start your life over."

"So for starting over on a new leaf, what are we drinking?"

"I'm gonna have me some apple Bacardi. What about you?"

I looked down at the Hennessy then pulled out the Grey Goose.

"Vodka, straight up."

DOING ME

Tavon

After speaking to David last period I found it very hard to stay focused. The conversation played over and over again in my brain. Everything he said haunted my mind, tormenting me purposely. My nerves had me fidgety. I couldn't stop shaking my leg and tapping my pen on the desk. She was doing everything he said. I even shared her around with my boys. Some of my friends actually paid her for video. We didn't need protection. It tore through my mind like the incredible Hulk, attacking everything in sight. It was painful to finally know the truth and the pain was settling in my heart and conscience. I was trying to stay calm and hold out to until the end of class but time seemed to go even slower than usual. My anger and frustrations built inside me transforming to rage. Calvin nudged me with his elbow.

"Yo, calm down and be patient. Class is almost over."

Thinking of how she had been pretending nothing ever happened, hugging me and saying she loved me. If Calvin knew the way I was feeling he would've held me down because I couldn't wait any longer. I stood up and walked out. I swiftly roamed the halls in search of Ariel as the footsteps behind me caught up.

"Hold up Tay, she's still a female. She did you dirty no lie but don't hurt her, at least not in school." Calvin said not helping the situation. We heard the familiar giggles behind us and we both knew exactly who it was. I quickly made a U-turn and sprinted in her direction. Ariel was walking in the halls with Jennifer. She saw me and waved but as I got closer to her smiled faded.

"What happen?" She asked as I approached her.

I gripped her arm roughly and dragged her away from Jennifer.

"Ouch that hurts." She said snatching her arm from me.

"What is this I hear about you messing around with mad dudes?"

"Who told you that?" She asked nervously.

"Oh, so it's true." I say raising my voice.

"I didn't say it was."

"So what are you saying?" I say looking her in the face. She dropped her head and looked away from me.

"This is so low for you. I can't believe you would do me like this. You're trifling and I trusted you, and you've been fucking David and his boys! You're a slut!"

She started crying and reached out to touch me and I snatched my arm away.

"Naw, don't you dare touch me."

"I'm sorry."

"I bet you are. Naw don't even cry because you weren't crying when you were cheating on me. And you had the nerve to kiss me!"

I spit on the floor.

"I love you Tavon, I'm sorry."

She grabbed me. I pushed her off me and punched the locker behind her. She covered her face with her hands and slid down the lockers to the floor.

"I hope it was worth it Ariel."

Before I could realize I was getting thrown up against the lockers by three security guards. They put handcuffs on me and dragged me to the main office as students stared in awe. I waited in the office for Principal Hale. An hour later my dad showed up asking me did I hit Ariel. I shook my head realizing the security guards put me in cuffs because they thought I was beating on Ariel. After the principal put me on suspension my dad signed me out of school. My right hand was swollen from punching the locker but the pain didn't settle in until I got to the hospital. The doctor told me I popped a knuckle out of place. So he pulled it back and bandaged it up for me. My dad drove me and the ride was silent like always. He would try to spark a conversation but I would just ignore him but today he didn't bother me with father and son talk. He pulled up in front of my building and got swiftly and shut the door behind me. As I began walking to my building I heard his car door open.

"Hey, Tavon." He said. I turned slightly and turned my head and watched him from the corner of my eye.

"If you ever need anything, my address hasn't changed."

I nod and continued to walk.

Carmen

Within the past three weeks I haven't really went to work. I probably missed three days every week. After buying my two bedroom condo out in Manhattan that was well furnished, for two hundred and fifty thousand dollars I have been appreciating it. Buying extra furniture and replacing the things I threw out. Now I was out looking for the right king size canopy bed that would fit my bedroom. I wanted mahogany wood with craved designs in the wood. So far I couldn't find one but I was determined to get one. After a week of searching I ran across a bed that almost fit my description.

"Excuse miss, I'm in need of assistance." I say to the sale's clerk. She smiled and came right over.

"Yes, how may I help you?"

"I would like to buy this bedroom set."

"Yes ma'am, this bed set is twenty-five hundred dollars."

I look at her and clear my throat.

"If I wanted the price I would've looked on the side of the mattress."

"But there's no price tag on this set."

"Okay, but if I wanted the price I would've called you over asking for it. But I believe I said I wanted to but the bed."

I look at her with my hand on my hip wondering if she was being racist.

"Yes of course, but I assumed . . . -"

"Well I really don't think you're getting paid to assume shit."

"How do I suppose to know your budget without asking?"

"Oh don't think just 'cause you have a budget when you go places mean I have a budget."

"Okay well the down payment is four hundred dollars."

"There you go assuming again. Maybe your broke ass make down payments but I buy shit out the same day so you better run and go get that billing receipt and warranty."

"Sorry for trying to save you from debt."

I laugh lightly and step closer to her. I look at her name tag and suck my teeth.

"Look Alice, you're about two seconds away from getting snatched up and leaving this place with a busted lip and black eye."

"I can't stand you people."

"You people?" I say raising my voice.

"Excuse ma'am, is there a problem?" I heard someone say from behind. I turn around abruptly.

"Are you the manager?"

"Yes I am."

"Well, Miss Alice over here is discriminating against me because my race. Assuming since I'm black I can't afford shit but I can afford a damn good lawyer. Now I want this bed, no down payments either."

"Yes of course. Alice you're fired, John please go get this young woman her sale billing receipt." He yelled across the store. I smile at him.

"Thank you sir."

"Oh no, thank you."

ANOTHER DAY, ANOTHER DOLLAR

Tavon

I sit in science class and stare at the clock above the chalk board. As it ticked closer and closer to the twelve it seemed to go slower. Only ten seconds left and it feels like ten minutes. The pain in my hand from punching the locker still remained but that was just an excuse not to do work. Tick, tock, tock, tick, tock, finally the bell rung. I went to pick up my books.

"Mr. Holmes stay behind I need to speak with you." Mrs. Smith said sternly. I put my books back on the desk and waited for the classroom to clear out. What did she want to talk about? There couldn't be a possible chance she wanted to finish the conversation we started weeks ago. As the last kid left the door shut. Mrs. Smith stood up and walked around to the front of her desk to lean on and looked me in my eyes. I gave her an unsure look as she stared.

"Tavon, I don't know what has come over you these past few weeks I've been gone but your grades are dropping again."

I look down at the desk and sighed.

"What's wrong?"

I sit up straight to make eye contact.

"I don't need to know how to dissect a frog to play football."

"This isn't just about football. This is your life you're throwing away."

"Man, whatever." I stood and picked up my books. As I lifted them a sharp pain went through my hand making my drop them. Mrs. Smith walked over to me and picked them up. She held them close to her chest and looked at me.

"Tavon, is there something going on? You can talk to me."

She seemed sincere. I knew I could talk to her about anything, but Ariel was a problem of the past.

"Mrs. Smith I got a long walk home, so it's best I start walking now."

"I got a car I could umm, you know drop you off if you want." She looked down at the ground as she asked unsurely. I would love to take a ride with her but she didn't say it like she meant it, she said it like it was the right thing to do.

"Naw, no thanks." I say frowning. She handed me my books and I went to door. As I turned the knob she called my name softly.

"Tay." I turn to face her.

"Yes."

She smiled.

"I would really appreciate it if you let me take you home."

I smiled too.

"Then I'll have to take you up on that offer."

After a few minutes we were in the car and she was driving down the streets of the Bronx. Soon after she was parking in front of my building complex. The whole ride here was silent and it was more awkward just sitting here.

"You know, most of the time when there's silence there is something to be said." She said looking at me. She was right because I had a lot to say.

"Actually, I want to say that my ego is hurt from your rejections. I keep coming on to you and you always push me away, but at the same time you seem interested. I don't know what you want but I know I want you. And since I got you for a science teacher, while you're teaching you're teasing me. Watching you pace the classroom is so mind blowing because of your automatic switch when you walk. Just talking to you makes me lose it. And I know my age is a problem but big things come in little packages, and umm . . . what I'm trying to ask is can I be your man or not?"

She blushed. I looked away hoping she wouldn't reject me once again.

"When you wrote me that poem about the flower what was the point of it?"

"The flower was you."

She took my hand in hers.

"Can you give me some time to think about this?"

I nod.

"Of course but just don't keep me waiting forever."

"I won't."

"But before I go, can I at least kiss you."

She nodded. I took her chin into my hand and leaned in to kiss her warm lips. When I pulled back I could still taste her strawberry chap stick. She grinned from ear to ear.

"Have a good evening Mrs. Smith."

"Call me Carmen, and have a great night also Tavon."

Carmen

I walk in the door of my condo blushing like a school girl. I don't know what came over me this afternoon offering him a ride home. A part of me knew this was wrong but the other side felt I needed a change and this could be what I needed. I touch my lips still feeling his soft moisturized lips. Even though it was only a tap kiss it was still mind blowing. I walked deeper inside my home and sighed. I took off my clothes and took a hot shower. The water ran down my body for what seemed like forever. Soon I lay across my bed staring blankly at the ceiling. It was great moment to think. Thoughts of Erin and Tavon filled my head. The decision would be epic but choosing would be fatal. Erin had done more wrong than right. And how fate would have it Tavon was the complete opposite. The only difference was the time spent. Erin had much more time to make his mistakes but could it make a difference. By the looks of it Tavon had won by a mile. Soon after I dazed deeper into my mind to only be pulled back into reality, by the doorbell. I got up and headed for the door.

"Who is it?" I asked unlocking my door.

"Tay." He said as I opened the door. He stood there holding out roses for me. I took them.

"Tavon, what are you doing here?"

"I came to give you what you been waiting for."

He stepped inside closing the door behind himself.

"What are you talking about?" I ask taking a step back.

"You know what I mean."

He pulled me into his strong built chest and nibbled on my neck. The roses quickly slipped from my hand and hit the floor. I stood on my tip toes to wrap my arms around him. He swept me off my feet to carry me over to the sofa.

"Tay wait, we shouldn't be doing this." I continued trying to reason. "This will only lead to consequences."

His hand traveled up my thigh.

"Baby do you want it or not?" He asked deeply. I knew then, I could not refuse. I nodded.

He climbed on top of me.

Ring. Ring. Ring. Ring. Ring. My head jerked off bed quickly, pulling me form my intense wet dream, knocking some of my pillows on the floor. I searched around my bed for the phone until my hand ran across it.

"Hello?" I asked trying to sound less irritated.

"Mrs. Smith." A heavy bass-like voice boomed on the other side of the line. My l eyes grew wide with worry.

"Hello Principal Hale."

"I'm not calling at a bad time am I?"

"No not all."

I sat up clearing my voice.

"Well, that's good because I would like to talk to you about something."

My heart pounded loudly in my chest. What if someone saw me give Tavon a ride home, and the kiss?

"Yes of course, what's wrong?" I asked nervously.

"Well it came to my attention that some time ago you and Dean Smith have had some problems. Problems that has come to the work area."

"Yes."

"Well it's very inappropriate for the school area. We as adults supposed to lead as an example and disorderly conduct in the school's hallway is out of line."

"Yes Principal Hale, I'm sorry for my behavior it was neither the time nor the place. My personal problems should have never made it to my work place. It will not happen again."

"Thank you Carmen. By the way you can write me a letter about what happened between Erin and Helen, and I will gladly send it to the board of education."

"Oh no thank you Sean, a divorce would be the best thing for me."

"Okay but if you need someone to talk to I'm here alright."

"Thanks."

"You're welcome, enjoy the rest of evening."

"Okay, you too."

"Bye." I hung up relieved. I had really thought he had found out about Tavon. I ran my hand through my hair and dialed Jasmine's number.

"Hello?" She answered.

"Hey Jazz."

"Hey girl, what you up to?"

"Nothing, just stressed."

"About what?"

"I don't know if I want to tell you."

"You acting like I'm going to judge you."

"Well, you just may after I tell you."

"Girl, tell me what's going on." She demanded.

"There's this guy at the school that I'm considering to have in my life."

"Okay, so what's the problem?"

"He's one of my students, he's eighteen."

"So, when are you going to get to the problem?"

"Jazz, come on this is serious for me."

"Okay I'm sorry, but it really doesn't seem like a big problem. Yeah he's really young but he's pretty much legal. I would tell you to be careful, but anyone's better than Erin."

I chuckled knowing that was the truth.

"Jazz, I feel like a preverted creep preying on children at the playground. All im missing is the deep heavy breathing voice."

She laughed. I sighed.

"I'm serious, he's so young and I'm suppose to be his teacher, counselor, and friend. I'm abandoning my dupities to him by allowing this circus freak show to continue."

"Well since you put it that that way, I'd advise against it, but real question is are you willing to sacrifice your job for him? And if this goes public could you deal with the media throwing dirt on your name and people giving you the dirty looks?"

"People already do that to me. So I don't I mind entertaining my haters, but my job is a little more important."

She laughed.

"Carmie, a job is just that . . . a job. You have a life outside of work and when you get home who's going to be there to listen to your day, help you relax and relieve your stress."

I sighed as she continued.

"I'm not saying dive in head first but this boy could give you a new meaning to love."

"I don't love him, I just like him."

"So what's this loverboy's name?"

"Tavon." I say smiling.

"Does he treat you right?"

"From what I can tell he wants to."

"I'm loving him already."

We chuckle.

"He's just so young." I say after a moment of silence.

"He's about to graduate."

"I know but I could get arrested for this."

"He isn't a minor anymore, he's grown."

"I know but it's still wrong to take advantage of him."

"I never heard of a guy not wanting a woman to take advantage of them." She said chuckling at her own joke. I shake my head.

"It's morally wrong."

"Okay, I get it you're his teacher but I see nothing wrong with two adults having a healthy relationship outside of the school area."

"It still bothers me."

"Well it shouldn't. I wish I could be in your shoes right now, I'll have that boy naked in my shower right now."

We both laugh.

"So does he have a big one?" Jazz asked bluntly. I laugh.

"Why do you want to know?" I say not believing she just asked that.

"So that means you haven't seen it yet?"

"No, no it doesn't mean anything."

"Does he have a big one?"

"I don't know, but I hope he does."

We both laugh again.

"And when we kissed it was so intense."

"So when you kissed him was it a peck or open mouth?"

"Just a peck really."

"Did he feel you up?"

"No."

"Sorry, just asking. So if Tavon's so perfect then just fuck all that other shit, and go get yo' man."

I shake my head and laugh.

"Alright."

"No, repeat after me. Fuck what people say."

"Fuck what people say."

"Fuck the consequences."

"Fuck the consequences."

"Fuck all the shit that ain't important."

"Fuck all the shit that ain't important."

"Fuck my job."

"What?!"

"Repeat it."

"Fuck my job."

"If I want to give it to Tavon it's my pussy."

I laugh.

"I'm not saying that."

"Fine, I was trying to get you hype."

"So if I'm going to fuck the whole world I should start looking for a new job."

"Shit don't ask me, you know how I do. Cause I'll be saying fuck that too."

CHRISTMAS LIST

Tavon

Detention with Carmen was like an everyday thing. I stayed behind to catch up on my work I missed and retook testes I failed. It's been amazing watching her teach me by myself. No students to take her attention. Every time she turned around to write on the board my eyes trailed down her curvy waistline to her long thick legs. We tried to keep it strictly professional but it was hard to do with her. And now that Christmas vacation was a week away I away I couldn't wait, knowing I would have her all to myself for two weeks. I walked a few blocks down from the school to the jewelry shop. I walked in and one the ladies behind the large glass case full jewelry told me to hold on. I came here a week ago and put a down payment for a gold necklace with a heart charm locket. I was planning on buying her something special for Christmas and this was a great idea. I finished paying for it and got it all wrapped and headed back to school. When I got there I put the necklace in my locker and headed to Carmen's room. As I turned I bumped into some one.

"Oh, my bad." I said quickly. As I looked up and noticed it was Ariel I regret saying sorry. I sucked my teeth and sighed. I leaned my back against the locker. Her stomach was starting to show. She put her hands on her hips and rolled her eyes.

"What do you want?" I ask looking away from her.

"Oh nothing, just wondering if you're going to take care of your baby." She said with an attitude.

I stood up and looked her in the eye.

"You know that baby ain't mine."

"Oh, so you're going to deny it because I had sex with David."

"Naw I'm denying it because we had condoms every time."

"Condoms break."

"But I didn't nut in you, and you know that."

"You know what, I don't care. But you'll care when you're paying child support."

"Whatever, I got shit to do and my woman's waiting for me." I said as I begin to walk away. She glared at me until I was out of sight.

Carmen

I hang up the phone and smile. I knew Tavon would be thrilled when he found out I got us a reservations on Christmas at a French style restaurant in Manhattan for his birthday. We'll have a steamy morning, a beautiful dinner, and a hot night. Just as I begin to wander off in my own world the classroom door opened. I looked and Tavon was walking in. I smiled as I stood and walked around my desk.

"Hey Carmie, what's crackin'?" He asked walking to me.

"Hey baby."

He kissed me and ran his fingers through my hair.

"I can't wait 'til Christmas." He said softly in my ear as he embraced me tightly. I pushed him back.

"Not in school." I say straightening my shirt.

"My bad, you look beautiful today."

"Thanks."

"Have you decided what you wanted to do yet?" He asked taking my hand.

"Yes, actual I have but it's a bit of a surprise."

"Alright, that's fair but I get the bill." He said sternly.

I sighed.

"No it's okay, I'll pay."

"No, I'll pay it's a Christmas dinner."

"No, I'll pay it's a birthday dinner."

"But the rules say the man supposed to pay so I got it."

"How about we just talk about it later?" I asked pulling him closer to me.

"No, let's talk about it now." He said trying to stay focused. I started kissing his neck.

"Okay, you let me pay for dinner and later on that night I'll pay you back."

He took a step back to look at me.

"Oh hell to the no, first you making me be the woman in this relationship and now you calling me a hoe." He said pretending to be a female. I rolled my eyes and laughed.

"Naw, but for real you should just let me pay this one then you get the next."

I sighed in defeat.

"Okay, fine."

"Good, finally I get to wear the pants."

I punched him softly in his chest as we both chuckled. He pretended to be hurt by holding his chest. I just stood there giggling at him. The classroom door then opened and Ms. Funnell walked in. I stopped laughing and looked up at her. She eyed Tavon then me.

"Hello Ms. Funnell." Tavon said looking at her.

"Hey Mr. Holmes. Mrs. Smith I'm having a Christmas party and I wanted to invite you if you didn't have any plans."

"Oh, sorry I would love to go but I do have plans." I say looking at her and glancing at Tavon.

"Okay, what you doing on Christmas?"

"I'm going out."

"With who?"

"This fine young man I've been talking to for the past two months and a half."

"Oh, your Christmas is going to be warm by the fire."

"Oh no it's going to be too hot for fire."

Ms. Funnell laughed and walked out. I looked at Tavon and the smirk on his face let me know he knew what was in store for our Christmas break. Once the door shut he grabbed me by the waist and pulled me into his chest.

"I can't wait 'til Christmas. I'm going to be one lucky man." He said with a grin.

"It's going to be hot and sticky."

"Wow, a dinner for Christmas and a special night with a special woman for my birthday."

He then kissed me sweetly.

ALL I WANT FOR X-MAS

Tavon

Carmen and I sat on the floor of her living room laughing. Carmen had been drinking eggnog and vodka ever since five this afternoon and now it was ten minutes to twelve. She was twisted and couldn't stop laughing at some of Christmas stories from my years ago.

"So my mom told me don't touch the gifts but Derek dared me to open all of them, so I waited until mom was sleep and I opened them all. I was so happy because all the things that I wanted my mom had bought me. So then I go back to my room and we go to sleep. We wake the next morning and all my gift wrappers were there but the gifts were gone."

"Where were they?" She asked smiling.

"Hold on, so my mom is like who opened the presents and I knew better than to tell the truth and get my ass whooped. So I told her it wasn't me, and she's like well then someone came in the house and opened my gifts and took them. But I knew I opened them so I just sat there in shock. And I started crying because I wanted to play with my airplane then my mom's like how did you know you had an airplane. So I was caught in a lie. So I told her the truth and she whipped my ass. Then had me believe Santa came and took my gifts. So the whole year I hated Santa."

She laughed.

"What happen to your presents?"

"My mom gave me them the next Christmas."

"So I got a question."

"What's that?" I asked staring into her eyes. She smiled causing me to smile too.

"Is it true that since you birthday is on Christmas that you get twice the gifts?"

"Hell nah." We both laughed.

"It's just another bullshit lie children thought up in their head and spread around."

She stood up and took my hand pulling me up off the floor. She pulled me toward the couch and I climbed up there with her. She laid her head on my chest as I held her close to me. I could smell her strawberry body wash lingering on her skin. She laid her hand on mine and I noticed a flicker of light and it brought my attention to the ring on her left hand. It shocked me to see her holding on to Erin's ring let alone wear it. I kiss her shoulder trying to take my mind off the ring and she turned her head to kiss my lips. As our lips locked on to one another she shifted her body around to face me. She pulled back and stared at me.

"I want you Tavon."

How she said my name was different. It was truly turning me on but I knew it was the liquor talking.

"Why do you want me?" I whispered in her ear.

"Cause, I'm tired of fantasizing about you. I want to know how good you are in reality."

She faced me and sat on my lap. I knew she could feel me growing beneath her.

"I thought you said you wanted to wait for my birthday?"

"I do, but why can't we have a little peek at your present." She said seductively in my ear.

"A little peek?"

"Just to see what you about to get."

I grinned.

"Okay."

She stood up and stumbled to the radio then cuts it on. She put in a cd and turned to a track. 112's song "Anywhere" flowed through the room. She pulled her shirt over her head and slowly moved her hips to the beat. Then her jeans slid down legs and stop at her ankles. She stepped out of them and walked back to me and sat on my lap. I looked down at my watch and it was midnight.

"Hey, Merry Christmas." I said putting my hands on her waist. She smiled.

"Happy birthday baby." She kissed me. I dug my hand in my pocket and pulled out the jewelry box.

"This is for you." I said opening it for her. She laid her hand on her chest as her eyes grew bigger.

"Oh my gosh, baby I love it." She said clapping cheerfully.

"Put it on me." She demanded as she pulled all her hair from her neck. I took it out the box and clasped it around her neck. She kissed me intensively then tugged on my shirt until it came over my head. Her hands ran down my abs until she reached my jeans and unbuckled them. I pulled her close to me and laid her back on the sofa. I stood up to finish taking off my jeans. As they dropped to the floor her eyes trailed down my body. She spread her legs and I got in between them. I looked down and chuckled.

"What?" She asked smiling.

"Baby, you still got your panties on."

She giggled as I pulled them down her legs. She spread her legs again. I slowly eased into her and she wrapped her arms around me pulling me closer to her. I started off with slow strokes taking in the greatest feeling I've ever had. She was already wet and I glided into her so easily. She was hot and tight. Every pull made my mind go blank. I tried to control myself from busting but it was hard. Her grip on me was strong. Carmen's breathing was unsteady as she tried to hold in her moans. I picked up my pace and she opened her legs wider giving me the ultimate access to her. She held me closer to her. I started to lose my breathe knowing I couldn't hold my climax no longer. Carmen tightened up underneath me and her legs loosen around my waist. I went limp on top of her and prompt myself up on my forearms. I looked in her eyes and kissed her softly. Somehow we managed to get to the bedroom to cuddle there. Weather Carmen knew it or not I was beginning to fall for her. As we laid there in silence for a while Carmen fell asleep. I played in her hair as she slept peacefully. Soon after my cell phone begin to ring. I slid from underneath her and went in the living room for my phone.

"Hello?" I said in a low whisper.

"Tay, you need to come home now." My mom said in a panic voice.

"Mom? What happened?"

"I don't know but Ariel's outside the door crying and she won't talk to me."

I sigh.

"I don't care. Tell her to go to David's door and cry."

"Tay, I think something is wrong with the baby."

Carmen

I lay in my bed pretending to be sleep. When Tavon got out of bed I had woke up. I heard him whispering to someone on the phone but I could barely make out the words he was saying. It all just sounded like muffles, but whoever it was must have been important because he was getting dressed. He walked back in the room and stood at the bedroom door for a moment before he left swiftly. I sat up and listened to the cold dead silence throughout my home. Before I could try to pull myself together tears were already falling from my eyes. I ran a hot bubble bath and soaked into it for hours. The bubbles had disappeared and the water was no longer warm. My tears probably took up twenty percent of the water. I laid there wondering what would make him leave after such a passionate night. When I finally got out my clock blinked eight o' clock. I crawled up in my bed and passed out. When my eyes opened again it was two in the afternoon. As I laid there all I could think about was Tavon. The phone rang and I jumped out of bed and ran to my phone knowing it was him. I grabbed my phone and answered.

"Hello?" I said trying to hide the fact I was crying.

"Hey Carmen." I hung up instantly. Why the hell couldn't Erin just leave me alone? The phone begins to ring again. I answered and hung up again. I walked back to my room and slung myself across the bed, and dialed Jasmine's number.

"Hello?" She said in a cheerful manner.

"Jazz." I said holding back my tears.

"Carmen? Is everything all right?" She asked recognizing the worry in my voice. I broke down again.

"He left Jazz. After we had sex he just left." I said in between sobs.

"Well, maybe something came up."

"Right after we're done?"

She sighed knowing I was right.

"Do you want me to come over?"

"No, your children need you. It's Christmas."

"I know but who will you have?"

"I got umm . . . a bottle whisky and a pint of ice cream."

She chuckled.

"Okay, but if you need company don't hesitate to call."

"I won't." I say sighing.

"Alright, Merry Christmas."

"Merry Christmas." I hung up feeling a little better. Sometimes jazz didn't need to hold a conversation with me for me to feel better. I got up to head towards the kitchen and the phone rang again.

"Hello?" I say hoping it wasn't Erin.

"Merry Christmas Carmie."

"Merry Christmas mom." I said continuing to the kitchen.

"Did you get something special this year?"

"Yeah, but I opened my gift early." I said pulling a cup out the cabinet.

"What did you get?"

"A charm necklace with a locket." I said touching my necklace.

"Aww, that sounds wonderful. What's in the locket?"

"A picture of me and Tavon."

I took down the bottle of whisky.

"Tavon? I haven't heard that name before."

"I know, because I haven't told you about him."

"Why not?"

"I just want to make sure he's sticking around."

I poured the liquor into my cup filling it to the top.

"Oh, okay. Well is he?"

"I don't think he is mom."

"Well that's his lost."

"Thanks."

"You're welcome. So are you coming over from dinner tonight."

I sigh.

"I don't feel like being around everybody right now but if I change my mind I'll let you know."

"Alright, suit yourself. Now I have to finish Christmas dinner so I'll call you later on."

"Okay." I hung up. I took a deep breath and gulped down the first cup, then poured another. I walked to the living room and sat on the sofa. I threw the phone beside me. Before it could hit the sofa it was ringing again.

"Hello?"

"Why are you being such a scrooge?" He said with an attitude.

"What the hell do you want Erin?"

"Why can't we just talk this through and get past this?"

"You just don't get it. I will never be with you again. Don't you think you fucked up my life enough? You always took my kindness for weakness.

You took my kind heart and turned it cold. I blame you for the way my life is!" I yelled at the phone. He went to say something and I hung up the phone. I gulped down my cup of whisky and went back to my room. I got into my bed and crawled up into a ball. My phone begins to ring again but I was tired of talking. The answering machine finally picked up and my voice echoed through the condo.

"You reached Carmen Sanderson. I'm not able to answer my phone at the time but if you leave me a message I will get back to you." Beep.

"Carmen, I truly am sorry. I know you've done a lot for me and I seem to not acknowledge it but I do. Baby I love you. I may not show it but I love you. An, I'm coming over, cause I need you in my life." He hung up. I laid there wondering if he really was coming over. I hadn't notice my tears until they ran down my face. A half hour later my doorbell rang. I got up, grabbed my robe, wrapped it around myself, and answered the door. Erin stood there smiling. He walked in and I closed the door behind him. He sat on the sofa as I went into the kitchen.

"Baby I meant it when I said I love you." He said loudly. I opened my bottle of Hennessy and took it to the head. I coughed as my throat burned. I walked back into the living room finally feeling the buzz from the liquor.

"I'm done talking." I said taking off my robe.

EVERYONE MAKES MISTAKES

Tavon

Whoever said you only spend New Year's Day with the person you love, lied. Christmas Eve David kicked Ariel out for another girl. Instead of Ariel going home she came to my mom's front door. When I got there I let her in. She told me how much she missed me and begged me to love her back. I called her parents. Her mother told me Ariel was suicidal and they were worried something was going to happen to her. So I spent Christmas day with her. I called Carmen only to get her answering machine but I didn't leave a message. New Year's Day finally came along and Carmen still wasn't answering her phone. I knew she was angry that I disappeared on her, but I just wasn't ready to let her know about Ariel. I didn't know how to tell her and if the baby isnt mine I wouldn't need to tell her. So I rather just wait for the results before I even bring it up. Since she didn't answer I went baby shopping with Ariel, then to her doctor's appointment. Afterwards I brought her home. She tried to kiss me but I moved away.

"It would be best if you just didn't try to come on to me. I understand how you feel but that chapter of my life is closed and I'm with someone else, and you know I don't cheat." She nodded. I waved good-bye then left. Once I got outside I flagged down a cab and went to Carmen's place. I tried calling once more but got her voicemail again. An hour later I was walking into her building lobby and pressing for the elevator. When I got to her floor I quickly walked to her door and knocked. I heard movement but no one came to the door so I knocked again but harder. I went for my cell phone, as I looked for her number the door swung open. Carmen stood there emotionless as she stared at me. She leaned against the door frame. She didn't seemed a bit surprised to see me.

"Carmen I am so sorry, I know you're probably mad at me and there's no excuse for what I did."

She rolled her eyes and sighed. I could smell alcohol on her breath strongly, so I knew she had been drinking.

"What are you doing here?" She asked faintly.

"Well, I've been calling you and you haven't your cell phone or house phone so I thought- . . ."

"Hurry up Carmen!" I heard the dean call from inside cutting me off.

Then I noticed Carmen's hair was out and she had on only a robe, and from what I could see she was naked underneath it. As I realized what was going on I took a step back to take the blow to the face like a man.

"Look Tavon, I'm sorry. But it wasn't like we were serious." She said folding her arms. I nodded.

"No, you're right we weren't. I guess you helped me pass and I gave you a good time."

Weather she knew it or not she ripped out my heart to play tennis.

After I picked up the remaining pieces of my heart I walked away.

Carmen

After Tavon got on the elevator I closed the door. I leaned against it and slid down to the floor as I bled internally from where he stabbed me. I put my hands over my face to cry. Once I saw him I wanted to hurt him like he hurt me but somehow he turned the tables around on me.

"Fuck!" I screamed as I banged my head on the door behind me. Even though he left me that morning I still wanted him to stick around, I just didn't think he was going to. I thought maybe he was just in it for the sex, but when he turned his back to me it was like I was sober. Erin came out of the room calling my name. I didn't even really know why I have been messing around with him. I probably just needed someone to hold my broken heart toegther to keep me from falling apart.

"Carmen, I've been waiting far too long I need you." He said standing over me.

"Erin I want you to leave." I said staring at him solemnly.

He arched his brow.

"What?"

I stood up.

"I want you to leave Erin."

He embraced me.

"I love you, I can't live without you. Don't you see that?"

I pushed him away from me roughly.

"Erin I said I want you out my house."

"Baby let's just stop and talk about this." I went in my bedroom and grabbed all his clothes. I opened my door and threw it out into the hallway.

"Erin get the fuck out." I said loudly. He hesitated so I started pushing him out the door.

"Wait let's talk about this." He said trying to convince me but my weak days were over. I slammed the door in his face. I looked at all the presents Erin brought me and started throwing them around. I could tell from the look on Tavon's face I hurt him. I should've never said we weren't serious. In my heart I knew he was more than a great orgasm. How could I mess this up so bad? I took off the necklace he gave me and looked at the picture of us. I remember that day. We went down to Central Park for a long walk. We talked about everything that crossed our minds. It was a nice first date. An as we were walking a guy stopped us and asked did we want our picture taken. We took two pictures one for him and one for me. Thinking about it I still had my picture of us in my top dresser draw. I put the necklace back on and sat there on the living room floor for a moment. I wiped my eyes from the tears and sighed. Did I love him?

LIFE IS TOO SHORT

Tavon

The first day back to school, I walked through the halls like a ghost. I didn't want to talk. I wanted to be left alone. I went to Principal Hale's office to get my science class changed, there was no point in staying in Carmen's class anymore. I lied about having an enemy in that class just so I wouldn't be able to see her. After what she said I'd be happy if I never saw her again. Principal Hale gave me Mr. Jones for a science teacher and I went on about my life. Two weeks later I was on my way to football practice and saw Carmen. She had her hair up and the sun glistened off her skin. She was talking to Ms. Funnell and she smiled. She looked in my direction and I looked away. I turned around and went the long way around just to avoid her. I went to the football field after I got geared up. Ariel sat in the bleachers with her friends cheering me on. I ignored them and did my plays. After a serious case of sore muscles and two hours of practice, it was over and I headed for the locker room. As I was on my way there coach walked up beside me. He patted me on the back and smiled.

"Hey, good job out there today. You were hauling ass."

We chuckled.

"Thanks coach."

"But there is one problem."

I looked at him with a rose eyebrow.

"What's that?"

"You need to stay focused. I know Ariel is pregnant and that can cause a lot of stress so I just need you to stay focused on the prize."

We stopped walking and faced one another.

"I don't understand." I say confused.

"Tay, I don't mean any harm but Ariel is a distraction and if you want to be in the NFL then cut the shit. She's trouble and you know it, your career is on the line." Then he walked off. I went to my gym locker room still thinking about what he said. He was right too. As I walked out the building I noticed Ariel waiting for me. I approached her and sighed.

"What do you want?"

"Nothing, I was going to walk you home."

"No thanks Ariel. I'd rather go alone."

"Okay."

"And if you wouldn't mind can you stop showing up at my football practices."

"I thought-"

"I know what you thought but it's not going to happen."

"Oh you're on your period again."

"What does that supposed to mean?"

"You're treating me like shit again."

"No, I just need my space."

"I'm giving you space."

"No, you're hovering."

"What do you want me to do then?"

"Leave me alone would be a start."

"And I guess next you're not going to want to be a father to your child."

"You don't even know if the baby is mine."

"Fuck you Tavon." I turned to walk away from her knowing she was about to go overboard. As I turned David was walking down the street to me. He looked mad as hell.

"What's going on with you and my baby's mama?"

"Nothing David, everything is fine." Ariel responded.

I laughed lightly.

"Shut the fuck up I'm talking to him." He quickly retorted. He put her head down. I shook my head and walked past him. He grabbed my shoulder.

"You ain't leaving." He said. I jerked from him and continued walking.

"Don't forget who you're talkng to." I said tunring to face. He clenched his jaw and nodded. I knew he wasn't as stupid as he looked. I had him by fifty pounds I didn't need my friends to help me beat him. As I turned around again I bumped into his friend. He chuckled as I notice it was the same man that Carmen threaten.

"I told you I was going to see you again pretty boy."

I sighed immediately. I turned back around to face David knowing it was no way out of this one.

"Where's yo' boys now Tay?" he said smiling. i smirked at him.

Ariel stopped in between me and David.

"David, please don't do this." She begged. He grabbed her arm and yanked her out the way. It was only two ways this going to go either I run down the block to Derek's building with them hot my heels and pray he's outside on his block or be bold and try to take them both on. Be a punk and run or talk shit and get my ass handed to me. Well my legs were already burning from pratice so I guess running was out of them question.

"It ain't my fault you can't control ya bitch, maybe you need a leash." I said laughing lightly remembering how just months ago the situation was in reverse. Oh what irony this turned out to be. I tighten my fist.

"You should've never said that." He said as he stepped to my face. I swung punching him as hard as I could in his jaw. He stumbled and fell back. As I turned the guy behind me punch me in my gut and I fell to my knees holding my stomach. I tried to breathe but he punched the wind out of me. As I looked up David's foot came across my face knocking me on my back. Through the kicks to the face and Ariel's piercing screams for a split second I saw Derek and Carmen standing over me in black. Then there was nothing.

Carmen

I sit at my desk looking at Tavon's attendance records making sure it wasn't just me that haven't seen him in class. It was true he was going to everyone's class but mine for two weeks straight. I knew he was mad at me but he needs to pass his classes so it was time to bring this to Principal Hale. I walked down to his office and knocked on his door.

"Come in." He said sternly through the door. I opened it and came in. He looked up and smiled.

"Hello Mrs. Smith, oh I mean Ms. Sanderson forgot you're getting a divorce."

"Yes it's almost finale. But umm that's not the reason I'm here. Tavon Holmes has missed two weeks of my class and I think it's time to call a parent teachers conference."

"No, that won't be necessary. Tavon switched his classes once he got back from break."

"Oh okay, I umm didn't know that." I turned around and walked out. I couldn't blame him for switching classes. Why would he want to look upon my face every day knowing what I did to him? There was no going back now. I knew how much of a big mistake I made and now I could only wait for Tavon to come find me.

It's been a few days and Tavon haven't been to school. I knew it was probably a good reason but in the back of my mind I believed I was the reason why. I sat in my classroom at my desk during lunch hoping any minute Tavon would walk through the door and I was soon regretting getting my hopes up. My classroom door opened and Ariel walked in.

"Hello Mrs. Smith. I know you tutor Tavon in science so I was hoping you could look over his homework before I hand it in."

I look at her and notice her stomach. She had a baby bump.

"Yes of course." I say holding out my hand for the work. I felt kind of hurt at the fact he couldn't come see me and sent Ariel instead. I knew I had it coming but it still hurt to see it happen. I look over the papers seeing all the work was correct and handed it back. She turned to leave but something came over me.

"Umm Ariel, may I ask you a question?"

She turned quickly.

"Yeah."

"How's Tavon? I mean I haven't seen him around in a few days."

"You haven't heard? He's in the hospital."

"What happened?" I asked trying to remain in my seat.

"He got jumped walking home from school a few days ago. He got beat up really bad."

"Is he conscience?"

"Yeah, he's doing a lot better that's why his mom sent me down here with his school work. But he can't move around too much that's why he hasn't been back."

"Did the doctors tell you what was the damage?"

"There was a lot. I can't remember all of them but I know one of his ribs was fractured."

Oh my God. The mere thought of him being injured tore me up inside. I put my hands over my mouth trying to cover my emotions.

"Will he be okay?" I mumbled through my fingers.

"Yeah, he'll be fine."

I sighed a bit relieved.

"That's good."

"I know because I couldn't bear the fact that I would be in the delivery room alone."

I arch my brow at her.

"Delivery room?"

"Yeah when I give birth to our child. I thought he wasn't going to make it to the due date but the doctors told me he would."

"He's the father of your baby?"

"He didn't want me to tell anyone until after the baby was born but yeah he is."

I watched her giggle and jump in joy as she waved good-bye and left my classroom. I couldn't believe she was pregnant with his baby and he didn't tell me. Even though I was worried I was mad as hell. After school ended I got my stuff packed and got ready to leave. I had plans on stopping by Lenox Hill Hospital and I didn't want to waste time. My classroom door opened and Erin strolled in. I sighed heavily and hurried up.

"Carmen, are you really going to give up on me? Do not notice all the history we've made with each other."

I put on my pea coat and buttoned it up then slipped on my scarf and gloves.

"Do you remember what we had on Christmas day until New Year's Day?"

I picked up my papers and put them in my briefcase and locked up my cabinets.

"Carmen I know you hear me."

As I locked the last cabinet he came up behind me and embraced me.

"Let me make tonight as special as Christmas was."

I pulled his arms from around me and turned to face him.

"Erin, sex with you is the most boring and unpleasing thing I've ever done in my life. I will never have sex with you ever again, even if my life depended on it." I said with a smile.

I walked around him and gather my things up in my hand.

"If it's so boring then why did you stay with me for so long?"

"First of all it was never about sex with us, second you were my first and I thought that's how it's supposed to be. But I'm dating someone else and the things he do to me, umm well let's just say you could never compete with."

He stood in front of me blocking my way.

"Dating, you're cheating on me."

I burst into laughter.

"Cheating, no cheating was when you were fucking around with Helen. You see, we're getting a divorce so I can do whatever the hell I please. So you can call this weighing my options."

"We're not getting a divorce."

"Yes we are."

"It's this new guy in your life isn't."

"What?"

"Who is he? Jeff? I knew that punk ass nigga use to come on to you."

"No it's not coach Jefferson. He's not a teacher at this school." I say rolling my eyes.

"Then who's the guy you've been fucking?"

"I don't have to tell you what's going on in my life no more."

I walked past him towards the door and he grabbed my arm roughly to turn me around and face him. I looked down at his hand on my arm.

"I won't let you just leave me."

I looked at him with hatred noticing how stupid he really was.

"If you ever put your hands on me again I will slap the shit out of you." I said snatching my arm from him.

"This conversation is over." I say walking out.

"No it isn't."

"Good-bye Erin."

Tavon

I lay on the hospital bed with a fractured rib, fractured arm, and dislocated shoulder. The pain relievers made me sleep all day, so I stop taking them. Now the pain was unbearable. What made it worst was the stern talk from my mom and boys. My mom had already left to eat but Derek was still digging in my ass about me not calling him.

"Nigga you knew I lived a few blocks away. I could've made it there in sixty seconds flat."

"Derek, I didn't have time to call."

"But you had time to talk shit." He said pacing the floor.

"Please Derek, don't do anything to him. Let's just leave it at this okay."

"Hell no, he gonna get his."

"I deserved this D. All the girls I did wrong, all the niggas I jumped. Like, how many times did we jump David? This has to be karma."

He stopped pacing and looked at me.

"Shut the fuck up, this wasn't no karma. David did this to you."

"I know but-"

"But nothing he gonna get what's coming to him."

The room door opened and we both looked up and Ariel walked in. I sighed lightly.

"Hey baby, how you doing?" She said softly.

"I know this grimy bitch didn't just come in this room to see you." Derek said glaring at her.

"How am I grimy?"

"You set my boy up."

"No the fuck I didn't."

"The only reason why my hands ain't around your throat yet is because we in a hospital but wait 'til we get outside."

"You ain't gon' put ya hands on me."

"Okay we gonna see."

"Derek stop talking to her and Ariel what are you doing here?" I ask tired of hearing them argue.

"I came to see you."

"You have to stop coming by to see me. I don't want nothing to do with you, don't you think I've suffered enough."

"Tay, how can you say that to me?"

"Your with David and I don't care but as long as your involved with him I don't want to be involved with you. I refuse to get into brawls for a girl that isnt important to me. So I don't want to see your face unless it's about the baby."

"I thought-"

"Well you thought wrong. We are nothing not even friends and the only reason why I tolerate you is because the baby. But if the baby turn out not to be mine, that's where our communication stops."

"Tavon you can't do that to me."

"I'm in too much pain to argue with you so just leave Ariel."

She turned and left quietly. Derek sat in the chair by the window and sighed.

"I'm ya best friend Tay, we are brothers fuck blood we thicker than that."

"I know." I say looking in his direction.

He stood up and smiled at me.

"Just remember that okay. I'll be back later on."

I nod as he threw up the deuces and walked out. I dazed out the window into the sky and dozed off.

Carmen

I stepped into the room quietly and Tavon lay on the hospital bed hooked up to a heart rate monitor, with ivy in his hand. His right arm was in a brace and bandages covered his left shoulder. His face was bruised up. It looked painful. I walked to the foot of his bed and watched him sleep. I didn't know if I should wake him but I was going to anyway.

"Tavon."

Once I spoke his name his eyes shot open. He watched me for a moment with a confused look on his face. To see him like this was truly priceless.

"What the hell are you doing here?" He asked with attitude.

"Don't curse at me Tay, I came to see if you were okay. I was worried about you."

"I can't believe you came all the way over here when you have a husband. What you caught him messing around with Ms. Drew again and decided to come and look for me?"

I smile at him as I take off my coat. I laid it across the arm of the chair.

"Tavon, you already knew he was still my husband."

"Why would you want to be with someone who doesn't give a damn about you?"

I leaned against the wall and glared at him.

"It's not like you cared."

"You don't know how much it irritated me to see you still wearing the ring he bought you."

"What?"

"Christmas Eve, when I was over. I saw the ring on your finger."

"How come if it bothered you, you didn't say anything?"

He tried to sit up and cried out in pain.

"Hold on let me help you." I ran to his side and pulled him up in sitting position.

I sat on the bed beside him.

"What was I suppose to say? Take off your husband's ring. It made me feel stupid for thinking- . . . never mind." He said shaking his head.

"Thinking what?"

He stared at me for a moment in silence.

"Thinking we was serious about each other."

"Were we serious?"

"That's what I thought."

"Then why did you say we weren't?"

"Because you said we weren't. And if I knew you felt that way, I wouldn't have put myself out there."

"I wasn't feeling like that."

"Then why would you say it?"

"Because I was angry."

"Angry about what?"

I stood up and began to pace the floor.

"About how you treated me that night. We made love and it was so passionate and mind blowing, then you left. Gone. You were out the door. It made me feel like a two cent hoe. Just another piece of ass. Then Christmas day you didn't even call so I had to cancel our reservations. Then to come and find out the whole time you've been expecting a baby. Yeah, Ms. Perky bitch Ariel is just flaunting the fact she carrying your baby, which you never mentioned."

"I was getting around to it." He said surprised to know I knew. I turned my back to him.

"Yeah, sure you were. It had me thinking maybe you are too young for me. Maybe I should stick with Erin and not get involved with you."

"But you've already made your decision." He said. I turned to look at him and he was staring at me.

"You made that decision for me." I said fighting back my tears.

"Oh wow, I doubt if what I did could even compare to what you did."

"You don't know how bad you hurt me."

"Enlighten me then. I left I know it was sudden but how come you didn't call me. Instead you called Erin."

"I didn't call him. he showed up and I was drunk and my emotions were running wild and I couldn't bear the empitiness I felt. And maybe if you were still with me he wouldn't have been the one in my bed."

"Yes, blame what you did on me."

"I'm not blaming you. I just wanted you to stay with me, was that too much to ask for."

He was silent for a moment as he watched me from across the room.

"You know I wanted to be with you. I had beg for you to even consider thinking about being with me."

I sat in the chair and held my head in my hands.

"I cant help to notice your speaking in past tense."

I looked up at him and his head hung low.

"Please don't tell me, that is where we end." I said looking away from him.

"I . . ."

He paused for a brief moment. As he opened his mouth to continue the room door open. A woman in her late thiries maybe even younger walked in. Her light brown hair was pulled back into a bun showing off her beautiful golden like skin. She had on a white button up blouse and black dress pants. Then pendant attached to her shirt confrmed she was a officer of the law.

"I brought you some . . . Oh sorry I didn't know you had a visitor." She said coming into the room.

"Hey mom, this is Carmen. Carmen this is my mom." Tavon said. I stood up to shake hands with her.

"Hello, you can call me Mary."

"Hello Mary." I say smiling.

"Well I have to be on my way." I say looking at Tavon. His eyes were telling me to stay but I couldn't. I wave good-bye and walked out. I scurry out the hospital to my car and close the door. I sit there for a moment as the tears flowed from my eyes and messed up my mascara. Then I cut on the engine to my car.

A FAVOR

Tavon

I leant on Carmen's car waiting for her to come out the school building. After hearing this disturbing news I needed a favor that only Carmen could help me with. It had been almost three weeks since I last spoke to her. She didn't come back by the hospital to see me after the first visit. There was nothing I would want more than to finish our conversation but this visit was not a social one. Just then she walked out the school heading straight in my direction. She didn't notice me until she was in ear shot distance. She looked surprised to see me as she paused then continued to walk.

"I wasn't expecting to see you for at least another week. Did you get released early?" She asked standing in front of me.

"Yeah, you could say that."

She sighed and folded her arms.

"So what makes you break out the hospital and come see me?"

"Actually Carmen I need a favor."

"What type of favor?" she asked arching her brow.

"I need you to take me out to Hartford."

"Hartford as in Hartford, Connecticut?"

"Yeah."

"What the hell is out there?"

"My dad."

"Miss your father?"

"No. I need 10 grand and I know he's good for it."

"Wow, that's a lot of cash. What makes you think he's going to give it to?"

"He'll give it to me because he thinks giving me anything I ask for makes him a better father."

"Okay, so what's the catch?"

"Mom will probably go crazy and probably have a heart attack."

"Hmm, sounds like she'll try and kill me if she knew I took you."

"She won't."

"Okay." She unlocked her doors and we both got in. She put the key in and pulled off. It took us a while to get there but when she pulled up in front of his house it seemed just a little too soon. I looked at her and I could tell she didn't want me to go but I opened the car door and got out anyway. I walked up to his door and knocked. I swallowed hard as I heard the door unlock. It swung open and my father stood there with a cigar in his mouth. He smiled.

"Hey." I said uneasy.

"Tavon, don't you live in the Bronx?"

"Yeah, I do but my girlfriend drove me out here."

He looked behind me and waved to Carmen.

"Dating an older woman I see."

"Yeah."

"Not bad, well bring her in Tay." He said moving aside.

"Umm, well I would but this is going to be a short visit. I actually gotta get back to the Bronx pronto."

"So what brought you all the way out here?"

"I need a favor Robert, and you said I could come to you if I needed anything." I said. He nodded.

"Come on aren't we past the first names son."

"No we're not." I said sighing knowing he was going to make a big thing about it.

"Come in Tay, let's finish this inside."

I stepped in and shut the door behind. He walked down the hallway and waved for me to follow him. I followed him to his office and took a seat. He sat at his desk and looked up at me.

"Tay I'm trying my best to be the father you need."

"You're about nineteen years too late for that."

"Then what do you want me to do. Huh? Tell me."

"I don't have time for this Robert. I need ten grand."

"Okay, what for?"

"Are you going to give it to me or not?"

"I will but there's one condition."

"Fuck it then I don't want your money." I stood up and headed for the door.

"You haven't even heard the condition."

I turn around to face him abruptly.

"I don't want to hear it. You're always trying to force yourself in my life and I'm fine on my own with mom." I said looking him in the eye. He sighed and opened his draw and pulled out his check book with a pen then began to write.

"So who am I writing this check out to?"

"Me."

He finished and held the check out for me. I walked over to him and took it.

"I didn't know it was ever too late to be a loving parent but I will not apologize for it."

"Thanks." I said and turned to leave.

"Don't you want to know what the condition was going to be?"

"What?"

"Come and have dinner with me and your step mother next weekend. Oh yeah and bring your girlfriend."

"What a shame, I don't think I'll be able to make it." I say as I quickly headed for the front door.

"I think you will make it or I'll be giving your mother a call on Sunday about this short visit." He yelled to me as I opened the front door.

"I think my schedule just opened this weekend." I said knowing this was blackmail. I knew he was smiling as I left. Once the breeze hit me I could finally breathe easy. I got in the car and sighed.

"Did you get what you needed?" Carmen said as she pulled off.

"Yeah. But we gotta come back next weekend."

She cut her eye at me.

"What do you mean by "we"?"

"We have a dinner date with my dad."

"You keep saying we."

"I kinda said we would come for dinner next weekend."

"You kinda said!" She said raising her voice.

"Look I was forced."

"Forced."

"If I said no he would've called my mother. And my mom would freak if she knew I came all the way out here to ask my dad for money. What the hell else could I say."

"Fine let's just hope that he doesn't know me."

Carmen

We finally hit the Bronx but most of the drive back we sat in silence listening to the radio. He didn't want to tell why he needed the money and I didn't want to push the conversation on him.

"So you want me to drop you off somewhere?" I said glancing at him.

"Umm, well I'm actually waiting for a phone call to let me know where I need to go."

"Oh, okay so you want to come to my place until then? So we can talk."

He nodded.

When we got to the condo I headed for the kitchen.

"You can make yourself at home. Are you thirsty?"

"Not really."

"Alright." I said opening my cabinet for a cup. As got some orange juice from the fridge and began to pour me some juice Tavon wrapped his arms around my waist. I turned around and he pulled me close to his body and kissed my neck as I begin to drink my juice.

"I thought we came to talk." I said putting my cup down. His hands traveled up my back to the front of my shirt and unbuttoned it then took it off.

"We have to talk Tavon." I said trying to maneuver myself away from him.

"I love the way you say my name." He said pulling me into his chest. He kissed my lips passionately as he unzipped my skirt and let it fall to the floor. He groped my behind and licked my neck.

"Say my name again."

He unsnapped my bra and slipped it off my shoulders.

"Tavon." I said breathing lightly as I felt shivers run down my back. He picked me up and put me on the counter. My mind was so wrapped up in him. I lay back as he slid my panties down and let it dangle on my left ankle.

"We have to talk." I said in a faint whisper.

"Then talk baby, I aint stopping you."

He pulled me closer to the edge of the counter.

"I know but I forgot what I wanted to say."

His tongue rubbed against my clitoris. I was already leaking but his quick tongue movements made a waterfall. He sucked on me and licked hard. His soft nibbles made my toes curl. I bit down on my lip and whimpered trying to stop the screams of pleasure that would send for the cops. Who would've thought he knew how to please a woman so well. He lifted his head and looked at me and licked his lips. He took me off the counter and I stood up.

"I would carry you to the room but my arm still hurts a bit." He said with his lips against mine. I lifted his shirt and he pulled it off. I walked backwards to my room while he followed me. I stopped in the living room and gotten down on my knees. He walked to me and I pulled him by his jeans closer to me. I unbuckled his jeans and they dropped heavily on to the floor. When I pulled down his boxers Tavon Jr. was ready to play. I gripped onto the base and licked from the bottom to the top and sucked on the head. Tavon threw his head back and closed his eyes. The further I had him in my mouth the more saliva formulated. As I sucked I massage him with my tongue. He started to tremble slightly. I knew none of these young girls he had before could make him feel the way I was making him feel now.

"Oh baby chill." He said stopping me. I stood up and we continued to the room and I lie back on the bed and spread my legs and he was swiftly in between them. Before I could inhale junior was all in my sugar and stretching my walls to fit his size. I couldn't hold in the moans anymore. He was big and his strokes were deep, passionate, with perfect rhythm. I held him close to my body as he as he thrust in to me. I could feel the muscles in his chest and back clench then release. I could feel my blood rushing, my muscles tensing, and my body began to stiffen and I clung onto him tighter. I arched my back and trembled underneath him. He was unbelievingly amazing. After he had his orgasm he laid on top of me for a moment then laid beside. I slung my arm over his chest and curled up beside him. I hadn't notice I dozed off until Tavon was tapping my shoulder. He had tuck me in and was fully dressed sitting on the edge of the bed next to me.

"Hey sleepy head I got to go okay." He said moving my hair from my face. I nodded. It felt as though he was leaving once again but I knew he had something to do.

"I promise we'll get to talk and finish our conversation okay."
He kissed my lips softly and rubbed the side of my face.
"Get some sleep babe. I'll call you later on."
"Okay." I said smiling weakly.
He kissed me once more and left.
"I love you." I said faintly and drifted off again.

More than Friends

Tavon

I had been sitting in the lobby of the court house waiting for Derek to be released since last night. When his lawyer finally showed up he told me to wait here while he and the D.A. spoke to Judge Winston in his office. I had been sitting here almost twenty minutes and I was hoping this Lawyer was as good as he said was. An as I sat here I couldn't help but remember when Derek was sitting in the very same seat I was now and I standing in front of the judge in the court room two years ago. I had gotten in to a fight with my ex-girlfriends man and in the mist of fighting she grabbed me and I punch her out of reflex and broke her nose. She had pressed charges and my mom couldn't afford a lawyer and my Dad was nowhere to be found. Derek begged his mom to use his money for college to get me a lawyer and she did. Yeah I got community service but even that was better than 3 years in a juvenile correctional facility. The door finally opened and I stood up. Derek walked out and the first person he saw was me.

He smiled causing me to chuckle.

"I guess we even huh?" He asked walking to me.

"Nah we boys, I had to get you the best damn lawyer I could find. I ain't shit without you."

"We more than boys, we brothers."

I hugged him and gave him pound on the back.

"Thanks man. Now, I'm ready to get my ass home and take a fucking a shower."

We both laughed.

"I'll walk you down stairs and get you cab." I said walking with him to the elevator.

"Okay, where you heading to?"

"I gotta drop by the school."

"School is almost over."

"I know but I gotta get my homework."

He lifted his brow and shrugged.

"Okay."

Carmen

My classroom door opened and I sighed. I turn around with an attitude tired of talking with Erin about the same thing.

"What do you want?"

"Damn, I thought we kind of made up yesterday." Tavon said smiling a bit uneasy.

"Oh it's you." I say relieved and embarrassed.

"Sorry about that I thought you were Erin so I just umm, well you know."

He walked to me and took my hand.

"I promised we would finish our talk so I'm here."

"Okay."

"Let me start by saying I'm sorry."

"No, I should've told you what was going on. There shouldn't have been secrets between us."

"I know."

"And about new years, with Erin."

As I looked away I took a deep breath and tried to continue, but my lips wouldn't move anymore. He took my chin in his hand. He guided my face to his as he stepped closer to me.

"I'm sorry that I walked out on you and there's no excuse for that."

I slightly nodded.

"I will never do that to you again, because you mean a lot to me."

"I know that now. I just hope you can forgive me."

"I wouldn't be here if I didn't."

I nodded once more. He pulled me closer and kissed my lips. He turned me around and bent me over my desk and pulled up my skirt over my hips. He slipped my panties down and unzipped his pants. He positioned his self behind me and I arched my back then poked my behind in the air. I bit my lip as he penetrated me so I wouldn't moan too loud.

He held my waist softly because his arm still hurt from getting jumped. As I threw my ass back on him he thrust into me. We met in the middle and the sound of our bodies slapping together turned me on even more. I held my moans in as much as I could but my muffles soon turned into hums. As I climaxed my legs began to shake and I couldn't stand up straight. I knocked my pencils and papers off my desk trying to stand up. He came right after me and leant over me trying to catch his breath."Damn" was all he could say. He eased out of me and pulled up my panties for me. I pulled down my skirt and straightened it down flat. I turned around and kissed him. He smiled and fixed my hair for me. Then I opened the windows and he helped me pick up the things I dropped off the desk. I looked at him and laughed. I couldn't believe I just had sex with him in the school building. My door opened and I picked my head up and looked over my desk and Erin stood there puzzled.

"Umm, what's going on?" He said noticing Tavon behind the desk with me. I stood up and patted the dirt from the floor off my skirt.

"Oh nothing, Tavon was helping me pick up some things I dropped off my desk." I said glancing at Tavon. I could see the anger written all over his face. I picked up Tavon's jacket and slipped my car keys in his pocket then passed it to him.

"See you tomorrow Ms. Sanderson." Tavon said walking past Erin to the door.

"Wait, do you have your keys?" I ask looking at him hoping he would understand when he saw my keys. He stuck his hand in his pocket and looked at me.

"Yeah."

"Okay, later."

My eyes diverted to Erin once the door closed.

"What the hell do you want Erin?" I said getting my bag and starting to pack my things to leave.

"You and Tavon seem to be getting very well acquainted."

"I don't have time for your bullshit today."

"Well maybe Principal Hale does."

I look at him.

"What are you trying to say?"

"If I find out something is going on between you two I'm bringing it to the Board of Ed. You'll never have a job as a teacher again."

I roll my eyes and finish gathering my items.

"Well become Detective Dumb-ass I hope you find what you're looking for." I say unmoved by his threats. I grab my bag and head for the door. As I walked past him, he grabbed my arm. I spun around and slapped him. I snatched my arm from him and fixed my bag on my shoulder.

"Don't put your hands on me, ever. Because I will tell Principal Hale you're a pedophile."

He stood silently.

"Oh did you forget? You were twenty-three having sex with a sixteen year old girl. I guess you didn't. And I hope you notice if it wasn't for me you would be sitting in jail, still homeless, and a broke-ass nigga. You are really a dumb ass."

I turned and left him standing there.

Meet the Family

Tavon

Carmen and I lay in the bed naked. Carmen lay across my chest entwining our fingers while I played in her hair.

"So tell me about your parents?" Carmen asked looking up at me.

"Well umm, there is not much to the story. My dad left my mom to be a football player when my mom was pregnant with me. She had to raise me on her own until I was seven. After my dad had to retire he stepped back in. But two years later he got married and he disappear again. I didn't see him again until I was in middle school. My football team had made the papers and he took an interest in me but it was too late by then to be a father to me because my mother had already done all the work."

"And what about now?" She asked.

"Now . . . he's just trying to force his way in my life."

"Okay. So why won't you forgive him."

I sighed and shrugged my shoulders.

"Maybe if he showed interest in me for being his son instead of a football player, I could forgive him. What about your dad?"

"My dad was abusive he use to beat my mother every day. He was a drunk, never was a good father. He died about four years ago. Even though he wasn't a good father I was there with him on his death bed. He begged for me to forgive him but I wouldn't speak to him. Even though I wanted to tell him that I was over all the pain he caused us, I couldn't betray my mother by telling him. But somehow he knew I forgave him. He tore my family apart but he was still my father and I loved him. When he past he gave me everything that was his in his will. That's how I know he knew I forgave him."

"Wow, your life was hard."

"Yup, and I've lived throughout all the hard ships and I know I'm stronger now than I've been."

"I do believe you are stronger, because tonight you were man handling me."

We both laughed as she pushed me slightly.

"Shut up." She said in between laughing.

"So what about your mom?"

"Oh she was a very strong independent woman. She took care of me my sister and my brother by herself after she got away from my father. She was very loving and always has been. Trust me, you would love her."

"Does that mean I'll be meeting her?"

"In the future, I think you will. So what about your step mom, I know you said your dad remarried."

"I hate her."

"Why?"

"When I was sixteen I brought my girlfriend over for the weekend to spend the night at my dad's house. She walked in on me having sex but she didn't anything to my dad. About two weeks later when I went to visit again she came on to me."

"Came on to you?" She asked sitting up.

"Baby its nothing." I said pulling her arm until she laid back on my chest.

"I just don't like her. She creeps me out." I said sighing.

"If I ever meet her."

"Baby let's just switch the topic."

"Fine. So, as a kid what did you always dream of being. And don't tell me football player or I'll poke you in the eyes."

I chuckle and continue to play in her hair.

"No actually, I wanted to be a pilot."

"So what happened?"

"My mom said she didn't want me to die in an airplane or be too far away from her. She thought the NFL would be best for me after she saw me play football."

"Do you still think of being a pilot?"

"All the time."

"Then maybe you should to go to college and take pilot lessons instead of going pro."

"I can't, my mom would kill me."

"I'm just saying if it's something you want to do you should do it. Some people never get a chance to fulfill their dreams and you have a chance to. I think you should do what you desire to do."

"But my mom . . . -"

"It's not your mom's life it's yours, and you only get one and I say you should go to training to become a pilot but it's your choice."

I chuckle.

"Okay Miss Bossy, so what did you want to become?"

"A painter."

"Why didn't you do it?"

"I went to school for it but Erin told me it was just a waste of money, so I never finished my course."

"Well I think Erin was stupid, if drawing is what you want to do then do it."

She climbed on top of me and kissed me softly on my lips. She yawned and sighed.

"What's the story of you and Derek?"

"He's like a brother I never had. We have been tight since sixth grade. He taught me everything I know. He was there for me when nobody else was."

She smiled at me.

"That sounds like my best friend Jasmine. We have been friends since elementary. When life happened we could depend on each other and that's how it's always been."

"Did you tell her about me?"

She chuckled.

"Actually I did."

"I bet you were like "girl he so cute and he be turning me on"."

She laughed.

"Yeah something like that."

She yawned again. I looked at the clock. It was nearly two-thirty in the morning.

"Are you tired?" I ask.

"Kinda."

"Then go to sleep baby."

"I don't want you to leave."

"Carmen I'm not going anywhere. When you wake up I'll still be here lying beside you, holding you."

"For how long?"

"For as long as you want."

"What if I say for years?"

"I'd lie beside you for an eternity."

She smiled. I kissed her forehead. It wasn't long before she was sleep on my chest. Then I was out like a light.

Carmen

9 AM

My doorbell rang waking me up. I could still hear Tavon's heartbeat in my ear. I sat up and looked at him as the sun was coming in through the window shining on him. I was happy to know throughout the whole night we were holding each other. The doorbell rang again. I jumped out of bed and put on my robe. Who the hell could be at my door so early in the morning? Whoever it was, was going to get a piece of my mind. I walked to the door and swung it open.

"Auntie Carmen!" Jordin and Anthony yelled in union as they bum rushed me. I hugged them back.

"Hey you guys." I said looking up at Jasmine standing behind them. They ran on past me to the living room.

"Hey Jazzy." I said moving aside for her to come in.

"Girl, get dressed I'm taking us all out for breakfast."

I remember Tavon was in the room as I shut the door.

"Umm . . . Today's not really a good day."

"I'm not going to repeat myself. Get yo ass in that room and get some clothes on." She said treating me like a child. I walk back into my room to wake up Tavon. I shake him a little.

"Tavon, baby wake up." He opened his eyes. He smiled at me and pulled me on the bed with him and kissed me. He started to rub my thighs and caress my ass.

"Baby stop." I said pushing him back.

"What's wrong?"

"I would love to but Jasmine's here with her kids, they're in the living room as we speak." He jumped up off the bed.

"Okay I want to meet her."

I smiled weakly. I was bit unsure about that idea.

"What now?" He said looking at me.

"Well, I don't know if you should."

He turned around and headed for the door. I hopped off the bed and jump in front of him to block his way.

"Hey, is everything okay in there?" Jasmine asked from the living room.

"Baby it's okay. She's your best friend she's not going to judge you."

"I know but I'm just not sure yet Tavon."

Jasmine knocked on the door.

"Carmen, what the hell is going on in there?"

"What are you so afraid of?" He asked taking my hands.

"I don't know."

"Can't you trust me on this one, please? I want to meet your best friend."

"Tavon, it's too soon."

"I'm going to meet her one day so why not now."

I sigh.

"Okay, fine."

"Do I hear another voice in there? You got that boy in there? Open up I want to meet him?"

I smile and shake my head.

"Okay, but first put some clothes on. I don't want you to meet her in your boxers." I said laughing. He picked up his jeans and put them on. He looked under the bed then looked at me.

"Where's my shirt?"

"The lamp." I say point to my night stand. He pulled his shirt off the lamp and put it on. I opened the door and Jasmine stood with her hands on her hips. She pushed past me and looked him up and down.

"Okay, he is looking good girl. Way better than punk ass Erin." She said bluntly. Tavon smiled. They shook hands.

"Hey Jasmine nice to meet you."

"Thanks, you too. Please call me Jazz."

Tavon

After IHOP I headed home to get ready for dinner with dad tonight. I unlocked the door and went to my room. Once I entered the room I immediately regretted it. Ariel was sitting on my bed wiping her tears with a napkin. I rolled my eyes and sighed heavily. I swiftly walked to my closet and looked for something nice to wear for dinner.

"I have been here all night waiting for you. Where have you been?" She asked sniffling. I pulled out my black button up shirt.

"I thought I told you at the hospital to stop coming by my house. If there's an emergency you can call my cell phone." I said coldly. I grabbed a pair of jeans and shut the closet door.

"I've missed you." She said looking me in the eye.

"Well I haven't missed you."

She stood up.

"Why are you acting like you don't love me anymore?" She replied.

"Because I don't."

She walked to me and wrapped her arms around my waist. She laid her head on my chest and held me tight.

"What you're feeling is just a phase baby. This girl is just a stepping stone to get over the break up, but you don't have to get over it . . . because I still love you and want to be with you." She said talking into my chest.

"No she's not. Ariel, I love her."

Her grip around me loosened. She looked up at me with watery eyes.

"Tavon, I love you."

I sighed and backed up from her.

"I told you at the hospital that we could never be together."

"You're still the father of my child."

"Speaking of the baby I want a D.N.A test, and if it comes back that I'm not the father then there will be nothing keeping me around. So I am going to leave you alone and I want you to do the same."

Her tears finally ran down her cheeks. She turned and headed for the door.

"This girl of yours doesn't know how lucky she is." She said under her breath before closing the door behind her. I tossed my clothes on the bed and rubbed my temples. I grabbed a towel and got in the shower. After I washed up I put on my clothes and sneakers. I came out my room and my mother called my name.

"Tavon, come in here."

I sighed and walked to the living room.

"Yeah mom."

She sat on the couch with the house phone in her hand.

"Where have you been all night? I waited up for you and you never made it home."

"I spent the night at my girlfriend's house."

"And you never thought to call." She said dropping the phone on the coffee table. I sighed and leaned on the wall.

"If you were really that worried you could've called my cell phone."

"Who's this so called girlfriend?"

"Her name is Carmen."

"Carmen sounds familiar."

I noticed my mistake too late. If she realized she had met Carmen before she may find out who she was. I had to switch the subject before she remembered.

"Look I gotta head out. I got plans for tonight."

She rolled her eyes.

"Just make sure you keep practicing your football."

I scratch my head and scrunched up my eyes.

"Well actually, I'm not going to do the football thing."

She tilted her head and narrowed her eyes at me.

"What do you mean by not going to do?" She replied baffled.

"I decided to become a pilot."

She stood up abruptly and swiftly walked to the kitchen. I followed her silently knowing she was going to make a big thing out of nothing. She begin pulling food from the cabinets and slamming them on the counter tops. She stopped for a brief second then continued.

"I thought we talked about this months ago." She said roughly through her teeth.

"Yeah we talked about it for a while but you stop the conversation. You never wanted to talk about it after that." I answered.

"I didn't have to talk about it again because I said no."

"Mom you don't have the right to say no because I make the last decision." I said firmly. She finally turned around to look at me.

"I will always love and respect you mom, but this is my life. And I want to do what I've always wanted to."

She put her head down and tapped her nails on the counter.

"Oh, you're a man now. You don't need my two cents."

I sighed.

"Mom I didn't say that."

She held out her hand to shush me and looked me in the eye.

"Obviously you're too grown for healthy guidance. You're always out running the streets, getting girls pregnant, and God knows what else."

"You're not guiding me. You're forcing my hand. And Carmen said if I have dreams I should follow them and that's exactly what I'm doing."

She slammed her hand on the counter.

"I'm your damn mother! And instead of listening to me you're following after some girl."

"You had your chance at life mom, why can't you just be happy for me and let me have mine."

She dropped her head to the floor and ran her hand through her hair.

"Because you're about to mess up everything I had planned for you."

"Exactly mom, you been planning everything since day one. It's time for me to map out my own life for a change." She kept her head down as she began slice up bell peppers. There was nothing left to say. I stepped out the kitchen and left out the front door. I hated to argue with my mom. I loved her too much and knew she deserved much more than that. Even though I couldn't shake the fact that there something she wasn't telling me. She was still my mother and I respected her to the highest.

When I got downstairs Carmen was already waiting for me. I jumped in the car and gave her a soft kissed. Then we were off to Robert's house. We finally pulled up and went to the door. As I rung the bell Carmen fluffed her hair.

"Baby, you look great." I said taking her hand. She smiled.

"Thanks."

I heard the door unlock from the inside and I turn to face it. It swung open and Dad stood there smiling.

"I thought you forgot. I was debating if I was really going to call your mother." He said eyeballing Carmen. If I didn't know any better I would say he was checking her out.

"Umm, Robert this is Carmen, Carmen this Robert."

Carmen waved and smiled uncomfortably.

"Come in you guys." He said grinning. He stepped aside. I walked in behind her so he wouldn't be tempted to look at her behind. He shut the door and escorted us to the dining room. The table was already set so we took our seats. I sat next to Carmen and Robert stepped out to go check on things in the kitchen.

"I think your father was checking me out." Carmen said looking at me.

"I thought he was too. I was hoping I was just being paranoid." I sighed with frustration.

"Baby if you feel uncomfortable then let's leave." I said backing my chair up. She took my hand and gave it a squeeze. She smiled warming up my heart.

"Tay, calm down. He probably didn't mean anything by it. I mean look at me, I'm an eye sight." She chuckled trying to lighten the mood.

"Fine, but if you feel the slightest bit of awkwardness we're leaving."

She nodded in agreement. I scooted back to the table. Dad walked back in with my step mom Trina trailing behind him. They sat across the table from us.

"Hey Tavonie, it's been far too long." Trina said as the butlers came into the room with our plates.

"Everyone calls me Tavon now Trina." I replied never making eye contact with her.

"Okay, so who's this marvelous woman? Your teacher?" She said laughing lightly at her own joke.

"No, this is my girlfriend. Her name is Carmen." I replied. I brought Carmen's hand to my lips and kissed it.

"She's hardly a girl Tavonie."

I finally looked at her and she smiled.

"That's the second time you have insulted me. I'm not going to let the next one slide." Carmen said glaring at Trina.

"I'm just saying you have to be close to my age because young girls don't look as sophisticated as yourself." Trina replied.

"Well you look around forty years old where I'm in my twenties. Yes I am intelligent and sophisticated but maybe I should be your teacher so you can learn that his name is Tavon not Tavonie." Carmen said smiling. I could tell she had an attitude and wasn't going to be long before she leaped across the table. Trina sighed in defeat and we begin to eat.

"So Tavonie, when did you two meet?" Trina said staring at me.

"Tavon." Carmen said looking at Trina. I cleared my throat and glanced at Carmen.

"That doesn't really matter, just know we're together now and we're happy."

"Does she have a job Tavonie?" Trina asked. I could tell she was purposely annoying Carmen.

"Tavon." Carmen said she before taking another bite of food. I looked at dad for help but he just continued to eat.

"Umm . . . well . . ."

"You don't have to ask him what I do when I'm sitting right here." Carmen said nonchalantly. I knew that Carmen didn't like her already from what I told her last night, so I didn't know how much longer she was going to patient with her.

"Tavonie, you have the worst taste in women."

And that was it.

"Excuse me bitch." Carmen said glaring at viciously. Carmen stood up abruptly. I jumped out of my seat swiftly and took her hand.

"I've asked Carmen to marry me." I said loudly getting everyone's attention.

My dad choked on his food. He finally looked up and gave me eye contact. Carmen looked at me and Trina stared with her mouth ajar.

"She's my fiancée and Trina I will not have you talk to her anyway you feel. You're not invited to the wedding. Goodbye." I pulled Carmen with me as I headed for the door. My dad was on his feet and following behind us.

"No, wait don't leave Tavon and Carmen. I know she can be a pest sometime but at least stay for me."

I turned to face him and caught him eyeing Carmen once again.

"You want to know why I hate being around you Robert? Because you and you're wife is a bunch of sick perverts. This will be the last time you ever see me so I hope you got enough mental pictures of Carmen's ass that'll last you a lifetime." I said then pulled Carmen out the door.

"Let's go baby. We can find a nice restaurant to eat dinner at."

REALITY

Tavon

I stood outside Carmen's door pacing with an engagement ring in my hand. I had been out here for about an hour trying to decide what to say and how present it. As I paced the elevator door opened. I quickly walked to the end table that held a few dozen roses in a vase. I pretended to smell them hoping whoever it was would soon be in their own condo. The person passed me by and approached Carmen's door. He rang her doorbell. I glanced behind me and immediately knew it was Dean Smith. I panicked inside knowing it would suspicious if the dean saw me here. I grabbed a few roses to cover my face and crept to the elevator. I pressed the button praying it would open before Erin noticed me. Carmen's door opened and she stood there. I watched her through the roses. She was stared at him irritated.

"What the hell are you doing here Erin?"

"I fucked up okay, I get it already."

"No you don't get it. I have moved on and you need to do the same."

"Helen was an accident. I know I've been an ass throughout our marriage but I'm a changed man now."

"I'm seeing other people Erin."

"No you're not."

"Yes I am. He's the best thing that ever happened to me, and I'm not risking my happiness for you. Not anymore."

"Remember prom night."

She sighed and shifted her weight to one side.

"You were really nervous about having our first time together."

"That was almost ten years ago."

"I told you "I love you" and you said it too. That same night I proposed to you and you said "yes". That's how I knew you loved me."

"I did love you. You just could never show me that you did too." Then pain in her voice shot through me. She still loved him. Just when I thought me and her could be happy together he swoops in once again.

"Then let me prove myself now."

"It's too late."

"Then why did we have sex all those times on Christmas to New Year's Day?"

The elevator doors finally opened and I stepped in without hesitation. I dropped the roses on the floor. The doors began to shut and I looked up to only catch Carmen's beautiful eyes on me. She pushed past Erin to make a run for the elevator. I put my head down unable to stare into her watery eyes.

Carmen

When the elevator doors opened I glanced over Erin's shoulder noticing someone had been waiting there the whole time for the elevator. The mysterious guy got on and suddenly dropped the flowers he had been holding. When I saw his face my heart jumped. No, it wasn't Tavon. I tried so hard to believe it wasn't because the sadness written on his face could only mean one thing. I no longer cared about Erin seeing the student and teacher love affair. My body reacted before my brain could. I pushed Erin to the side and dashed for the closing elevator. I hadn't noticed the tears in my eyes until my body slammed against the closed elevator doors. My heart was sinking further in my chest. Soon it would be pushing up against my back.

"What are you doing?' Erin asked confused. I ignored him and took the stairs. The tears were falling from my face. Once I made it to the ground floor I ran through the lobby out the front door and looked both ways. It was raining hard but I saw him walking fast down the street. I ran to catch up with him. I called his name and he stopped walking. I stopped running when I got directly behind him.

"What?" He said with his back still to me. As I ran after him I didn't think of what to say to him.

"What were you doing here?" I said panting. He turned around and opened his hand. A beautiful ring glistened in his palm.

"I came to make you my fiancée. For real this time. So you could be my wife someday."

I stared him in the eyes. They were so empty, so emotionless.

"How long were you outside my door?"

He chuckled.

"For an hour."

He probably didn't notice that I was crying because of the rain.

"Then please, propose to me." I said stepping closer to him. He shook his head.

"I don't think I want to anymore Carmen."

He took a step back.

"Why not?"

I tried so hard to sound strong but my voice cracked as I spoke.

"I don't think I can take the fact he had you first."

"Please don't do this Tay. I . . . love you."

"But as long as you love him, he'll always be standing in my way."

"You're too young to understand."

"Then make me understand Mrs. Smith, you're the teacher. Help me understand what I'm missing."

"That's not fair."

"No, it's not fair what you're doing to me."

"What am I doing to you?"

"You're making me fall for you with my eyes closed."

I couldn't breathe. For a second I couldn't hear the rain anymore.

"You're the only woman that exists in my world. You're the reason I went to school, just so I could hear your voice. Or maybe it was the way you said my name for attendance and smiled warming my soul like always, staring at me with your sunset eyes. It made me feel no one could come between that. But you're still in love with him and I can't compete with him no more, because it's killing me Carmen. I can't live knowing you love him."

"I don't love Erin anymore. Tavon I love you. It's just that simple."

He stared at me.

"You love me?" He asked stepping closer to verify my words.

"I love you Tavon."

He stepped closer and I held up my hand to stop him.

"You say that you love me . . . so propose."

He smiled lightly.

"Go on, get on one knee." I said pointing to the ground. He got down and took my hand in his.

"Well I pretty much already told you everything I thought of in the hallway so I'll just ask you. Will you marry me Carmen?" He said.

"Yes Tavon, I will marry you." He stood up and slid the ring on my finger. He pulled me into his strong arms held me close to his chest and kissed me. As our lips met it felt as though he switched hearts, so we'd be forever with each other.

"Can we get the hell out of the rain now?" I asked.

We both laughed. I took his hand and walked back to the building lobby. Once we got on the elevator Tavon pushed me up against the wall. He rubbed all over my body and sucked on my neck. I wrapped my arms around him and closed my eyes as I enjoyed the feeling he gave me.

As the door opened I pushed him back lightly. He took my hand guided me out the elevator. As we approached my condo I realized I had left my door open. We walked in and I closed the door behind us. As I turned around I walked into Tavon that was standing in front of me. I didn't know what made him stop so suddenly, but I should have never asked.

"Baby is there something wrong?" I ask rubbing his back.

"Yeah, actually there's a lot wrong. A lot wrong with you." I heard Erin's voice say.

Immediately I knew why Tavon had come to a halt. I walked around to the front of him and stood face to face with Erin. I felt it would be better if I stood in between them. Erin's face was full of disgust as he watched me.

"Why the hell are you in my house?" I ask sternly. He sighed.

"Well, I thought we could finish our conversation. Now I know why you didn't want me back. You were too busy fucking a boy."

He said raising his voice.

"Excuse me." Tavon said stepping closer to him. I pushed Tavon back slightly.

"Erin, he's not the reason I left you. The only person you can blame for that is yourself." I replied.

"The hell it is, you been fucking him the whole time!" He yelled stepping closer.

"You better watch your tone when you talk my woman." Tavon said gently pushing me out the way.

"Your woman." Erin said angrily.

"Calm down Tavon." I said trying my best to keep him behind me. Erin reached out to grab me but Tavon pulled me into his chest.

"Don't you put your hands her!" Tavon yelled. I shoved Tavon into the door behind him with all my strength.

"Erin I think it's time for you to leave." I said sharply. Before I knew it Tavon tucked me under his arm and pushed me behind him.

"Yeah, I think you need to get the fuck out now." Tavon said.

"Are you forgetting that legally she is still my wife?" He asked staring Tavon down.

"Not for long." Tavon replied smiling wickedly. I knew that the worst was about to happen.

"What makes you so sure?" Erin said.

"I guess you haven't seen the engagement ring on her finger yet." Tavon said. The anger on Erin's face was unreal. I have never seen him so livid. Erin searched the ground lost of words. When he looked up he tackled Tavon. I knew he wasn't a match for Erin since he hadn't fully healed. He was just fresh out the hospital a few days prior and the doctor told him to take it easy. Too much pressure on his chest could tear his stitches. Just as I shove Erin off him, he punched Tavon in the face. I was enraged at the thought of Erin even touching Tavon. Once he stood up off the floor I punched Erin square in the face. His head jerked back. When he looked at me his nose begin to bleed. He stared in disbelief. I walked to the door and opened it wide.

"I want you out, now." I said glaring at him.

Tavon pulled himself off the floor slowly. Erin walked past him and out the door. He turned to face me.

"You're really going to choose a child over me."

"No Erin, you're the child. The only man I see standing is Tavon."

"Carmen, please. If you close that door I'll have to bring this to the board of education. You will be fired."

"That's okay, because I quit." With that said I shut the door in his face. I stood there for a second to gather myself. I turned around and Tavon was walking to the living room. I went to the kitchen and got an ice pack, then followed behind him. He sat down and I sat beside him then passed him the ice pack. He took it and put it against his ribs. He laid his head back and sighed.

"Are you okay?" I ask remorseful.

"I'm not dying if that's what you mean."

"Is there anything I can do to help?"

"No, I'm just going to take a cold bath."

He stood up and headed for the back.

"You're not hungry? It is dinner time."

"Nope. I just had a real big knuckle sandwich and that was enough for the night." He chuckled at his joke. I smiled. At least he wasn't angry anymore. I walked to the kitchen and pulled out my champagne and two glasses. I know he was under the drinking age but we had to celebrate our engagement. I heard the bath water start running. I grabbed the glasses and champagne then walked to the bedroom. I placed everything on my dresser and got naked. I pulled my hair up into a bun so it wouldn't get wet but messing around with Tavon, anything was possible. I picked everything up and headed for the bathroom. "He lay in the tub with the ice pack on his forehead. I sat on the edge of the tub and poured him a glass.

"This will help." I said getting his attention. I held out the cup and he took it. He threw it back and laid his head back on the edge. He handed me back the glass.

"You got anything stronger?" He asked with his eyes closed. I dipped my hand in the bath water and slung water on his chest. He smiled.

"I do but when you're celebrating something this life changing, you suppose to drink something soft." I say tilting my head as I watched him. He peeked at me from the corner of his eye then closed them again.

"The only thing soft enough to drink for this celebration is you." He said grinning. I chuckled.

"I would never turn that down, but I want to do something else tonight."

He opened his eyes and propped himself up.

"Like what?" He said with curious eyes.

"Intimacy." I said standing up.

"Baby I always show you affection." He said confused.

"We've been having sex so much that we're not intimate anymore."

He stood up and stepped out the tub. I picked up a towel from the rack and tossed it to him. He tied it around his waist and walked pass me. I followed him into the bedroom and watched him put on his boxers and shorts. He looked at me for a moment and gently pulled me closer to him.

"Carmen I love you, and if it ever felt like I didn't I apologize." He said into my ear. He held me for a while then brought me over to the bed. We lay beside each other. He held my face in his hands and kissed me. His kisses were never ending, one after another. It felt as though I was falling in love with him all over again. His hands slowly made their way to the edge of my shirt and partly lifted the rim and caressed my back. His tongue wrapped around mine continuously. I closed my eyes and tightened my grip around his waist. His rubbed my thighs and pulled me even closer to him. The warmth of his body sent chills throughout my body. The passion in his touch was unlike anything I've ever felt. When he stopped kissing me I laid my head on his chest.

"Without sex, loving you would still be the best thing in the world. All I need is you, and that would be enough for me." He said putting his chin on the top of my head. I smiled. It was amazing to finally know that he fell for me just like I had fallen for him, and incredible to hear him say it. This couldn't be real. Maybe I was having one of my daydreams again. I put my ear to his chest and listen to the soft melody of his heart. There was no way this was a dream. Tavon loves me and we're getting married. Nothing else mattered, because right here and right now only we existed.

Tavon

The next day in school it seemed like everyone's eyes were on me. I quickly made it to my locker and pretended not to notice the hundreds of piercing eyes. As I pulled out my books I heard Derek behind me.

"Tay, you a grimy dude." He said approaching me.

I turn to face him.

"Not you too." I say sighing.

"How you not gonna tell your brother you fucking the hottest teacher on the damn planet."

"Look man, it was personal. I didn't want to talk about it." I said shutting my locker.

"Why the hell not? I mean she fine as hell."

"Can you stop saying that?"

"Oh my bad, I didn't mean to check your girl out. Oh wait I didn't know she was ya girl 'cause you didn't fucking tell me."

I sighed and leaned against my locker.

"I love her D. She's the best thing that could ever happen to me, so I had to keep it secret because I didn't want her to lose her job."

He nodded.

"Okay. Well you could've told me you were getting married."

"How the hell do you know?"

"Dean Smith gotta big ass mouth so he told the teachers and students over heard it and the word got back to me."

"Well I was going to tell you regardless. I mean who else was going to be my best man." He laughed and gave me a pound.

"A'right. So it's time to spill the beans, is she as good as she looks?"

I push him playfully and laugh.

"Shut up man."

"It was worth a try though." He said in between laughs.

"Tavon Holmes, you are needed in Principal Hale's office immediately. Tavon Holmes." We heard Ms. Clomber say over the loud speaker. I sigh and head for Principal Hale's office. Once I got to the main desk Ms. Clomber stared me down as she pointed to Hale's door. I roll my eyes and go inside. Once I open the door I regretted not going to class. Principal Hale and Erin sat in there waiting for me.

"Please Tavon, sit down." Hale said pointing to the seat next to Erin.

"I rather not."

"Fine, stand. I called you in to get this situation handled. This morning Ms. Sanderson called in and quit and Dean Smith is accusing you and Ms. Sanderson of having an affair, and that is the reason that she quit."

"If Ms. Sanderson quit I don't know nothing of it. No we are not having an affair. I don't know what Dean Smith is talking about." I said acting surprised about the situation.

"Don't you fucking lie. You were at her house last night talking a whole lot of hot shit, saying you two are engaged."

"Mr. Smith!" Hale said standing up.

I inhaled loudly and opened my eyes wide.

"That is not true. Everyone knows me and Ariel is together. Did you forget Ariel is pregnant with my baby?"

I deserve an Oscar for the best lie ever performed.

"He's lying Sean, he's fucking my wife."

"Okay, sorry to have bothered you Tavon please go to class." Hale said coming around his desk to escort me out.

"Sean don't let him leave he's bullshitting!" Erin yelled. Hale opened the door and I left to go to class. I smiled walking down the hallway. The vein bulging from his neck had to be the funniest part of the conversation.

"Tavon, you're a liar." I heard Erin say walking up behind me. I turned around to face him smiling.

"A good one, wouldn't you say."

"You better stay away from Carmen or next time you'll be walking away bloody." He said stopping in my face.

"Since I just got out the hospital I'll give you the upper hand but you better believe when I recover, I'll be counting it." I said not bothered by his words.

"You talk tough but you keep forgetting I been all up and through Carmen for years."

I chuckle and step back.

"Damn all those years of practice and I still out shine you."

The look on his face was priceless. I hated him and he hated me. It was funny to think that he thought he was in competition with me. He wasn't even a contestant.

"I have to go to class. So have a horrible day Erin. Oh yeah burn in hell." I said laughing lightly as I walked away.

MY LIFE WITH YOU

Carmen

It's been a couple of months since I quit and I knew Tavon was having a hard time at school because he never wanted to talk about it. He pretty much moved in with me but some days his mother wanted him home and he went. Ariel was a few days past her due date and was calling Tavon for every little thing. Lately he was stressed out and I could tell because all he ever did was sleep. I understood he was tired but it had been over two weeks since we even had a conversation. Last time we spoke he told me to do the wedding plans to stay occupied, but how can a bride have a wedding without a groom. I sat in my bedroom on my bed with a wedding dress, cake, church, and decoration books. I had on a lacy bra and panties as I waited for Tavon to get home. I was determined to get his mind off everything and put it on me. I was flipping through my books as the front door unlocked. I sat up quickly and knocked them all on the floor and spread out on the bed. He walked in and dropped his keys on the night stand.

"Hey baby, how was your day?" I asked seductively.

"A repeat of yesterday." He said lying on top of me. He kissed my neck. I knew he was tired. I rolled him over on his beck and got on him.

"Baby I need you." I said lifting his shirt to rub on his chest. He took my hands and kissed them.

"You know I need you too."

He smiled.

"Baby, not like that. I mean I want you." I whined.

He sat up and kissed my lips.

"I want you too."

"Then have sex with me."

He chuckled.

"Okay. But let me jump in the shower first."

I pout and fold my arms. He rolled me over and got off the bed.

"It'll be a quick shower."

"Fuck that, I'm horny."

He laughed.

"Baby, you can't wait five minutes?"

"Hell no, I've waited two weeks already."

"Five minutes won't hurt."

"Fine, get in the damn shower."

He blew me a kiss and went to the bathroom. I lay back on the bed with my arms still folded. I lie there for a few minutes listening to the water run. I smiled wickedly and stood up. I took off my bra and panties and headed for the shower. As I stepped in the tub he turned around and smiled.

"I knew you couldn't wait." He said backing me up against the tiled wall. I wrapped my arms around his neck as he sucked on my lips and tongue. His hand traveled down my body until he reached my sugar cookie jar. He stroked my clitoris continuously and licked my neck.

"Oh baby, give it to me." I begged.

"Say my name first." He said grinning.

"Tavon." I replied without hesitation.

"Damn right girl, you better remember it too."

"Tavon, Tavon. Tavon give it to me."

"Okay, okay."

He kissed me then turned off the water. He picked me up in his strong hands and brought me to the bed. He put me down and I pulled him on the bed with me and climbed on top of him. I pushed off his chest as he held on top my hips guiding me up and down on his shaft. As I came down on him he would thrust into me causing me to moan louder. I couldn't even say his name without a pause.

"Ta . . . hmm . . . von."

He must have loved it because he continued. I could feel the shivers go up my back as my toes curled. I quivered on top of him as he held me tightly and grunt. I could feel our warm sticky fluids slowly slid down my thighs. I lay on his chest to catch my breath.

Erin

"Then get me an officer who can help me because it seems as though, you don't comprehend." I say to the officer sitting at the desk in front of me. She sighed as she rolled her eyes.

"Sir, lower your voice and I'll see if I can get somebody to help you."

"Thank you." I say calmly. She stood up and walked away leaving me at the main desk.

"I couldn't help but over hear your problem and I think I can help you." A female cop said walking towards me. I turned to face her. She looked well over thirty years old. She was pretty. Her brown hair pulled back into a ponytail. She was petite. I smile.

"Is there a price involved?" I ask leaning on the desk.

"Nothing's free."

"Okay, is that the only reason why would you help me?"

"No, actually I know Tavon Holmes very well and it seems as though Carmen needs to learn her lesson. She is way too old to be dating an eighteen year old boy."

"Finally someone understands me."

"Follow me, so we can talk in private."

"Yes of course. I never got your name." I say following behind her.

"Just call me Mary."

Carmen

It had been a few days after Ariel had her baby and I hadn't seen Tavon since. I knew he was hurt to find out the baby wasn't his but I was beginning to worry about him. I had taken a pregnancy test and it was positive. I knew he would be thrilled to find out about it but he wasn't answering his phone for me. I knew he probably needed some time but I felt a bit impatient. I started to get dressed. I decided to go to Jasmine's house for a while to pass time. I grabbed my keys and purse and headed for the door. As I grabbed the knob the doorbell rang. I opened it and two police officers stood at my door.

"May I help you officers?" I ask as my heart sank in my chest. My first thought was something happened to Tavon and they found my address on him.

"Yes, we're looking for a Carmen Sanderson."

"I'm Carmen." I reply arching my eye brow. The heavy set cop grabbed my arm and pulled me out my condo and pushed me up on the wall.

"You're under arrest for statutory rape." The officer said as he cuffed me.

I knew this was bound to happen but I didn't expect it to happen so soon. The tall, slender officer took my purse and keys.

"Would you like me to put this in your house or bring it down to the station?" He said waving my belongings.

"I only need my keys." I reply calmly. He tossed my purse inside and closed my door. They brought me downstairs and put me in the back of their police cruiser. In all my years of living I have never sat in a police car. I was always the civilian standing on the sidewalk staring at the criminal in the back. Maybe all those times I was wrong. Maybe they were innocent just as I am today. After a few minutes we pulled up in front of a precinct and the chubby officer was yanking me out the car. He walked me inside and took down my information then put me in a holding cell. I sat on the bench and put my head between my legs and held my face. My unborn child's life without me would be cold, lonely, and far. No distance could be further than the relationship with a parent in prison.

Tavon

I spent the night at Derek's place for a few days so I could clear my mind. I knew the baby wasn't mine but a part of me wanted it to be. I felt guilty for wanting to be the father of Ariel's baby and I couldn't face Carmen. I knew she would notice my feelings and I didn't want her to. Though I missed her so much I wasn't ready to approach her head on. Derek kept telling to at least call her but I couldn't get up the courage for that. Plus what would I say to her. I knew she was probably worried about me but I wanted to go back to her with a clear head. I heard all her voice messages and she was practically begging me to come home, and it hurt to know I wasn't man enough to call her back. Derek walked into the living room and looked at me lying on the couch. I glanced at him.

"You need to get over the fact that Ariel lied to you this whole time. I know you're hurt but you can't leave Carmen home alone worried about you like this." Derek said. I coughed.

"I feel sick." I reply avoiding the conversation.

"Because you're sick mentally."

"No I'm serious. I think I have a virus."

"So go home to Carmen. She can take care of you."

"I can't move."

"What are you so afraid of that you don't want Carmen to find out about?"

"I'm not afraid of anything, and if I was I wouldn't care if Carmen found out about it."

"Then why are you hiding it from her?"

"I'm not."

"Yes you are."

"No I'm not."

"Then why the hell are you still here? Huh? Why haven't you answered your phone once? I call that hiding."

I sat up on the couch and put my feet on the floor. Derek looked worried for me. I dropped my head in my hands.

"What should I do then?" I said looking back up at him. He tossed me my keys.

"Go check up on your girl."

Erin

I sit in my house in the living room on the sofa, sweating. The basketball game was on but I paid it no attention. I knew getting Carmen arrested was wrong but it would be the only way to get her back. When we were married I knew whatever I did she would still stay with me, but since Tavon stepped in the picture . . . I could tell from the look in her eyes that she wasn't coming back this time. She was always beautiful to me, even after she gained a little weight. I didn't know what I had until she packed her bags. I knew she would be alright in the precinct with Tavon's mother because she knew how much Carmen meant to Tavon. Though I couldn't believe she would choose a child over me. I could forgive her a thousand times just as long as she forgives me. My house phone begins to ring and I picked it up quickly.

"Hello?" I say eagerly.

"She's here." Mary said.

"Okay are you about to talk to her?"

"Yes I am."

"Okay call me afterwards and tell me what she says."

"Alright."

Then the line went dead.

Carmen

After sitting in a holding cell for two hours with three other females that were spread out on the floor, a female officer came over and pulled out a piece of paper.

"Carmen Smith." She said loudly. I stand up and she unlocked the cell. I stepped out and she locked the cell back. She took by the arm and escorted to a room with a table and two chairs. She pushed me in and shut the door.

"Sit." She demanded as she pointed to a chair. I sat down and sighed. She sat down across from and looked me in the eye.

"What is this all about?" I ask looking around the small room.

"This is about you and Tavon Holmes?" She said folding her arms. I arch my eye brow at her. She looked very familiar but I couldn't remember where I knew her from.

"What about me and Tavon?"

"You're looking at three years or more." She said ignoring the question.

"What about me and Tavon?"

"I'll let you out of these handcuffs and let you off scot-free and we can forget this all happened. If you leave Tavon alone, or I can make your life a living hell."

"What does Tavon and I have to do with you?"

"Tavon is my son."

The light bulb went off in my head. It was Mary from the hospital, Tavon's mother. I smile and notice what she was trying to do.

"Why do you want me to leave Tavon alone? I'm only making him better."

"No, you're ruining his career but that stops here and now."

"If Tavon wants to be with me then I can't change that. You can try to pull us away from each other but it's not going to change how we feel about each other."

She grinned.

"I'm not going to make him do anything, you are."

"No I am not."

She stood up and leaned into my face.

"Actually you are and you will realize that in a while, when your back is up against the wall and this is the only direction to turn." She said coldly.

CAGED

Tavon

It tore me into pieces finding out Carmen had gotten arrested. I had gone by her condo and the bell hop downstairs told me she was cuffed and put in a police car. What hurt worse than that was when I couldn't find her. Every precinct in her area they said she wasn't in their system. I called up the correctional facilities but she was never booked. I laid on my mother's sofa for a week dying inside. My mom seemed happy but I shrugged it off. My mom said she was doing everything she could to find Carmen but that didn't take away the pain. Carmen's mom Renee had called me to find out where she was and I gave all her all the information I had. We spoke for an hour. She asked me about myself and my intentions with her daughter but I think I stayed on her good side. It took my mom a week to find out where Carmen was, and once I had the information I was on my way to queens to visit her. On the bus ride into Rikers Island I closed my eyes and wished I was superman, so I could break through the barbwire and steel doors to rescue her. When I opened my eyes, I wasn't Clark Kent. I was still Tavon Holmes. After being searched it took almost a half an hour to get on the bus to go to Carmen's building. When I got inside the next building I was searched again, twice, then had to wait twenty more minutes to be called. When I was finally called I sat at a table and waited for Carmen to come into the visiting room. I watched the door on the other side of the room and waited. It opened and women wearing orange jump suits walked through it. Carmen was one of the last in the line. She was still beautiful as always. She saw me and her eyes seem to sparkle but her expression told another story. I stood up and embraced her tightly, then we both sat down. I took her hand and held it gently.

"Are you a'right? I been worried sick about you. My mind been racing with negative thoughts and I couldn't bare it if it were true."

She watched me with a cold look.

"I'm fine." She said with no emotion.

"Did something happen to you?"

"No."

I searched her eyes trying to understand her. We sat there silent for a moment as I tried to figure out why I wasn't feeling any love in our conversation from her side.

"Why did you get arrested?"

"Statutory rape and right about now it's looking true. You should've never came Tavon."

She took her hand back slowly and placed her hand in her lap.

"I'm sorry but I had to see you. I love you Carmen."

She looked down at her lap and played with her fingers.

"Tavon, you have this bright future ahead of you with a contract. Once you sign your name you're scot-free and that life you're going for isn't for me."

"What are you talking about? I already decided to be a pilot, you know that."

"No, don't waste your time. Become a football player, you're so good at it."

"I don't understand where you're coming from. What are you getting at?"

"I can't be with you anymore more."

Her words were like swords and they pierced my heart. I wanted to speak but my voice was stuck in my throat. I wanted to be strong about it but I could feel the tears formulating. Her head was still down.

"You're too young for me and now I realize that. This publicity wouldn't look good when recruiters are watching you at your games."

She finally looked up and saw the tears leaking from my face. She looked away.

"It was a mistake that day in the car. I'm sorry for leading you on this far but it's time we both take a step back and notice where we need to be. I am truly sorry but you have to understand where I am sitting."

"I do understand but I can't live . . . without you."

"Yes you can."

"But I don't want to."

"You have to."

"Give me one good reason why I should."

"Because I'm not divorcing Erin. I'm going to stay with him and work things out."

"And what if it doesn't work out?"

"Then I'm going to continue my life without him."

"But can you continue your life without me?"

She looked at me and I knew she didn't want to leave me but I couldn't understand why she would if she didn't want to.

"Yes I can."

"I . . . thought you loved me."

"I did but all that changed. I don't love you anymore."

The correctional officer yelled fifteen minutes left.

We sat silently for a moment. She couldn't even look me in the eye. Depression was beginning to settle itself deep into my heart.

"What has Erin done for you that I haven't done triple times better, that would make you want to leave me?"

"You're too young you wouldn't understand?"

"Don't give me that bullshit." I said leaning closer to her.

"Can you please not make this hard for me? I've made up my mind."

"Was I not good to you? Is it because I disappeared for a few days? If it is I'm sorry. I just needed to clear my head from Ariel so I can come back to you with no baggage, just me."

"You don't need to explain anymore because it doesn't matter."

"It does matter, you matter to me."

She place her hands back the table and focused on them.

"You know how Erin used to treat you. I would never disrespect you the way he did, or degrade you like you're not important to me. You've gave him his chance and he lost it. Why can't I get a chance to show you how you should be treated? Let me prove to you that I can be better than him."

"Tavon, some decisions in life will seem outrages and it may hurt people but have great outcomes."

"What if this is a mistake?"

"Then I'll learn from it."

"Are you really willing to lose me forever?"

"Tavon it was good while it lasted but now it's time for me to go home to my husband. You were just a fantasy and I don't have time to be chasing after a dream. You're young, you can easily find a beautiful young lady."

"But I want you."

"Want is a desire, and everything you desire you don't need."

Silence crowded us again.

The officer yelled five minutes.

"So I guess this good-bye." She said dropping her head.

"Do you really have no more feelings for me?"

"No."

"Carmen, I love you." I said taking her hand roughly. She turned her head away me.

"I'm begging you not to leave me. I know in your heart you still love me. Please don't make the biggest mistake of your life."

"I love Erin . . . and I have since junior year of high school. I can't leave him. We have too much history together."

"Carmen if you let me walk out of your life I won't turn back. I'll walk away and be gone forever. I will never take you back."

She sat there silently. She looked down into her lap and that was all the answer I needed.

The officer yelled time. I stood up and she looked me in the eyes.

"I wish you the best Carmen. And I pray Erin doesn't hurt you the way you just hurt me."

I turned around and went to the exit. My mind told me to walk away and forget but my heart said to look back at her for the last time and remember her forever. I thought walking away and forgetting seemed easier and painless, but to prove to myself that I would never turn back for her I didn't turn around I just walked out.

Carmen

After getting released Mary escorted me out to the front gate.

"You're doing the right thing." She said smiling. The pain in my chest hurt too much to even pay attention to her. I could still see him through my stinging teary eyes walking away from me. He didn't look back once as he left, but I wish he would have, maybe he would have saw me mouth to him "I love you". As I walked out Erin stood by the parking lot waiting for me. Mary told me I should consider getting back with him. Knowing no man could compete with Tavon, I'd settle for anyone. I walked with him back to his car and he drove me to his house. I got out and he brought me inside the prison that was worse than Rikers Island. As he made dinner he told me how he was a changed man. He promised me that everything was going to be different and he was going to put me first. I didn't speak the entire time. Nothing I could have said would change my situation so I chose to stay quiet. After dinner we went to bed. Erin fell asleep on my chest. I lay in bed awake unable to sleep. I pushed him off me gently and got out of bed. I got his car keys and headed out to Central Park. When I got there I walked down the same path me and Tavon had taken on our date. When I finally got to the part where we took our picture I stopped and took a seat on the park bench. I pulled out my locket and kissed it.

"Oh Tavon if you only knew." I said looking up into the starry sky.

I sat in a room at Rikers similar to one Mary had me in before at the precinct. She stood in front of me with the table between us. She dropped the folder in her hand on the table.

"I spoke with the doctor that did your check up here, and he told me something very interesting about you Carmen." Mary said smiling. I folded my arms.

"He said you were pregnant."

She glanced at me and began to pace the floor.

"Something tells me this baby is Tavon's."

I sighed.

"What of it?"

She giggled.

"Well you haven't told Tavon yet and that gives me the perfect opportunity I need."

I glared at her.

"You see, if I keep you locked up your child will be forced into the system. And if Tavon doesn't know you're pregnant, he wouldn't know to even fight for custody."

"Then I'll tell him." I said rolling my eyes.

"But you cheated on him." She laughed.

"You think Tavon wants to be put in another Ariel situation. Not knowing if the woman he loves is carrying someone else's child. All I have to do is lie about how far along you are in your pregnancy." She said stopping to watch my expression. The disgust written on my face gave her joy.

"Now it's time for you to choose, Tavon or your unborn child. It's your call."

I held my face as I shook my head. This couldn't be happening.

"There are conditions though. When Tavon visits you have to wear a wire, if you tell him about our little deal when you get out I get you arrested for real, and you can't tell Tavon the baby is his until he goes pro."

I looked her in the eye.

"So do we have ourselves a deal?"

I nodded slowly.

For some reason the stars seemed brighter tonight. I walked backed the way I came and drove back to Erin's. When I got back he hadn't moved an inch. I got back in bed and tried to sleep, but I just felt boxed in like a caged animal.

STARTING OVER

Tavon

6 Months Later

I had gotten recruited to college out in Los Angeles. After finishing high school I went straight to college. I couldn't stay home with my mom another minute. All she did was try and talk me into going pro early. Derek had gotten his main chick, Brittany, pregnant and broke up with all his other chicks and was staying faithful. All my other friends didn't stay in contact with me over the months. I was too focused on school for anything else anyway. I laid on my bed finishing up my homework and my phone rang. I picked up.

"Hello?"

"Hey Tay."

"Hey mom."

"I was calling to ask if you wanted to go to a New Year's party with me this year."

"Yeah, sure I'll go."

"Okay, I spoke to your father the other day."

"Oh yeah, how did that go?"

"Okay, he had mentioned you getting married."

"Yeah I was thinking about it before but that's a thing of the past."

"With who? Ariel?"

"No, umm . . . with Carmen."

It had been a while since I spoke her name, and that's how I liked it. It was painful to reminisce about her. A few months ago she use to call but never said anything. After while I stopped answering the phone for her. I guess she had gotten the hint because she stopped calling.

Mom had gotten so quiet on the phone I had almost forgotten we were even talking.

"Well I'm starting dinner so I have to go." She said quickly and then hung up. Talk about being rushed off the phone. A hard knock came to my door and I went to answer. My friend Carlos stood there with a party banner. I shook my head.

"You know I don't go to parties."

"Come on man, just this once. You never get out your room, you need this." He said coming into my room. I chuckle and close the door behind him.

"If I go you're going to talk me into drinking, a girl is going to wanna dance with me, then her boyfriend is going to beat the shit outta me, then I'll be going to class with a busted lip for a week. Thanks, but no."

"I bet you fifty bucks that's not going to happen."

"You never win a bet with me."

"You never know tonight might be my lucky night."

I smile.

"Okay give me ten minutes."

The club was packed out. It seemed like everybody from the college was at the party tonight. The lights flashed on and off over the dance floor. I leaned up against the bar besides Carlos. He knew almost everybody in the club, because every time someone passed by they were waving hi to him. He passed me a cup. I smiled as I looked at him.

"Don't ask what it is. Just drink it. It will help you loosen up a bit." He said after downing his drink.

"You literally make it too easy to win a bet with you."

"Just drink it."

I sighed and shrugged my shoulders.

"What's the worst that could happen?"

I threw it back. It burned my chest as it went down. I coughed. Carlos laughed as he pat my back.

"What the fuck was that?" I said leaning over to catch my breath.

"I call it a "Fuck You Up"." He said in between his laughter.

"Why?" I ask standing up straight.

"Because it fucks you up."

"What the hell is in it?"

"Everything."

I push him playfully.

"Are you trying to kill me?" I asked after I started to breathe normally.

"Just wait until it hits you, you won't even understand what the fuck is going on." We both laugh. A girl walked up to us and begins to rub Carlos chest. She wore a tight fitting strapless dress that stopped at her thighs. The white girl had it going on.

"Hey Carlos, you wanna dance?" She asked pushing up on him. He looked at me.

"Go ahead, I'm gonna stay by the bar." I said waving him away. She took his hand and led him to the dance floor. I grabbed the stool next to me and sat down. The music was great but the flashing lights were giving me a head. I sat the bar for ten minutes and couldn't focus on anything. My vision was a bit blurry, and I was beginning to feel slightly amused.

"Aren't you from one of my classes?" A female asked getting my attention. I hadn't noticed she even sat beside me. I assumed she was from the Islands from her strange accent. She had on a spaghetti strap silky shirt, a mini skirt, and heels with straps the crisscrossed around her ankle. Her orange—like hair was pulled into a bun with long bangs. I turned to face her.

"I'm so fucked right now I wouldn't know." I said laughing. She chuckled.

"Okay, do you at least remember your name?"

"Yeah, I'm Tavon but everybody calls me Tay."

"Hi Tay, I'm Violet."

I held out my hand and she shook it.

"Hi Vi-o-let." I said pronouncing every syllable in her name.

"I would ask you to dance but I don't think that's safe." She said smiling at me.

"I don't think so either."

She scooted her chair over and leaned in closer to me.

"So are you single?"

I sighed.

"Yeah, but I'm not looking for a relationship."

She took my hand and held it.

"Me neither. How about we get out here and go somewhere quieter?"

I nodded. She stood up and pulled me along with her. I didn't realize how wasted I was until I stood up and couldn't walk straight. It was a bit cooler outside but it didn't help sober me up. I knew the school was in walking distance so I just trailed behind Violet. When we got back to the dorms something looked at bit different. The hallway didn't look the same, I was sure of it.

"Where are we going?" I ask. She turned around and put her finger to her lips. She stopped at the next door and pulled out a key.

"Boys aren't allowed in the girl dorms so you have to be quiet." She whispered as she unlocked her door. She pulled me into the dark room and closed the door. The shades on her window were open letting in the moonlight, but I still managed to trip over a few things. She pushed me back on her bed and started to strip. I didn't know if I wanted to go through with this or not but Violet was already naked and unbuckling my pants. I didn't know her, but I was hard and ready to play. She pushed me back and I lay down.

"Don't worry Tay, I'm going to take care of you." She whispered.

I nodded out of reflex but I was still undecided. Before I knew it her mouth went to work and I loved the familiar feeling I hadn't had in so long. Then she climbed on top of me and pulled out her hair. She reached over me to her desk and pulled out a condom then she rolled it on. She leaned on my chest and bounced up and down on me as I held onto her thighs. Her breathing was uneven as her head hung down with her eyes closed. I didn't know how long it lasted but after a while she laid on my chest motionless.

"I really hope you didn't fall asleep on me." She said breathing heavy.

"No, I'm still up."

"Did you enjoy that as much as I did?"

"I think so."

She started laughing making me laugh with her. She rolled over and started to get dressed. I pulled up my jeans and buckled them back up.

"I know you're kinda drunk still, so I'll take you back to your dorm."

I stood up.

"Okay."

After she walked me to the boy's side we stopped at the bottom of the stairs. I leaned against the wall and watched her. She smiled and pulled her hair out her face.

"You look beautiful in the moonlight." I said smiling. She stepped closer to me.

"It was just sex Tay."

"I know, but I was never a one night stand kind of guy."

She giggled.

"Don't tell me you want to be my man."

"Well, no. But we can be friends."

She stood on her tippy toes and kissed my lips.

"I'd like that. Plus I already got a boyfriend."

I laughed.

"What's so funny?" She asked stepping back.

"Nothing, umm does your boyfriend go to college here?"

She nodded.

"Violet." Someone called from a distance. She backed up from me and shook her head.

"As a matter of fact, that's him calling me right now." She said sighing.

"Oh, okay. So are you and him serious?" I ask smiling.

"No not really." She said lifting her eye brow at me.

"Hey Tay, I found you." Carlos said as he approached us.

"Just the guy I wanted to see." I said.

"Why did you leave the party?" He asked eyeing Violet.

"It was getting too crowded." I said looking past him. I saw a guy coming up behind him looking straight at Violet. Everything was falling into place.

"You owe me fifty bucks." I said pulling him beside me.

"Don't tell me you got in a fight." He said throwing his head back.

"Not yet."

"Violet, where the hell have you been?" The guy said grabbing Violet's arm.

"Get the hell off me Daniel." She said yanking her arm back. I pulled her into my chest.

"She has been with me. So who the fuck are you?" I said getting his attention.

"I'm her boyfriend." He said stepping closer.

"Well I'm her new body guard." I say challenging him.

"No he was just kidding." Carlos said stepping in between us.

"Tay chill out." Violet said looking at me. Daniel pushed Carlos aside.

"No Violet, he can't just grab you up like that while I'm standing here. He's a punk ass bitch and I'd fuck him up."

He punched me in my face knocking me over on the stairs. Carlos stood in front of him.

"Okay, you got it man. Damn, now I owe him fifty bucks 'cause of you." Carlos said frustrated. As I lay on the ground I burst into laughter. Any other day I would've got up and beat the shit out of him but it seem so funny. It had to be the liquor still in my system. I wiped my lip from the blood and got up. Daniel stormed off angry with Violet as Carlos helped me to my room. When I finally got into my bed I stared up at the ceiling laughing. It took a while for the senseless humor to fade, and to get some sleep.

Carmen

I was seven months pregnant and my stomach was huge. It looked as though I had a basketball hidden under my shirt. I was at a baby store buying some things I felt I hadn't bought already. Jasmine felt everything I had picked up so far was unnecessary, but not to me. When we finally got outside we rushed to the car. Ever since it hit the news last month about the teacher and student affair reporters had been stalking me. So to avoid the outrages questions of the press, I'd never stay one place too long. I popped my trunk and Jasmine helped me put my things inside. Just as I turned around I saw the crowd of cameras and desperate reporters rushing to my car. I sighed knowing I couldn't make it to the passenger's side in time to get away from them. I held on to Jasmine and she helped me around to get inside. The crowd huddled around me moving with every step I took.

"Is it true Tavon Holmes went away to college to get away from you?" The first reporter said shoving the microphone in my face.

"Fuck off!" Jasmine yelled giving him the middle finger.

"Is it true you had sex with Tavon Holmes without his consent?" Another one yelled. I turned to face them and they got silent.

"Are you saying I raped him?" I asked.

"No, but I am asking."

"No I didn't rape him."

"Was he at legal age?"

"Yes he was."

"Why did you and Tavon Holmes break up?"

I looked at the female reporter and rubbed my belly. I took a deep breath and clenched my jaw. She put her mic to my mouth eager to hear my statement.

"We departed for reasons I can't even explain."

"Is the baby you're carrying Tavon's?"

I quickly turned to my car and opened the door. Jasmine shut it behind me.

"Okay that's enough questions, she's pregnant give her some space." She yelled pushing past them. She got in the driver's seat and pulled off. She helped me get all my things inside my condo then I poured her a drink.

"So does Erin know you still got this condo?" She asked taking a sip.

I shook my head.

"I told him I sold it."

"Why did you lie about it?"

"I need privacy sometimes, and I hate it when he comes over here."

She nodded.

"Okay."

We walked into the living room and sat down. She looked around the room.

"Everything looks pretty much the same, besides the pictures that are missing."

I sighed.

"Yeah, I couldn't even face Tavon's pictures anymore after what I did to him."

She took my hand.

"Carmen, you had no other choice."

"I know."

She finished her drink and placed the cup on the coffee table.

"So did you tell Erin that Tavon is the father?"

I shook my head.

"No, I let him assume it's his."

"Damn girl, you can't do that."

"I'm trying to make us work, but it will only make matters worse if I tell him the truth."

She nodded. She looked at the receipts on the tabled and opened her mouth wide.

"What?" I asked following her eyes. She picked them and went through them.

"Carmen you can't be just spending money like this." She said shoving the receipts in my face. I pushed her hand away.

"What's been going on with you? You never acted like this." She said. I stood and went to my second bedroom I never really used. Jasmine followed in behind me. Baby items filled the middle of the room. Everything was piled up on each other. I sat down in the rocking chair at the window and stared out into the sky.

"My child is going to grow up without knowing its real father . . . so . . . the least I can do is make sure it gets everything it needs. Because I will not allow our child to miss out on anything else." I said wanting to cry. Jasmine ran to my side and embraced me tightly. She cried the tears I couldn't cry anymore. She stood up and wiped her face and smiled. She looked around the room then back at me.

"So let's get started on the baby's room. You only got two more months before it's here."

A Ghost from My Past

Tavon

I didn't really want to go home for thanksgiving but I had already told my mom yes. The plan was to have dinner at Robert's, but I knew dinner was going end with a bang. My mom never got along with my step mom so a disaster was bound to happen. I brought Violet with me since her parents were going on a vacation for the holiday. She turned out to be a lot fun and a best friend, so we were always together like we were joined at the hip. I told her to prepare for the worse thanksgiving of her life, so for just in case we needed a quick getaway we rented a car and drove to Connecticut ourselves. I knocked on the door and Trina answered with a big smile.

"Hey Tay, come on in."

I stared at her suspiciously, because my first thought was she was an imposter. We both stepped in and she closed the door.

"Hi Trina, this is my friend Violet. Violet this is my step mom Trina."

They shook hands and then Trina escorted us to the dining room. Mom was sitting across from dad leaving four available seats. One seat beside the both of them and the two end of the table seats. No matter what no seat was safe. I sat next to mom and Violet took the end of the table seat by Trina that sat next to dad.

Mom and dad smiled at me.

"Hey everybody this is Violet, Violet this is my mom Mary and my dad Robert." I said smiling uncomfortably. She waved hello.

"Hey Violet." Mom said politely.

"Hi." Dad said.

Then the butlers came in and placed the food on the table. They made our plates and we all begin to eat in silence. My dad cleared his throat and smiled at me.

"So son, why haven't you brought Carmen?" He said cheerfully. I glared at him. Even if I was still with her he knew damn well I would never bring her around him.

"We broke up dad. Months ago." I said stuffing my face.

"Sad to hear, I thought you two were . . ."

"Violet, Tavon has told me so much about you." Mom said cutting dad off. I was relieved she did, because I didn't think I could bear talking about it.

"Oh he has." Violet said nudging me under the table. I looked at her and smiled.

"I hope it was nothing but good things." She said smiling.

"Yes, of course they were lovely things. So why haven't you two started dating."

I looked at mom embarrassed. Violet chuckled.

"Well umm relationships complicate things, plus we need to stay focused on school." Violet said nodding.

"Yes, an education important." Trina said smiling at her.

"You didn't seem to take things slow with Carmen." Dad said bluntly. I stared at him coldly.

"Can you stop talking about her, please?" I ask him.

"No I can't. I thought for months I wouldn't see you ever again, miss your wedding, miss your children growing up, everything. So I made a lot of changes for you. Then you come back without the woman you claim to love dearly what the hell happened!" He said as he slammed his fist on the table. I dropped my head into my hand.

"Robert, don't you see he doesn't want to talk about it." Mom said raising her voice.

"I bet you didn't even realize Trina stopped calling you Tavonie." He said standing up.

"Dad, she didn't want to be with me anymore and I wasn't going to beg her to be somewhere she didn't want to be."

Dad stared at me for a moment then sat back down to eat.

"So Violet, do you know what you're doing after college?" Trina asked trying to lighten the mood. Dad and I sat there quietly for the remainder of the night. Before anyone was near finish I excused myself from the table and sat in the living room and dad followed me soon after. He sat across from me and stared at me.

"Son, I am truly sorry. I didn't know . . ."

"I know dad, now let's just drop it." I said cutting him off.

He sighed.

"Well just so you know Trina and I went and got some help from a shrink, and we went to parenting classes. I promise I am going to be there for you for now on. I don't care if you want to a bug collector or a gangsta rapper just as long as I can be in your life."

I nodded.

"I've been waiting for you to say that for so long dad." I said smiling lightly.

When Violet and I finally got to our hotel she was exhausted. She fell asleep once she hit the mattress, but my eyes wouldn't shut for no longer than a millisecond. It had been so long since I thought about Carmen, and she was trespassing in my thoughts again. I was starting to feel that gut wrenching pain again. I got out of bed and took a drive. I ended up where my thoughts were. I was driving aimlessly but subliminally I wounded up here in front of Carmen's building. I looked out the car window into her building lobby. I cut the engine off and got out the car. I went inside and got on the elevator to her floor. When I got off I stared at her door wondering why I even came this far. I put my ear to her door and listened to the lifelessly condo. She was probably sleeping with her hair over her face like she always did. This time though, Erin was the one moving it from her face as she slept peacefully on his chest. I backed up from the door and parted ways. She got what she wanted and I promised myself I wouldn't turn back for her, but in my heart she was above all things and I'd take her back before she could apologize.

Carmen

Thanksgiving with Erin's family wasn't entirely boring. I just wished it hadn't lasted as long as it did. Since I couldn't sleep I decided to go to my condo. I was always restlessly at Erin's house, because it only reminded me why I left. He had fixed the house up from the shambles I left it in, but it was still the same hell hole. I got out of bed and slipped in my sweat pants and sneakers. As I turned around to get my car keys off the night stand Erin was sitting up. I jumped in fear not realizing he was up. I held my chest as I exhaled deeply.

"You scared me."

"Where are you going?" He asked completely ignoring me.

"I can't sleep, so I was going for a drive."

"Are you sure that's all because you seem to take a drive every night."

I dropped my head and sighed.

"I know it's going to take time to adjust but it's only going to take longer if you don't give a little effort."

"I am making an effort but these fast changes are stressing me out, and I'm pregnant so my moods swings are only making things worst. So you're going to have to bear with me."

"I'm trying to but you hardly ever tell me how you're feeling and you won't let me touch you."

"After I have the baby we will have the rest of our lives to touch but right now I just need my space."

"And I respect your feelings but how about tonight you don't go for a drive and let me hold you." He said sincerely. I nod and take off my sneakers to get back into bed. He wrapped his arms around me and rubbed my belly. Soon he was sound asleep. I removed his arms from around me and snuck out the house. I got in my car and went to my condo. I could tell this time around Erin had changed but, I wasn't over Tavon yet and I didn't want to open a door without closing the last one. When I got home I went to baby's room. I found out I was having a girl so Jasmine and I painted the room lilac and pink. We put life size princess stickers on the walls and ceilings. We set up the crib and the swing set, filled up both toy chests, put away the baby clothes in the dresser and closet, and put the diapers I brought in the corner of the room. I sat in the rocking chair for a while rubbing my stomach, then crawled up in my bed. I held onto the pillow Tavon use to lie on and cried. I knew if he found out why I left him he would understand and take me back, but I couldn't be too sure. The day he walked away from he never looked back just reassure that I had made up my mind. He walked away too easily. He was over me. He had to be and I needed to move on. I cried myself to sleep.

When I woke up I jumped in the shower. As I got out Erin called my cell phone. I tossed my phone on the bed and got dressed. I tried on a few shirts but none would cover the bottom of my belly. So I decided to go shopping. I grabbed my pea coat and scarf as I called Jasmine. I told her where to meet me at Yonkers mall and made my way there. I made it to the store before Jasmine could so I was already trying on a sweater in the fitting room. I looked at myself in mirror and did a 360. The material was felt soft on my skin and it covered my belly. I had to get this sweater. I stared at myself in the mirror and rubbed my stomach.

"Anutie Carmie! Anutie Carmie!" I heard Anthony and Jordin calling me in union. I smiled and came out the fitting room. They ran to me hugging my leg. I put my arms over them and gave them both a kiss.

"Hey you guys, where's your mommy?" I asked searching the store for Jazz.

"She's outside talking to Tay." Anthony said pointing to the door. My heart stopped. I looked at the door and there he was. He wore a gray Nike Tech Pack Bonded Fleece Bomber jacket over his white shirt, and black jeans. He was smiling showing off his handsome features as he spoke with Jazz. I put my hand on my chest and tried to breathe. The butterflies fluttered in my heart. I so badly wanted to run to him, jump into his arms, kiss his lips, tell him everything, and beg him to take me back. It's just that my legs wouldn't move.

"We were walking from the parking lot and we saw him at the food court so he walked us here." Jordin said. I nod. His smile soon faded. Jazz pointed into the store and his eyes followed. Once he looked in we had direct eye contact with one another. He didn't look happy to see me but I was satisfied with just looking in his eyes. He walked in the store with Jazz watching me with every step. He stopped in front of me and tucked his hands in his pants pocket. My mind raced with some many memories of us.

"Hey." I said under my breath.

His eyes studied my body quietly making me uncomfortable. I knew he had to be thinking about my baby because his eyes stopped on my belly for a brief moment. Then he looked up at me.

"Carmen, I would've never thought I'd run into you here . . . and pregnant."

I put my head down wondering if I should tell him about everything.

"Life is full of surprises." I said looking back up.

"Yeah, it is . . . but the only surprises that are coming from you are negative. You never cease to amaze me."

Jazz took Anthony and Jordin by the hand and led them out the store to give us privacy.

"I see you're not going to hold back on me."

"Are you still with Erin?"

"Yes."

"After everything you did to better yourself, you still settle for less."

"I'm so happy to see you." I said stepping closer. His insults only showed how much I really hurt him, but I knew better than to hurt him worse by playing his childish games.

Tavon

I could tell by the look on her face she was happy to see me and deep inside I felt the same way. I just didn't want her to know. How she left hurt me, and I just wanted her to know how I felt.

"Did you ever go to college?" She asked smiling her same beautiful warming smile.

"Yes, I did and I'm passing. My tutor actually teachers me because it's her job."

"That's good."

I could tell her life was perfect. She was happily married, pregnant, with no worries and the more she smiled the angrier I became.

"So, Erin hasn't cheated on you lately?" I ask trying to provoke her.

"No, we're making it just fine. How's your dad?"

"He's great."

"And your step mom?"

"Better."

"Does she still call you Tavonie?"

I chuckled then regretted it. I started to get mad at myself for giving in to her kindness and joyful jokes.

"No she doesn't." I said with an attitude. She stepped closer to me. Her sweet breath brushed across my face. I inhaled her wonderful fragrance. She was glowing in front of me, even with the large stomach.

"I've missed you Tavon."

I was taken aback by her bluntness. She couldn't have just said that.

"What?" I asked confused. Before I could realize her arms were around my neck. Her body was pressed up against mine. She smothered her face into my chest. I wanted to hug her back and lift her up into my arms, but she was no longer my woman. I stood there motionless until her grip loosened. I took a step back. I didn't really know what to say. I turned around swiftly and rushed out the store using all the power in my body not to turn around. I walked pass Jasmine quickly and continued down the street towards the food court.

"Tavon." Violet said grabbing my attention. I looked up and walked over to her and my mother. I smiled as I took a seat at their table. They both looked at me oddly. I tried to maintain my smile and pretend everything was fine.

Carmen

I watched him leave the store with my heart. I couldn't speak as he I watched him leave again in my mind. He just proved that he was done with me by walking out. I walked back into the fitting room and put my back to the door and slid down it onto the floor. The tears fell before I could I even understand the feeling I was having. A knock came to the door.

"Carmie, are you okay?" Jazz said. I ignored her. The baby started to move around, I rubbed my belly.

I've tried my best but he doesn't want to be with me anymore. I'm so sorry that I hurt your daddy this bad. But I won't mess up no more. Not like this. You will be able to depend on me for anything. Tavon would love you. He would love you so much. He just doesn't know about you yet, and I can't tell him. But when I do, he will show you how much he really loves you. You just have to trust mommy on this one. Just give me some time.

Tavon

After spending a day with mom, Violet and I headed back to the hotel. Violet had been acting differently the whole afternoon, but I didn't want to bring up in front of mom. I sat on the bed as Violet got undressed.

"Violet, what's wrong?"
She looked at me.
"Who's Carmen to you?"
I arched my eye brow.
"She's just an ex-girlfriend."

"Your dad didn't seem to think so."

"Me and Carmen broke up a few months before I started college that's it."

"So you didn't propose to her?"

I sighed.

"Where is this going Violet?"

"I just want to know who she is to you."

"She's my past."

"Do you still love her?"

"No."

She put her hands on her hips.

"You're lying."

"Why are you even asking about her? I don't ask you about your ex-boyfriends."

"I want to know the real reason why you don't do relationships, because I don't want to be your best friend forever."

"We're not dating because you don't even trust me."

"I do trust you, but you never tell me about your life without closing up on me."

I got up and headed for the door. I'd rather not argue.

"Where are you going?" She asks sighing.

"It doesn't matter because I won't close up on you after I'm gone." I said grabbing my jacket off the back of the chair. She grabbed my arm. I stopped and threw my head back as I sighed. She stood in front of me and grabbed my face and forced me to look at her.

"I don't want you to leave, I'm sorry okay."

I nod.

"Okay."

She kissed me.

"I was just freaking out because your mom told me she played a big role in your life. So I was beginning to think she still had a hold on you and that was the reason why you didn't want to start a relationship with me."

She kissed me once more then went to take a shower. Why the hell would my mother tell her about Carmen? I pull out my cell phone and call my mom.

"Hello?"

"Mom, why did you tell Violet about Carmen?"

She sighed.

"She needed to know."

"No she didn't. Carmen and I are history, so keep your thoughts about her to yourself."

"Carmen is standing in your way even though you two broke up. She's stopping you from getting involved with someone else so I was just giving Violet a heads up."

I rubbed my temples.

"I want you to stay out of my love life mom. And stop talking about Carmen because you don't even know her."

"I know she filled your head up with fake dreams."

"Good-bye mom."

I hung up before she could say anything else. I tossed my phone on the nightstand and lay on the bed. Wondering about Carmen, remembering how she hugged me like she used to.

"I've missed you Tavon." She had said it with so much passion, but why. I promised myself I would never get involved with her again. When she left the first few months was devastating. I didn't think I could ever feel whole again. Now I will never deny my love for her, but I could never open myself like that again for no one. Not even for Carmen, but I would just hate myself forever for it.

No News is Good News

Carmen

7am

My cell phone began to ring waking me up. I rub my hand across the bed searching for the phone. I sit up and look around and see the phone on my night stand. I pick it up.

"Hello?" I say groggy.

"Carmen! Have you seen the news?" Jasmine yelled panicky. I wiped my eyes and looked at the clock.

"Yeah I have, because it's a Saturday morning and I'm pregnant but ready to go to a job that I don't have." I said putting my feet on the floor as I yawn.

"Wake the hell up and go check the damn news." She said ignoring my sarcasm.

I stand up and head to the living room. I picked up the television remote and cut it on. Then a knock came to my door. I sigh and get up.

"Weather has dropped rapidly for the beginning of December . . ." The weather man said on the television.

"Who the hell is at my door this early?" I said approaching the door.

"No! Don't . . . it" Jasmine said getting cut off by the incoming call beep. I look at the phone and see Erin's face.

"Hold on." I said to Jazz then switched to the other line.

"Hello?"

"Where the hell are you Carmen?" Erin asked with an attitude. I looked at the phone then put back to my ear.

"Why are you mad?"

"Oh you haven't heard?" He said.

"Hold on." I said. I opened the door and the news reporters flashed their cameras and shoved their microphones in my face.

"Tavon Holmes, the student that was having an affair with one of his teachers . . ." I heard the reporters on the TV say. I turned around to see what they were talking about. The video of me going to my car that day came on.

"We departed for reasons I can't even explain." My voice said echoing from the TV.

"A baby could be too much pressure for a football star." The reporter said smiling on the TV. I started to hyperventilate. I turned back to the door.

"Are you pregnant with Tavon Holmes baby?"

"Are you torn between who's the father of your child?"

"Did Tavon Holmes leave after you told him you were pregnant?"

They yelled question on top of question. I looked down and saw my newspaper on the floor. "Tavon Holmes Jr. or Erin Smith Jr." was the headline. My phone slipped from grasp. I slammed my door shut. Who knows what Tavon was thinking and what was Mary going to do?

Tavon

My cellphone rang. I woke up and reached over Violet for my phone on my desk.

"Hello?" I said after clearing my throat.

"Tavon, how you seen the news or New York Times?" mom said.

I wiped the sleep from my eyes.

"No."

"Oh, okay. Has Carmen called you?"

I sigh.

"Why would Carmen call me?"

"Umm . . . no reason."

I sit up and look at the time.

"Is there something going on?" I asked curious.

"No, not at all."

"Okay." I said slowly. I got out bed and went to my computer.

"But umm, if Carmen calls . . . never mind. I'll talk to you later." She hung up. I put the phone down. I cut it on and waited for it to load. My phone began to ring again. I answered quickly.

"Hello?"

"Yo, my dude have you seen the news? Well you are out in Los Angeles but this has to have gotten to you." Derek said overexcited.

"What's going on, on the news that got everybody up early calling me?"

"You gotta see it to believe it."

My computer finally finished loading and I got on the web. I pulled up the New York Times website and my eyes widened.

"Tavon Holmes Jr . . . , what are they talking about?" I ask confused.

"Their saying Carmen is pregnant and the baby maybe yours."

I shook my head still not understanding.

"She can't be pregnant with my baby. Can she?"

"She is eight months."

"It can't be mine. The last time we were together . . . it just doesn't add up." I said trying to remember the last time we were together.

"Hey baby what's going?" Violet said sitting up. I rubbed my temples tuning her out. I couldn't remember. If the baby was mine, Carmen would've told me. She wouldn't keep something this important from me. Plus when we broke up she got with Erin right after so it's impossible to even say that the baby was mine.

"She can't be pregnant with my kid. She can't be." I said deep in thought.

"Someone is pregnant with your baby?" Violet said walking over to me.

"If the baby is yours, what are you going to do?" Derek asked.

Violet started to get dressed. I sighed.

"I'm going to call you back D." I said to Derek then hung up.

"Why are you getting dressed?"

"Don't talk to me." She said.

"Why are you leaving?" I ask standing up.

"Because of her." She said paying me no attention.

"What does that mean?"

"I thought I could do this, you know wait for you to come around. But I can see that you're not, so whats the point of wasting my time on you."

"You said you didn't want a relationship."

"That's how I felt before I got to know you. I changed my mind. I don't want to share you with anyone."

"From day one I said I didn't want any strings attached because I didn't want to be tied down."

"Im not trying to tie you down, I just asking you to be faithful."

"I am faithful."

"And love me, that's not so hard."

"Yes it is very hard to love."

"Well if it's that hard let me make it easy for you."

She walked to the door. I took her hand gently. She looked back at me.

"I'm not going to run after you if you leave. You'll just walk out and that'll be it."

She turned around.

"I don't want to walk out on you." She said wiping her tears before they could run down her face.

"Then don't."

She embraced me tightly and shoved her face into my chest.

Carmen

I sit in the living room of Erin's house on the sofa while he stood at the window. I knew he was angry because this morning's shocking news. I was still deciding if I wanted to tell him the truth or lie about it all.

"When were you going to tell me or were you going to keep it to yourself." He said as he continued to stare out the window.

"I was going to . . . let you believe what you wanted."

He looked at me briefly with sadness then went back to staring out the window.

"Would you rather have me crush the beautiful dreams you were setting for my unborn child and yourself as a father?" I said looking at the floor.

"So you would have let me believe for years that this child was mine?"

I didn't respond. I knew I made the wrong decision to not tell him the truth.

"Well, I already knew." He said.

"For how long?" I ask looking back at him.

"Since the day you told me you were pregnant. You see, if the baby was mine you would have given birth in September. Here it is December, we had sex in January. Did you forget?"

"How come you didn't say anything?"

"Maybe I just wanted to believe that it was. But at least you didn't lie about it now. When were you going to tell me about the condo? I remember you saying you sold it months ago."

"I wasn't."

"So I guess you weren't going to tell me anything. Carmen I've changed for you and you don't seem to care."

I remembered the days when I felt the same way.

"Does it hurt?" I asked seeing how the tables turned.

"Yes it does."

"Good, because that's exactly how I used to feel."

He turned around and looked me in the eyes.

"Feels like you have nothing else to give?"

He nodded.

"Don't ever make me feel that type of way again."

He nodded.

"I promise I won't."

He walked over to me and took my hand then helped me off the sofa. We walked to the door together and the way I used to feel about Erin many years ago came rushing back. He looked at me and I smiled.

"No matter what the test results say the baby is my mine. Now are you ready."

I nod. He grabbed the knob and I took a deep breathe. He opened the door and crowd of reporters threw questions around. Erin gave my hand a squeeze.

"Erin, is it true the baby is not yours?"

"It is not true, the baby girl my wife Carmen Smith is having is mine."

Who has Skeletons?

Tavon

Christmas was three days away and I was dreading the day's arrival. Violet and I had come down early to New York for the New Year Eve's party my mom invited me to. I had dropped Violet off at the hotel while I went to surprise my mother. I got in the door and crept to her room. I pushed her door open slowly hoping she wouldn't notice me until I was already near her. I looked in and she wasn't in her room. Papers were spread all over bed. I walked inside to see what was going on. All the papers were unpaid bills that mom had accumulated over the years. I always knew my mom was in debt, but not like this. Credit cards, clothing stores, medical bills. You name it and she had it. Something thumped in the kitchen making me turn my head towards the door. I walked to the living room and overheard mom on the phone.

"You're not worried because you got what you wanted but what about me . . . I told you if he wasn't working by now you'd have to pay up . . . You haven't kept your side of the deal . . . I don't care what you've been going through. Yeah I saw the news . . . If I tell her how you got her set up you think she'll want you . . . Yeah exactly . . . well if you tell Tavon he'll still be my son, but she won't be your wife."

I stepped into the kitchen.

"Tell me what?"

She jumped back quickly holding her chest.

"I'm going to have to call you back." She said then hung up the phone.

"Tavon, you scared me. I didn't know you were coming this early."

"I know. I wanted to surprise you."

"Well that sure was a surprise."

"Yeah." I sighed and continued. "I was just in your room, and what are all those overdue bills on your bed?"

"What were you doing in my room?"

"Mom, I didn't know you were in debt like that."

"Well, taking care of a kid starts to add up."

"Some of them were hospital bills for you, what were those about?"

"Don't worry yourself about it, they are my problems. So, are you hungry?"

"No, I'm not. I'm concerned about you mom."

"This is why I never told you about it."

"These types of problems you don't keep to yourself."

"I'm a grown woman I don't need you worrying about me."

"And who were you on the phone with?"

"None of your business."

"Because it sounds like you were blackmailing someone."

"Oh, so you're going through my stuff and listening in on my calls."

"I just want to know what's going on."

"Tavon you're crossing the line. I'm your mother you need to stay in your place."

"What are you hiding?"

"I'm not hiding anything."

"Then why are you getting defensive?"

"I'm no longer having this conversation with you."

"Why is it so hard for you to tell me what's going on?"

"Tavon that is enough!" She yelled. "If you were really worried about me you would have already went pro."

I looked at her confused.

"What does me going pro has to do with anything?"

"Right now, you won't understand but in time you will."

Nothing she said made any sense to me. She opened the fridge and began to pull out food to make preparations.

"I'm only trying to help."

She sighed.

"Tavon, just go pro. If not for you . . . for me."

"Okay mom, I'll do the sign ups. But I still don't think it's going to help."

I turned and walked out. I had to go buy an outfit for the New Year's Eve party and Derek was probably already there waiting for me.

I stood in front of the mirror wearing a black suit, black buttoned up shirt, and a red tie. The guy from the store checked the suit and measured it up as I stood there. Derek sat in the chair behind reading a magazine

"What could she be hiding though?" I asked continuing our conversation.

"I don't know bro, just watch out because I think the reason why she wants you to go pro it because of the money."

I nodded.

"I think that too, but I know my mom and she's not like that. At least I think she's not."

"I'm only going by the obvious. But maybe you need to realize that your mother always been a shady person."

I cut my eye at him.

"No she's hasn't."

"Keep lying to yourself then. I'm just saying you want to be a pilot, but your mom wants you to be a football player. What mother would strip their child of their dreams?"

"She has her reasons."

"Yeah her reason is to keep you closer to her. If you were a pilot you would always be traveling never settling in one place. So that means she won't be able to control you or your money, but if you're a football player . . . that's just a seasonal thing you'd come home all the time."

I looked at him through the mirror.

"You really believe she could be after my money?"

He nodded.

"Maybe." I said unconvinced. He looked up from the magazine.

"Maybe you need to ask your dad how your mother was when he went pro."

"He wasn't around."

"Maybe there's a reason why." i nodded in agreement.

The guy stood up and picked up his measuring tape.

"Okay come back in three days it should be done by then."

I nodded.

After I finished up at the store Derek and I departed and went our separate ways. I picked up Violet and we went to a restaurant for dinner. We didn't really speak until our waiter came with our food.

"You seem kind of distant tonight, you alright?" Violet said pulling me from my thoughts.

"Umm . . . yeah I'm fine."

I continued to eat.

"So I think it's time you meet my parents."

I looked at her.

"Huh?"

"Well, I've met yours so I thought . . ."

"I don't know about that." I said shaking my head.

She clenched her jaw.

"Why not?"

"I really don't feel like arguing." she put her fork down on the table.

"We're not I just want to know why not."

"I can sense you're getting angry so let's leave it alone." i said glancing up at her then continuing to eat.

"No let's not."

I sigh and rub my temples.

"You're not even trying to get us anywhere."

"What happened to the girl at the party that night? I liked her much better."

"Oh so you only like it when I'm drunk and horny."

I closed my eyes and regretted ever saying anything.

"No I wasn't saying that."

"Well that night isn't that what I was, drunk and horny?"

I dropped my head in my hands. She waved her hand for the waiter and he walked over.

"Is there something I can do for you?" He asked politely.

"Yes, can I get the strongest liquor you serve here?" She said glaring at me.

"Right away." He trailed off into the back of the restaurant. I prayed she wouldn't do anything outrages. He came back with a cup on his tray. He placed it in front of her.

"Would you like anything else?" He asked looking at me then back at her. She picked up the glass and downed it like water. She exhaled and cleared her throat.

"Yes, can you bring me two more?" She said smiling. He nodded and walked away. She fluffed her hair and leaned forward over the table.

"If you want I can drop my fork under the table and give you the best blow job you've ever had."

I shook my head.

"Violet, please can you stop."

"I'm doing what you want me to do." She said flicking her tongue at me. The waiter came back with two more drinks and placed them on the table.

"Will that be it?" He asked looking only at me.

"Check please." I said going into my pocket. He nodded and left. Violet gulped down the two extra drinks. She threw her head back and begins to fondle herself. I threw sixty bucks on the table and left. I walk down the street zipping up my coat. I stopped at the street corner and waited for the light to change.

"Tavon!" I heard Violet yelling behind. I turn around watch her approach me. I dug my hands in my pocket.

"What do you want me to do? Not care about, not love you. Well I can't. I want to make you happy but I don't know how to. Won't you just tell me how to be the right woman for you? Just tell me and I will be her." She said begged. Tears ran down her cheeks.

"Violet, you can't be the woman I want because she's not someone you can just mimic. And even if you could, why would you? Because that means I wouldn't love you, I'd only love what you've become and I wouldn't want you to live like that."

She put her hand over her mouth and tried to hold in her sobs.

"I am uncontrollably in love with someone else. I've been trying for months now to get over her by forgetting and moving on but it doesn't help. And now that I can admit that to myself I know I can't be with you the way you want me to. I don't want to hurt you anymore by holding onto you. So I'm going to buy you a ticket back to college, okay."

She nodded. I wiped the tears from her face and pulled her into me. She held me tightly and wept.

"I want you to take care of yourself Tay." She said into my chest. I nodded.

"I always do."

It had been a few days since Violet left but I wish she would have stayed. The day I had been wishing would never come was here. It was Christmas, my birthday, and the worst day of my life. I didn't want to think about Carmen but this whole day was based on me and her. All I could remember was that night we spent together and I hated my thoughts for torturing me. After sitting around half the day cursing at myself I went to Derek's apartment. His girlfriend was out doing some shopping for the baby so it left us with nothing to do but stare at each other. I lay on his love seat looking everywhere but in Derek's direction. His eyes were piercing and I couldn't take looking at him.

"Why aren't you out doing something?" he asked slouching back on the sofa across from me.

"I don't feel the Christmas joy this year, i just wish this day would hurry up and be over."

"Come on man, it's your birthday."

"I'd rather not celebrate this year."

He sat up and leaned his elbows on his knees.

"It's about Carmen isn't it?" he asked.

I shook my head in denial.

"No, hell no. I ain't worried about her."

He sighed and sat back as he rubbed his legs.

"Okay, whatever you say."

I sat up and rubbed my head before I looked at him.

"Alright, she's been on my mind all day. Just a year ago we were perfect and now we don't even communicate. She's pregnant by her husband and happy while I'm afraid commit to anyone."

He chuckled.

"I knew you weren't over her."

I slouched back.

"Yes, I was over her. I was in college and I was focused then I saw her and she been stuck in my brain ever since. I try to forget about her but somehow she keeps popping back up."

"Then stop trying to forget her and go get her."

I shook my head.

"Naw man, she hurt me."

"You sound like a female."She hurt me", so fucking what. She loved you Tay I mean she really loved you. So I know she must be regretting her decision."

"No she doesn't."

He threw a couch pillow at me. i smiled lightly.

"For real man, she loved you. No woman would ever quit her job for a guy she didn't truly care about. Now she probably has her reasons on why she broke it off with you but we all know how Dean Smith used to treat her so there is no way in hell she wants to be with him."

I dropped my head in my hands.

"So what do i do?"

He sighed.

"Well you can start by finding out why she broke up with you so you can resolve the issue. Then next time you see her . . . put your cards on the table and tell her how you feel."

I looked at him.

"And how you know that's going to work."

"I don't, but it's worth a try."

I nod.

"She's worth a try." I say laying back down on the love seat.

When I finally got home I was happy mom was out. We hadn't been on good terms since I told her I was dropping out of college. So we did the best to avoid each other. Just as I laid down my cell phone rang. I looked at the number and didn't believe what I saw. This house number couldn't be calling me. My heart stopped as I answered. I put the phone to my ear and listened to the dead silence. I had almost forgotten how to speak.

"Hello?"

Carmen

"So have you decided on what you're wearing to the New Year's Eve party?" Jasmine asked me over the phone. I lay in the bed at Erin's house.

"Yeah, I'm going to wear my pink cashmere sweater that folds at the top and hangs off my shoulders with a plain black dress skirt that stops at my knees."

"Okay, that sounds cute."

"It's the most comfortable thing I could fine that was decent enough."

"Well, you are pregnant. I don't think anyone would be expecting you to be too flashy. I mean come on, you can give birth any day now."

I nodded in agreement.

"You're right about that."

I heard Erin pulling up in the drive way. I peeked out the curtains and watch him take bags out the backseat of his car.

"Okay Erin's here, so I'm going to call you later on."

"Okay, bye babe."

"Bye." I hung up and went downstairs to greet him. As he shut the door behind himself I came down stairs. He held a few bags in his hand. I wrapped my arms around him and brushed my lips against his. He smiled.

"Hey honey, how was your day?" He asked walking to the living room. I followed behind him.

"It was good and yours?"

He placed his bags on the coffee table.

"Great. I bought some new baby stuff this afternoon."

I clapped in excitement.

"But you can't open anything until the baby is born."

I fold my arms and pout. He kissed my forehead.

"Why not?" I said sitting on the sofa. He sat beside me.

"Because that's a surprise for the baby."

"I want something."

He stood up suddenly and held out his finger.

"I've already got you something."

He got down on one knee as he went into his pocket. I knew what he was doing. It was no surprise that he wanted to call off the divorce. In a way I wanted to call it off too, but I was trapped between a rock and a hard place. Yes, Tavon had moved on and was over me but only because he didn't know the truth. If I told him the truth I would go to jail and risk losing my child to the system. Since I held the truth from him so long he probably wouldn't believe me, and how could I put him in another situation like Ariel did. I couldn't hurt him anymore; I didn't have the strength to.

"Carmen Smith, I know I had lost sight of what I had in the past but I'm ready to start over. I have done wrong but I want to make them right again. So will you like to renew our vows?" He said taking my hand.

I started at him blankly. I knew taking this step would force me to never turn back for Tavon. If I took this route, I would never tell him about his child . . . but he needed to live his life to the fullest. Mary was right; a child would hold him back from his goals. Maybe it was for the best.

"Yes Erin, I want to renew our vows." I said putting on million dollar smile. He slid my wedding band on finger and hugged me.

"Trust me, you won't regret this." He said in my ear.

He kissed me sweetly and tucked my hair behind my ear. I rubbed the side of his face as he stared at me intently. He stood up and pulled out his phone.

"I'm going to call up my parents and tell them the good news."

I nodded.

"Okay." he gave my hand a squeeze then walked in to the kitchen. I lifted my hand in the air and sighed as I looked at my wedding band. My eyes shifted to the coffee table and locked on my car keys. I picked them up and headed out the door to my car. I sped off hoping Erin hadn't realized I was gone yet. After an hour and a half I drove into my building parking lot and went upstairs to my condo. Once I got in the door I felt the wave of depression sweep over me as I walked pass my living room to my daughter's room. I ran my fingers over the back of my sofa. When I got to her room I stood at the doorway and leaned against the door frame. Her room was beautiful. It was pink with lilac trimming, life-size princess stickers covered the walls, the sunset and butterflies were painted on the ceiling, and her belongs were neatly put away. I closed her door and went to my bedroom. I opened my closet and pulled down the box on the top shelf. I brought it to my bed and dumped everything out. The pictures of Tavon and I, and Tavon's clothes was spread out on my bed. I lay on top of it all. I picked up the picture of us at the park and held it to my chest. His cologne still smelt fresh on his clothes. I ran my hand across the bed and felt the small jewelry box full of love and heartache. I sat up and brought it to my lap. I opened it gazed at my necklace that held my locket and engagement ring from Tavon. The stitches that held my heart together was beginning to rip open. I closed the box quickly and placed it back on the bed. I looked at the house phone and picked it up. I dialed the all too familiar number that was forbidden and put my hand over the receiver. I had to hear his voice, just once more.

"Hello." he said with hesitation. I closed my eyes and listened to his uneasy breathing.

"Carmen, are you there?" he asked.

"Yeah I'm here." I said wishing I was strong enough to actually talk to him.

"I just was calling to hear your voice again before I . . . let you go." I whispered.

"Carmen, if you're there please talk to me." he begged.

"I know not telling you is one of the biggest mistakes I'll ever make, but hopefully you'll fulfill your dreams with no pressure."

"Please talk to me."

"I'm truly sorry. I love you Tavon, forever and always."

I hung up. I hadn't noticed I was crying until the tears dripped onto my arm. I wiped my face and grabbed my keys as I stood up. I was ready to say goodbye this time. I was sure of it. I took the spare keys to my condo with me. On my way back home to Erin I dropped by my bank. I put both my keys to my condo in a safe deposit box with intentions to not come back for them. I'd keep the condo because I didn't have the strength to give it up, but mostly because Tavon would always have a secret place in my heart. I didn't get a chance to get out of my car before Erin was at the front door waiting for me. As I approached him I could read worry all over his face.

"Where did you go?" he asked stepping aside. I walked in.

"I needed some air."

He shut the door behind me.

"It took you almost six hours to get some air."

I kissed his lips.

"Don't worry Erin, I won't disappear anymore. I promise."

He nodded and pulled me closer to him.

PARTY CRASHERS

Carmen

10:45 pm

New Year's Eve

The party was finally starting to pick up. The Deejay began to play party music and picked up the tempo. Erin was the host and was keeping everyone on their toes. Most of the guests were beginning to arrive all at once while Jazz and I sat a table far from the crowd of noise. She sipped on an apple martini and I had apple juice. Jazz was having a great time but any time would be great to her when she didn't have to watch her children. She had left her husband home with the kids for the night to hang out with me.

"So just get things cleared up, I am going to be in the delivery room with you right?" Jazz asked gulping down the rest of her drink.

I giggled.

"Well my mom is coming over to my house tomorrow so she'll be here when i go into labor so she'll be in the room. Erin said he wanted to be in the room but only two people can be in the delivery room with me."

She waved her glass in the air at the waitress and rolled her eyes.

"Well, since i respect your mother i ain't going to throw her out so it only leaves Erin. sorry but he will be in the waiting room."

I laughed.

"Well you take that up with him."

The waitress finally made it over to us and dropped off two glasses.

"You know I will." She said sternly. I laughed knowing she was serious about it. As I scanned the room my eyes stopped at the door. I felt a cold chill of fear overcome me. I pulled my hair over my face trying to hide from the angel and devil that walked in.

"What are you doing?" Jazz said after finishing off the two drinks the waitress just gave her.

"Mary and Tavon just walked in."

She swiftly turned around in her seat to look. I put my head on the table hoping Mary wouldn't notice me. I knew if Tavon saw me he would come over to talk to me and I was okay with that, but if Mary saw me talking to him I didn't know what would happen.

"That's Mary." Jazz said sizing her up.

"She aint got shit on me." she said staring at her. I grabbed her hand.

"Please dont start nothing." she snatched her hand from me.

"What the fuck she goning to do? Get me arrested . . . by the time back up gets here I'd already have that bitch bloody."

"Did you forget that I could lose my child to the system?" I ask hoping that would persuade her not to get hype. She turned around to look at me.

"Well if you tell him right now that he's the father what could she do." I picked my head up off the table.

"No, I've decided not to tell him." she sat back in her chair.

"And why the hell not?" she said with an attitude. I looked away from her.

"Dont tell me you trying to stay with Erin, because you said that this was only temporailary." she said starting to raise her voice.

"We've decided to renew our vows."

"With Erin? Did you bump your head and get amnesia?"

I looked at her.

"No."

"Then your going to take him back after all the shit he did to you." her attitude was starting to piss me off.

"He cheated, I cheated we forgave each other and now we moved past that. he's not the same guy he used to be he's changed."

"I wouldn't believe that shit if it was a tenth commandment."

"This is not your life Jazz, its mine and I might still want and probably need Tavon but if being with Tavon means life time of pain and misery for our child then I chose Erin. So either your going to support me or leave me alone, your decision."

She exhaled deeply and tried to calm down.

"Carmie, I've never said I don't support your decision because I do. But I will not stand around watch you get hurt because that wouldn't make me a good sister. I love you and thats why I won't let you settle for less than you deserve. Now I don't care what the hell you have to say because you know I'm damn right about this. So you sit here and I'm going to go get Tavon for you and I want you to talk to him."

I watched her stand up.

"Now I'm not going to tell him anything about your situation because its not my place to, but I am going to tell him to come over here. So if you decide to talk to him or not that is totally up to you."

She turned around walked towards him. I love her and I knew she was only doing what she believed was best for me. I watched her appraoch him and exchange hugs. Before she could point in my direction his eyes were already on me. He smiled at me and walked over. I played with my fingers as he sat across from me where Jazz had been.

"Hey." he said smiling showing his deep dimples. I nodded.

"Hi."

"You look beautiful." I glanced at him.

"I'm pregnant."

"Which makes you look even better." I sigh.

"Tavon, what is this about?" he reached for my hand and I sat them on my lap away from him.

"Carmen I miss you." i looked in his eyes. i knew what he was about to say.

"Tavon please dont." i begged.

"No, let me finish. i love you and i want you to be with me." i put my hand on my forehead and covered my eyes.

"Why are you doing this to me?" i asked trying my best not to break down in tears.

"I know its been months and you're pregnant but I'm not the same young boy you knew. I've matured."

"I cant Tavon."

"Why not?"

"Erin and I decided to renew our vows." he sat there quietly for a moment.

"Why did you break up with me?"

"Tavon, some things are better left alone."

He took my hand from my face and held it tightly.

"I love you, shouldnt that be enough."

"I'm married." i said looking everywhere excpect at him.

"That wasnt problem before."

"I'm pregnant."

"About that, we never got talk about it. how do you know he's the father?"

"Because . . . i just do."

"Carmen . . . look at me." he said softly. i looked at him.

"So you're telling me . . . that you're four moths past your due or your only seven to eight moths pregnant. when's your due date?" i couldnt hold my tears any longer. he was finding out the truth on his own. i stood up and walked away. i had to find the back room that Erin put my coat in so i could leave.

"Carmen." he said calling after me. i continued to walk. If i cried in front of him he would know something was wrong. as i walked down the hallway looking in the rooms Tavon followed behind me. it wasnt until i got towards the ending of the hallway before i could the right the right room. i walked in and picked up my coat for the stack of coats and jackets on the table. i turned around and bumped right into his chest. i missed the scent of his cologne. i wrapped my arms around his waist.

"Carmen?" he said confused.

"I dont mean to push you away. i just . . . i need . . ." i pressed my ear against his abs and listened to the long forgotten melody in his chest. he hugged me back.

"What do you need?" i closed my eyes.

"i dont know anymore." i begin to sob heavily.

"Why are you crying?" he asked.

"because . . . i cant be with you."

"Yes you can, im right here."

"Its more complicated than that."

"no you're making it complicated." i loosened my embrace and gazed into his eyes. he took my chin in his hand and brought my lips to his. the passion i've been missing for so long caused me to cry more. for the moment everything was perfect, but the secret bearing on my shoulders and i couldnt be alone with him.

"I have to go." i said walking around him to the door.

"Carmen please." i walked out and the door shut behind. my tears were stinging my eyes as i made my way for the exit.

Tavon i stood there for a minute thinking before i had decieded i wasnt going to sit back and watch her leave me. i ran out the room and down the hallway into the ballroom area. i saw her slip through the crowd and out the door.

"Hey Tavon." Jasmine called to me. i turned and walked over to her.

"yeah."

"Where is Carmen going?"

"she's leaving but im going to stop her."

"Okay i have to find my coat but I have to get through this crowd but i'll be out in a minute dont let her leave." i gave her a thumbs up and ran to the exit. i stepped outside and looked down the street. she hand her hand out in the street trying to hail down a cab. i walked over to her.

"Catching a cab on New Year's Eve an hour before the ball drops downtown is impossible." she turned around to look at me. i whistled loudly to get the valet's attention. he walked over to me and i gave him my card to get my car. i looked back at Carmen.

"We can leave, just you and me. Nobody has to know where we are, and we can love each other in peace. just you and me." her tears were constant. i took her hand.

"The baby is yours okay. it's yours. youre the father of my unborn child." she said under her breath. inside of me i knew it was my child. i wiped the tears from her eyes.

"Why didnt you just tell me?" i said tilting my head to meet her gaze.

"How could i?"

"I dont know, how about just saying it."

"I couldn't."

"Hey Carmen, where are you going?" Erin said getting our attention. my blood boiled as i looked at him.

"Umm . . . im not feeling to good so im going to head home." she said backing away from me.

"You want me to drive you home?" he said stepping in front of me. i took a step back.

"Why are you still with him?" i asked in disgust.

"Tavon." Carmen said cutting her eye at me.

"No, no, he has a right to his opinion. But tavon no matter what you say it doesnt change anything." i grinned.

"Are you sure about that?" he turned around to look at me.

"I'm postive about that."

"Tavon i've been looking all over for you." My mom said as she walked up beside me. i ignored her.

"Oh hello Dean Smith." she said smiling. Carmen put her head and took a step back.

"Hello Mrs. Holmes." Erin said shaking mom's hand. i stare at them in confusion. there was no way. i took a step back to look at mom.

"How do you know Erin?" I asked.

"He's your Dean from high school."

"I know that but i'm wondering how you know that."

"Oh we met at a parent and teachers conference." Erin said.

"You're lying." i said not understanding why they would be lying about knowing each other.

"You dont remember Tavon." Mom said touching my arm. i moved away from her.

"Why are you lying mom? Dad always came to my parent and teachers confrences not you. Mom you've never step foot in my high school before. i bet you dont even know my prinicpal's name."

Mom smiled weakily.

"Tavon." Erin said assuring.

"No, how the hell do you know my mother?"

"We've met at school."

"Just give it up Erin. There's no sense in lying anymore. Tavon i was tired of this old bitch messing around with you and filling your head with the stupid dreams." my mom said sighing. i turn to my mother in dibelief.

"My dream of being a pilot is not stupid. i wanted to take pilot training instead of going to college because i wanted to, not because she told me to."

"There's no money in that." she said rasing her voice.

"The money doesnt matter."

"Well it matters to me. you promised you would take care of me so i need the money. i am up to my neck in debt and i need you to pay off what your father wouldn't."

"Mary, i cant believe you. your selfish and full of shit. im not giving you a dime of my money." The valet pulled up beside up with my car and got out. he walked around to the sidewalk and passed me my keys.

"Tavon, you dont mean that." she said grabbing my arm. i pulled away from her.

"You can find your own ride home tonight." suddenly she pushed past Erin roughly and shoved Carmen into the side of my car.

"You bitch i told you to stay away from him, your going to get yours." She yelled. i grabbed my mother and pulled her off Carmen. she stumbled back and fell. Carmen grabbed my arm roughly as she slid down the car towards the ground. i grabbed her and pressed her against the car for support. she held her stomach as she stared down at her feet. i stared at her not knowing if i should pick her up or leave her crouched over the sidewalk.

"Carmen, are you alright?" i said in her ear.

Her eyes met mine in an instant. i shook my head in disbelief. she nodded.

"My water broke." she whispered. Maybe if I wasn't enraged I would have panicked.

"Get in my car, I'll drive you." I said calmly.

Her breathing was uneasy. As Carmen shifted her body onto me Erin grabbed my arm.

"You're not taking my wife anywhere." He said. I looked at glared at him.

"If you don't get your hand off me, you will regret it."

"Please don't argue right now." Carmen said reminding me that Erin was not important at the moment.

"What the hell is going on? Carmen? Are you okay!" Jazz yelled in a panic. She rushed to my side as she shoved Erin out her way.

"Her water broke." I explained as I helped Carmen into my car. Jasmine told the valet to get her car.

I shut the car door and Erin stood in my way.

"You are not taking Carmen." He said.

"Erin we don't have time for your bullshit. So if you don't move I will beat the shit out of you." Jazz said stepping in between us. Carmen knocked on the car window getting our attention. Erin stared at me furious. I sighed and gave Jasmine my keys.

"Jazz, just take my car and I'll take yours."

She nodded and walked around Erin to the driver's side and got in. As she pulled off Erin and my mom just stared at me. I couldn't believe my mother was really this person I was looking at. The person in front of me was a money-hungry-selfish-bitch, not a loving independent mother I thought she was.

"Just because you're the father of her child doesn't mean she wants to be with you." Erin said grinning.

The valet drove up with Jasmine's car.

"You believe that?"

Erin shoved his hands in his pocket and pulled out his car keys.

"Tavon please." My mom said taking a step closer to me.

"You watched me suffer for two months after our break up, and then tried to force me to go pro all because you needed money. You never cared about me, but Carmen did. I can never forgive you for what you have done."

She held out her hand trying to reason with me but I just got in Jasmine's car and drove off in the direction Jasmine and Carmen had gone.

Carmen

Everything had been moving too fast for me to keep up. My mom had already gotten to the hospital and I was hooked up to machines, with tubes plugged in holes I never knew I had. The contractions were getting closer together every five minutes. I would have taken the epidural but I was a little too late for that. I was almost 10 centimeters and the nurse was preparing my delivery room. Since only two people could be in the room with me Tavon said he would just wait in the waiting room for me. Mom went to grab something to drink before it was time to move me to the next room. Jasmine sat beside me holding my hand. I know she was trying to help but her support wasn't changing anything. The nurse knocked on the door before poking her head inside jasmine lifted up her head swiftly focusing towards the door

"There's a man here to see you his name is Erin should I let him in." the nurse said. I looked at Jasmine and nod.

"Yeah sure let him in." Jasmine said.

The nurse opened the door letting Erin in and closed it behind him. He rushed to my side taking my hand. I snatched my hand from his grasp in mid-contraction. I closed my eyes trying to cope with the pain. He cleared his throat, but before he had the chance to speak I cut him off.

"How the hell did you know Tavon's mother, because I didn't meet Mary until I ran into her at the hospital after Tavon got jumped. She never came to the school before but yet you were on a first name basis."

"Do we really have to talk about this now you're in labor we can talk about his after?" Erin said.

The contractions stopped me from arguing so I gave Jasmine's hand a squeeze and she knew to speak for me.

"Hell no, let's settle this shit now." Jazz said standing up.

"Jasmine, this is between me and my wife." He said rolling his eyes.

"I know I haven't been saying anything about ya'll relationship in the past but those times have changed I'm not going to let you dog her no more. So either you're going to tell her what she wants to know or get the fuck out"

He put his head down and sighed.

"I went to the precinct after you kicked me out of your house for Tavon while I was there I ran into Mary and she made a deal with me. She said she would arrest you with no charges and blackmail you into leaving Tavon and I took the deal. I took it because I loved you and I wanted you back and I'd do anything to be with you. But I never knew you were pregnant, she never told me!"

I took a deep breathe watching the man I once loved throw me under the bus.

"I sat in Rikers well over two weeks because you were so selfish you wouldn't let me love another man for my own happiness." I said

"Baby I'm sorry" he said

"There's only room for two people in the delivery room. Jazz and mom are going to be in there with me." I said closing my eyes.

"Carmen please." He begged. The room door opened and the nurses and doctor walked in.

"Are you ready Ms. Sanderson?" Doctor Milberg said studying my chart.

"Yes I am." I said as I smiled and looked at Jasmine.

"Jazz go find mom." I said faintly. She nodded. I closed my eyes again as they rolled me out my room into the hallway passing by Erin. The tears fell from my eyelashes running to the back of my head. Maybe I could have cried because of the pain from the contractions but the pain from my heartache brought me to tears.

HAPPY NEW YEAR

Tavon

After sitting in the waiting area all night and most of the morning I was finally getting tired. Even though I spent my first day of the New Year in a hospital's waiting room I knew it would be the best day I had all year. It bothered me a little not being in the room with Carmen but waiting would have to do. I sat beside Jasmine's husband Jacob and the kids. Erin sat in the waiting room with us with his parents and Carmen's siblings. Melissa, Bella, and Dennis warmed up to me quickly. I could tell they thought I was too young to be with Carmen but no one said a word about it. Erin sat across the room the whole time hating everyone that spoke to me. I could tell it was killing him to watch everyone take my side. Jasmine walked into the waiting room and we stood up. She held out her hand trying to calm everyone down.

"Carmie told me to tell everyone to wait a few minutes so she can be alone with Tavon." She said looking at me. I nodded and headed down the long hall to her room. The door was ajar so I pushed the door open and walked in. Carmen lay on the bed holding a baby wrapped in pink blankets. Renee noticed it was me immediately. She smiled at me as I walked over to her and gave her a hug.

"Hey, how are all of my beautiful ladies?" I ask looking at Carmen.

"See for yourself." Renee said slightly pushing me closer to Carmen as she walked pass me and left the room. Carmen sat up and lifted the baby in my direction. I didn't hesitate to take my daughter. As I looked at her yellow complexion and her round eyes I could see Carmen in her. I couldn't believe i was holding such a small person in my arms. I didn't know how to feel or if I was even feeling but I knew this beautiful baby girl was mine. She wrapped her small fingers around my index finger and held on. I finally started breathing again as I looked up at Carmen and caught her staring at me.

"Have you named her already?" I ask giving my attention to my daughter again.

"I was waiting for you to come so we could decide together."

I nod.

"Okay, what names were you thinking of?"

"Tarina." She said laying back.

"Tarina, I love it."

I began to rock her back and forth.

"Daddy loves you Tarina." I whispered in her ear. I looked up and Carmen laid there smiling her warming smile.

"How about Tarina Renee Holmes?" She asked tilting her head.

"You want to give her my last name?"

"You're going to be in her life, right?"

I nod.

"I plan to be."

"Then that's all that matters."

I paced the floor rocking Tarina gently.

"So I'm assuming you're not leaving him."

She sighed.

"This isn't the time or the place."

"So when is?"

"Tavon, I just got out of labor."

"I know because I sat in the waiting room waiting for you to get out of the delivery room. Carmen, and I know why you left me my mom told me everything. I understand why you didn't tell me but there's one thing I don't understand. Why you don't want me back."

"Erin changed . . . for me and during the time I spent with him I fell in love again. Last night really got me stressed out and confused. I'm not in the right state of mind to make those types of decisions right now."

I gave Tarina back to Carmen after I kissed her small hand.

"Look I got to get out of here I have appointment to go to but I have to ask . . . just tell me if I will ever have a chance at being with you again?"

She shook her head and look away from me.

"I need time."

I nodded.

"Sure, take all the time you need because I wouldn't just lay beside you for eternity . . . I'd also wait for you."

I smiled and gave her hand a squeeze before walking out the door.

Carmen

As Tavon walked out mom walked back in closing the door behind her. She smiled at me as she sat back down. I lay back on the bed holding onto Tarina tightly.

"I like the way that boy thinks." Mom said chuckling.

"Mom, that's not helping." I said turning my head to look at her.

"You gave Erin chance after chance after chance and still he took it for granted. Then walks in your knight in shining armor and let him leave."

"I never was expecting a knight maybe the rag boy that worked behind the scenes and no one knew his name."

Mom patted my hand.

"You already had the rag boy princess. When are you going to realize that you deserve better."

I could feel heat in my cheeks and the tears building in my eye sockets.

"Mom please, I don't need this right now."

"Every time you want advice I don't have it but when you need it you don't take it. I will never understand how your brain works."

I giggled.

"When I understand it myself I'll let you know."

We both laughed. The door crept opened and we both turned to see who was coming in. Erin and his parents walked in. I sat up with an attitude.

"Hello Carmen, it's been too long." Erin's mother Karen said in her uppity voice. I rolled my eyes.

"Not long enough Karen." I said not holding back my arrogance. Erin stood in front of his mother trying to avoid the argument that was bound to happen.

"May I hold the baby?" he asked coming closer. I held her out and he took her gently. He rocked her and smiled. He showed Tarina to Karen and she backed away.

"Just because you have a problem with my daughter doesn't mean you take out on my grandchild." My mom said standing up. I was happy mom stood up first because I was about to leap off this hospital bed.

"Well I'm not sure if she's been cleaned so I'm just keeping my distance." Karen said. Erin's father Larry grabbed Karen's arm.

"You promised you wouldn't be rude." Larry said.

"Give me my daughter." I said in between my teeth. Erin gave her back and lowered his head. I hated when he allowed his mother to say whatever the hell she wanted.

"If you don't get the fuck out of this room I will call the nurse and get you escorted out the damn building." Mom said walking around the bed to Karen.

"Sorry, we'll leave." Larry said pulling Karen out the room. Mom looked at me in disbelief.

"Did she really just come up in her with nasty ass attitude?" my mom asked.

"Renee please excuse my mother sometimes she can't control herself." Erin said.

"First of all to you my name is Ms. Sanderson second why apologize she was only following her animalistic instincts, but then again the apple doesn't fall far from the tree. I know how you have treated my daughter and I don't care how much you claim to have changed, in my eyes you will never be good enough for Carmen. So every apology you came up with before you came in here you can shove up your ass because I will not accept them, not now not ever."

Mom stood for a moment grilling a hole in Erin's head before she stormed out the room. I couldn't blame her and I sure wasn't mad that she shut him down like a rat infested restaurant. He cleared his throat.

"So, have you named her?"

"Her name is Tarina Renee Holmes."

"Tarina doesn't really fit her. I thought you said you would think about Rochelle."

"I did think about it and I didn't like it."

"Well I don't like Tarina."

"I don't care what you like because she's not your daughter."

He stepped back and sighed.

"Okay, I deserved that."

"No you don't, actually you deserve a lot more but I'm tired and I don't have the strength to get out this bed and beat the shit out of you. I can't believe you got me arrested and pretended it never happened."

"Baby, I can't take back what I did."

"You're not even sorry you did it."

"Yes I'm sorry about the way I went about it but I'll never be sorry for loving you."

"That's not love."

"I just couldn't sit back and lose you to him."

"Exactly you just couldn't sit back and lose to Tavon."

"That's not true."

"Then what is it? Did you want me because I'm not weak and naive anymore? I showed you I could make it without you and you decided to make a change."

"Carmen I always loved you."

"How could you have loved me when you were so busy fucking Helen. You didn't want me anymore and you know it but now that Tavon and I love each other you changed your mind."

"Ever since you left me I've been trying to get you back."

"You didn't wanted me back you just thought I was going to expose you to Principal Hale. You didn't want me until you knew someone else had me."

"I'm only human, I make mistakes."

"You're not human . . . you're a fucking savage."

"Why can't we just move past this? Baby I know we can get through this, I know we can."

"Who ever said I wanted work this out? Whatever this is?" I said looking at him with my eyebrow arched.

"Carmen come on. We can patch this up."

"Ha, 20 construction companies couldn't even build the dam we need to patch this hole you made in my life and my heart. I've been suffering for seven long ass months not knowing that you were the person who caused all this shit. Then you expect me to smile and give you another chance, what damn planet do you think you're on?"

"Carmen, I meant it when I said I'd do anything to get you back and that's exactly what I did. I did this out of love."

He had to be stupid. At some point in his life his brain must've lost oxygen and cut off all common sense because he was mentally challenged. I nodded.

"Well I hope that we can get through this because I don't want to regret choosing you."

He exhaled as he walked over to me taking my hand.

"Trust me you won't regret this." He said sitting on the edge of the bed.

I closed my eyes and lay back, because little did he know he would regret this.

New Year Same Shit

Tavon

I look down at my watch as i sped through the streets of Manhattan in my new Dodge Charger my dad brought me racing with time. it had been three days since Tarina was born and Carmen and her were finally getting released. i had another I five minutes to be there before i was late and i'd be damned if Erin thought he was going to make it there before me. carmen told me he was working but something in my gut told me he would try to pick her up before i could. i had moving into my new apartment today with my dad's help, but i didn't think it would've took as long as it did. i pulled up in front of the hospital as Renee, Carmen, and Tarina strolled out. i put the car in park and got out.

"I'm not late am i?" i asked approaching them. they shook their heads no.

"Actually, you're right on time." Renee said giving me a hug. i hugged her back and gave Carmen a kiss on the cheek.

"Got yourself a car i see." Carmen said eyeing me. i smiled.

"Yeah, my dad got it for my birthday."

"Very sexy, maybe i should get one." she said. i looked at her amused.

"Okay then, lets get you girls out of here." i took the car seat Tarina was in that Carmen was holding and open the back door. i put Tarina in the backseat and strapped her in. as i got out the car to move out the way for Renee to get in a Mercedes swiftly parked behind my car. i straighten up knowing who it was already. Erin jumped out the car and walked around to it to us.

"What are you doing here?" Carmen asked him.

"Well i got off early, so i decided to come pick you up myself so you wouldn't have to take a cab, but i can see he beat me to the punch." he said glaring at me. i smirked.

"You were late, thats not my fault."

"Well its okay Erin, i'll just meet you at home." she said.

"Why when I'm here now?"

"Tarina is already strapped in and momma don't want you to drive her home."

"Fine she can get a ride from him but i can take you and Tarina."

"Excuse me." Renee said. Carmen touched Renee's hand as she stepped in front of her.

"Why would i leave my mother with just anyone, no offense Tavon."

"None taken." i said leaning on my car.

"Just tell the truth Carmen, you just want a ride from him." he sad pointing at me.

"So what if she does?" i say.

"Tavon stop." Carmen said looking back at me.

"Please she'd pick me over you anyway." he said stepping closer. Carmen pushed him back. i sighed.

"And what makes you so sure?"

"Because im a man and your just a boy." i laugh.

"Wow, thats funny. so since your a man now did you ever fix that problem you were having?" i could tell he was heated.

"What problem?"

"Tavon! just stop already." Carmen said.

"You know, that problem with your dick." i responded.

"Tavon, you're taking things too far." Carmen said. Erin walked up to me and got in my face.

"Well i must have if she's planning to stay." i pushed off my car and stood up.

"Are you trying to insinuate something?"

"I don't know, do you think i am?"

"If you are, then just say it if you got heart."

"I don't have to say it, because you already know."

Carmen shoved us away from each other.

"Okay, thats enough! Unstrap Tarina now!" i looked at Carmen with disbelief.

"Just unstrap her Tay." Renee said touching my arm. i nodded.

"Fine." i got back in the car and unbuckled the seat beats and unstrapped the car seat. i pulled it out and Carmen took her from my hands.

"Okay, now lets go." Erin said as he begin to walk to his car.

"You're really going to go with him?" i asked Carmen.

"You thought she wasn't." Erin said turning back around. i clenched my fist and exhaled deeply.

"I'm getting tired of you." i say stepping closer to him.

"And what are you going to do about it?"

"Oh, trust me I been waiting to get another chance to fuck you up." he smiled knowing he was getting under my skin.

"Come on then."

I take step closer ready to approach him and Carmen shoved me in my chest.

"Why must you two always act like children?" She yelled.

I straightened my shirt and crack my neck as I stared at him.

"Well, according to you two I am a child so I'm just acting my age."

"No, let him come." Erin said stepping closer.

"Fine! Act like children I don't care anymore." She yelled as she stormed off. I stared him down wanting to take off his head. I turned to leave knowing going any farther with him wouldn't get me anywhere.

"Yeah, I fucked her while she pregnant with your daughter." He whispered. I looked at him from the corner of my eye and saw his twisted grin and lost my mind. As I turned around to face him I swung my fist as hard as I could. When my fist connected to the side of his face the sound was sickening. He lost his balance and fell back. I grab his shirt and pulled him back up to me and hit him with my left. He went down fast. I jumped on top of him and went to town on his face. He grabbed my neck and punched me off him. I get up off the floor and Erin tackled me shoving me back down. Before I knew it the security from the hospital was holding me back and pushing Erin into the hospital.

"Just calm down sir." The guard said letting me go as I stopped struggling to get to Erin. I put my hands up to surrender.

"Okay, I'm calm." I say breathing hard. I looked around searching for Carmen and caught her getting into a taxi. She turned around for a brief second to look at me and closed the door. The taxi pulled off as my head hung low. Damn, how could I have let him get to me like that? I knew I let my anger get the best of me.

"Look, if you leave the premises we won't call the police." The guard said getting my attention. I nodded.

"I'm leaving now." I said looking back at him. I slammed my back door and walked around to the front and got in. I left swiftly noticing all the people that had circled around me watching the fight. I drove to Derek's place and went upstairs to his apartment. I knocked on the door and he opened up the door staring at me with his eye brow arched.

"What happened to your lip?" he asked moving aside. I touched my lip and looked down at my hand saw blood. I hadn't even realized I was hurt. I wiped my lip as I walked in and headed for the living room.

"Erin happened." I said as I sat down and sighed. I laid back and closed my eyes.

"Who's Erin?" he asked standing over me.

"Dean Smith."

"The dean? Then what the fuck are we doing here? Let's go get his ass." He said grabbing his keys. I sat and looked at him.

"Sit yo' hype ass down. I swung first."

He sat down across from me and tossed his keys on the coffee table.

"Why the hell were you fighting anyway?"

"He always saying shit."

"Like what?"

I sighed.

"He told me . . . he said he that he . . . umm."

"Just say it."

"He been fucking Carmen . . . while she was carrying Tarina."

Derek sat back as he shook his head.

"Wow, that's really foul. But come on, you knew they were together."

I nod.

"Yeah I knew, but is it wrong to want her to be happy with me?"

I laid back.

"Well, it all depends. Is she really happy with you?"

"She was before."

"Then just give her time, you've done all you can do. You have to be patient now, but if she really made up her mind then you know you have to move on."

I just lay there while silence fell over us.

Carmen

I had drop Tarina off with mom and came home to grab some things I would need while I spent some time with her. I didn't want to see Erin's face after what he did outside of the hospital earlier. I couldn't believe how childish he was. The front door opened and closed. I heard him coming upstairs and I hurried. He stood at the doorway of the room and watched me. I looked at him for a brief moment and continued to pack.

"Baby, I'm sorry." He said softly.

"Sorry doesn't cut it." I say sternly.

"You're not leaving me, are you?"

I turn around to look at him and throw everything in my hands on the floor.

"You're so selfish. Your only worried about me being with you. What about me? Do you ever care about me?"

"I do care about you."

"You got into a fight with my daughter's father once I got out the hospital."

"He swung at me." He said walking to me. I pushed him away from me roughly.

"I heard what you told him Erin!"

He was speechless. I nod knowing he wouldn't have nothing to say to that. I turn around and put my back to him.

"You can't whisper for shit. I can't even believe you would tell him something like that. Why would you even say something so ignorant?"

"I don't know." He said.

I turn back around.

"You know damn well we haven't had sex once since we got back together."

"I know and I respect that."

"Obviously you don't if you have to lie about it."

"Baby, I'm trying my best."

"Well if this is your best, than your best isn't enough for me."

I continued to pack. He grabbed my arm turned me around.

"I have a feeling I'm not the real reason why your leaving." He said. I snatched my arm from him.

"What are you talking about?"

"You're still in love with Tavon and that's the reason why you won't stay."

"Tavon doesn't have anything to do with this."

He got in my face.

"Don't you see he's just a child?"

I jerked my neck and tilted my head.

"And you're not."

He ran his fingers through my hair and pulled me into his chest.

"He will never be man enough for you, and if can't see that . . . your blind."

With that said he turned and walked out. I sat on the bed for a moment before I decided to unpack.

The Grass Isn't Always Greener

3 Months Later

Tavon

I walk in the door from class and toss my keys on the couch. It had been a long day for me and my back was sore. My piloting course was coming to an end, but I was too stressed out worrying if I'd pass my required exams to rest. And if that wasn't frustrating enough I still had to deal with Carmen's bullshit. She invited me to her vow renewal ceremony, and insisted I be there to support her decision. After weeks of back and forth arguing I gave in and accepted her invitation. Now the weekend I'd been dreading was here. On Monday morning I would be sitting in a church watching Erin make more empty promises to the woman I love. I drop my head as I walked in my bedroom. I got in the shower and washed up, jumped out and I laid across my bed. My phone rang and I looked at it deciding if I should answer or pretend I wasn't home. I sighed heavily and got up to answer.

"Hello?"

"Hey Tay, it's been like forever. How you been?" Violet said excited. Once I heard her voice a smile crept on to my face.

"Hey Vi, I've been hanging in there. What about you?"

"Same old, same old."

"Okay, so what can I do for you?"

"Well actually I'm in the city. I'm on Broadway to be exact, and I wanted to know if you can use some company."

I rubbed my temples.

"I just got home and im kind of tired."

She groaned.

"Come on Tay. I haven't seen you in months, plus all the hotels are booked and I got my friend with me and we need a place to crash for the night."

I sighed.

"Please." She whined.

I closed my eyes and sighed. I gave her my address and hung up. I put on my shorts and grabbed some blankets from the closet. I didn't even know if her friend was a girl or not but I decided I'd give them the bed and I sleep in the living room. I laid down some sheets on the couch and folded the blankets and placed them on the coffee table. I knew if I laid down I'd fall asleep and I didn't want to leave them outside all night if I didn't hear them. I turned on the television and watched the news. After a while I couldn't keep my eyes open. I looked at the time and yawned. It was nearly midnight so they should've been popping up any minute. Finally a knock came to the door. I went to the door and opened it. Before I could say hello Violet rushed into me wrapping her arms around my neck. I laughed at how excited she was to see me. I hugged her back then let her down. She kissed my cheek as she smiled.

"It's been way too long." She said. I nodded in agreement.

She moved aside showing off her friend.

"This is Stacy. Stacy this is the amazing Tavon." She said taking Stacy's bags. I moved out of Violet's way so she could bring the bags inside. Stacy looked Brazilian, and was at least 5'7, with long reddish hair, light brown skin, and hour glass shape. She wasn't thick but her breast was extra-large. Her jacket was unzipped showing her v-cut shirt that left nothing to the imagination.

"Hey." I said waving tiredly.

She stepped into the house and placed her hand on my naked chest.

"Nice to finally meet you Tay." She said seductively as she ran her hand down my chest and walked inside. I raised my eye brows at her surprised at how forward she was with flirting with me. I closed the door behind her.

"I'm giving you guys the bed so you can just bring your bags into the room." I said helping Violet with her luggage.

"And ummm, just make yourselves at home." I continued.

They both nodded as I led them to my room. I dropped the bags by the bed and turned to face them.

"Well, I'm going to sleep but the bathroom is right down the hall and the kitchen is connected to the living room. If you need anything don't hesitate to ask, okay?"

"Okay." They said in union. I walked pass them and went back to the living room. Once my head hit the pillows I was gone. I hadn't even realized I was sleep until I heard my name in the distance. I shifted and pulled the blankets over my head. I felt someone tapping me and I gained consciousness as I lifted my head.

"Yeah." I said groggy.

"Wake up." Violet said. I sat up and wiped my eyes trying to adjust to the light. I looked up and Stacy stood beside Violet. I looked around for the time wondering why I still felt so tired.

"What time is it?" I asked rubbing my eyes.

"Two o'clock."

"In the afternoon?" I asked surprised.

She giggled.

"No silly, in the morning."

"Oh."

Finally everything was beginning to look clear but my brain must of still been in sleep mode because Violet and Stacy were naked. I tried my best to understand what was happening but I was convinced that I was still sleeping.

"Why are naked?" I asked.

"I haven't told you but Stacy and I are lovers and we want to have a threesome with you."

I shake my head.

"Impossible, number one you're not a lesbian number two shit like this doesn't really happen in real life."

They laughed.

"Then why would we both be naked in front of you if we weren't serious?"

"Because I'm dreaming, this isn't really happening."

Stacy sat on my lap and took my hands and put them on her breast. She squeezed my hand making me caress her. Her skin was warm on mine and her breast felt too real too be dreaming.

"Let's just fuck." Stacy whispered in my ear.

"I can't." I say looking away.

"I can feel your dick getting hard and I haven't even done anything. I know you want to so stop fighting it. You got two fine ass bitches in their birthday suits, so what you going to do?"

I knew this was wrong but these girls were too sexy to reject. A faithful married Christian man couldn't say no to this temptation. Stacy stood up and took Violet by the hand and led her to the room.

"Come on Tavon." Stacy said. I stood and followed behind them. I stood at the door while Stacy threw Violet on the bed and climbed on top her. Violet stuck her tongue in Stacy's mouth and pinched her nipples. Stacy rubbed Violets clitoris while her she poked her ass in the air. My jaw dropped as I watched these girls going in like porn stars. My phone begins to ring and walked over to it and picked it up. I shushed them and answered.

"Hello?" I say clearing my throat.

"Oh, you're up. I was going to leave a message but guess now I can just tell you." Carmen said.

"Tell me what?" I ask. Stacy grabbed my hand pulled me closer to the bed.

"Well there are two things I wanted to discuss. First I told Derek to pick up your Tuxedo for Monday."

"Okay." I responded. Violet pulled down my shorts and I began to lick one side while Stacy licked the other. I dropped my head and watched them do what they wanted to me.

"Second I wanted to ask you, would you walk Tarina down the aisle?"

My eyes widened. Had she lost her damn mind? Why the hell would I want, or Tarina for that matter, to be a part of her stupid ceremony with Erin. Just as I was about tell Carmen off Stacy put my whole dick in her mouth. Before I could stop myself I groaned. I knew Carmen heard me over everything. The silence on the phone was crucial. I didn't know if I should speak or just hang up. What made it worst was the slurping sounds that Violet and Stacy made. I pull away from them as I tried to control my breathing.

"What the hell are you doing?" Carmen said calmly. I didn't know how to react. Maybe if she would have screamed or cursed I would be ready to defend myself but the calmness in her voice was overwhelmingly brutal.

"Nothing." I say nervously.

"I never knew you as a liar Tavon."

Stacy walks over to me and started kissing my neck.

"I never lying, no I mean I don't . . . ugh I meant to say I'm not lying to you."

She laughed sending shivers down my spine.

"The funny thing about men is . . . when they get caught doing something they never know how to respond. They either lashes out in anger, lie, or most of all they state the obvious."

I swallowed hard as she continued.

"So which do you think I've caught on to?"

I pushed Stacy slightly. I pulled up my shorts and left the room.

"I'm not doing anything." I denied.

"Whatever, it's not like I'm even worry about what you're up to." She yelled.

"Then why would you even ask?"

"I don't know why but trust me Tavon I don't care."

"Obviously you do if you called me so damn late, which is something you never do."

"I didn't even think you were up. I thought I'd get the voicemail. Plus you didn't have to answer the phone for me."

"You're damn right I didn't but I did so if I was really doing something why the fuck would I answer."

"I don't know, but that doesn't matter. This conversation doesn't even matter."

"If it doesn't why are you even still talking to me?"

"Sometimes I just hate you so much that it kills me."

"Don't think you're such a walk in the fucking park Carmen. You piss me off too all the damn time. You think I want my daughter living with Erin? Huh? Hell no, so I fucking hate you too. And since you're still breathing you must not hate me as much as you say."

"Fuck you."

"I already have."

"I'm so happy that I didn't choose you! I'd just regret it, and then I'll be stuck in a marriage just like I was with Erin! At least now I know I made the right choice."

I could tell by her voice she was crying, and this time it was because of me.

"I'm sorry, okay. I didn't mean that." I said sincerely.

"Just make sure your on time on Monday."

"Please Carmen, I didn't know you were- . . ." Before I could finish she hung up.

I threw the phone across the room. Damn I was so stupid. Why would I say such foolish things to her? I got caught but yet I'm the one that's mad? Why did I even answer the phone? What's wrong with me? My fist clenched and the anger in my chest felt like a bomb ready to explode.

"Tay is everything alright?" Violet said getting my attention. I nodded.

"I just need some fresh air." I said. I grabbed my keys and walked towards the door.

"Aren't you going to get dressed first, its pneumonia season?" Stacy said.

I opened the door and walked out.

Carmen

I slammed the phone back on the base. I was so frustrated I could scream. I knew Tavon had the right to date whomever he pleases but I couldn't bear the thought of him loving someone else. I knew I didn't have the right to feel this way knowing I'm with Erin, but I couldn't shake this feeling.

"Why are you screaming at two in the morning? You know Tarina's sleep." Mom scolded. I pulled my hair out of my face and held my head as I closed my eyes to breathe.

"Are you crying?" mom asked as she rushed to my side. I nodded slowly.

"What happened?"

I looked at her and pulled myself together.

"Besides Tavon having sex with some bitch while I was on the phone with him, nothing."

"How do you know if he's having sex?"

"I know what he sounds like when he's fucking mother." I said slouching back on to the sofa.

"Of course you do sweetie."

I glared at her.

"What does that supposed to mean?"

"Nothing. So why are you so upset about him having sex?"

"I'm not it's just he wanted to argue with me because he knows that I know he was cheating . . . -"

I stopped talking once the word left my mouth. I looked away from my mother embarrassed and corrected myself.

"I mean having sex."

She nodded.

"Do you still love him Carmen?" she asked taking my hand.

"I don't know." I said sitting up. She patted my hand and stood up.

"Would it be wrong if I did?" I ask dropping my head into my hands.

"Baby, I don't think love could ever be wrong."

Mom walked to the stairs and stopped at the bottom.

"You never told me you loved to paint. Looking now though, I know you could be great at it."

I looked at her and somehow we spoke without words. She shook her head.

"Carmen, what are you doing here?" she asked. I laid back and sighed as she walked upstairs.

"I don't know mom, I don't know." I whispered to myself. I looked at the phone and picked it up.

"This will be the last time, I promise." I say as I dial this too familiar number.

A Little Too Late

Tavon

I tried to put the key in the keyhole once again and the keyhole moved. I laughed and wiped my eyes and tried it once more. The hole moved again. I was losing my mind, I had to be. I grab the door knob and notice the keyhole was never moving I was leaning too far over. I laughed even harder. The door swung open and I leaned back trying to keep my balance.

"Tavon! Where the hell have you been?" Stacy yelled as she yanked me inside. Once she let me go I tripped forward and landed on my face. I turned over on my back and tried to stop laughing. Stacy shook her head as she stared at me.

"Violet! Tavon's here and I think he's drunk." Stacy yelled toward the back of the apartment. Violet rushed into the living room and stood over me.

"Oh my gosh, Derek is going to kill him. Okay umm, help me get him to the couch." She said to Stacy. She nodded and they dragged me to the couch and pulled me up on it. I looked around at the spinning room and sat back.

"Where the hell were you?" Violet asked.

"I went for a walk." I responded.

"That was a long ass walk." Stacy said. I laughed. Violet smelled me.

"You have been drinking. I'm so mad at you." She said.

"You should've called me." I said. Stacy threw my phone at my chest.

"I did but you left it."

I picked it up and saw my missed calls and voicemails. I called my voicemail and put the phone to my ear. Someone knocked on the door and violet went to answer it. The first message was from Derek: "Yo, come on I called ya' house phone and you ain't answering. It's eight o'clock you know the wedding is at ten and I still have your tux. I'm coming over and you better be home."

The second message was from him again: "Man where are you? I got your suit so hit me up and let me know when you want me to bring it to you. Later."

"Dude we have thirty minutes and if you're late Carmen is going to kill me and torture you." Derek said as he walked in the door. He threw the tuxedo at me.

"I'm giving two minutes to get ready then I'm going to beat the shit out of you and dress you myself. Now let's go, move it move it." He said. Just as I began to speak Carmen's voice flowed through my ears cutting off all my body functions.

"I'm sorry that I just went crazy on you but you make me this way. I love you so much that it makes me kind of crazy sometimes. I know I have been saying I don't love you but I was trying to make sure you got everything you wanted out of life before I slow you down, but I can't live knowing you're loving someone else. I know that's kind of selfish, but it's true. As we both know Monday I'm renewing my vows, but if you still want me back then call me. But if you don't call me then I'll know what your answer is for sure." The silence after that was heavy. Derek was in my face yelling but I couldn't hear him over the silence. Violet pulled him back and he pushed her off him. Stacy walked up to me and slapped me clear across my face. The ringing in my ear brought the sound back.

"I don't care you still don't have to get in his face his drunk." Violet yelled at Derek.

"This is my brother and I can do what ever the fuck I please. And why the fuck you even here bitch?"

"I was fucking invited."

"Violet! Chill out." I say standing up. I was still a little twisted but I had to make it to the wedding and fast. Derek grabbed my shirt and pulled it on me. He looked at Stacy and Violet.

"Well are you going to help me?" he said. They grabbed my clothes and helped dress me. Before I knew it I was in my car and Derek was driving recklessly down the streets.

"I can't believe you got drunk before the wedding."

"I got drunk on Friday night and passed out at a hotel and been there ever since. I just got in this morning. I had forgotten all about today."

"Carmen was pissed off this morning."

"I have to talk to her before she walks down that aisle."

He looked at me for a brief moment.

"What?" he asked confused.

"She left me a message Friday after our argument."

"You guys got into an argument?"

"Yeah, and she left a message saying she love me. I gotta at least try to stop her from doing this. She has to know I still love her."

He pulled up in front of the church and looked at his watch.

"Okay, you got fifteen minutes so you better haul ass." He said. I jumped out the car and ran up the church steps to the entrance. Renee stood at the door.

"Where is she?" I said quickly. She point to the left.

"Down the hall to your left there's a staircase leading downstairs, follow the bridesmaids." She said pushing me slightly. I took off down the hallway and raced down the steps. Once I hit the last step all the ladies in the hall moved aside. I raced past them to the last door and Melissa stood there guarding it.

"Please Melissa I have to see her."

"Tavon, you hurt her so bad."

"Please." I begged. She stared at me for a moment and gave in. she moved aside and I walked in. Carmen sat in front of the vanity mirror. I looked at her through it and she wiped her nose. Her tears were constantly falling from her chin.

"Give me a few more minutes Melissa." She said without looking up.

"It's Tavon."

She looked in the mirror and met my glaze. She turned around and stood up. Then walk over to me and slapped me exactly were Stacy did.

"I can't stand you. I hate you so much. I wish I never met you." She said in between her sobs. I smiled.

"I love you too."

She wiped her tears.

"Why didn't you return my call?"

"I just got your message thirty minutes ago."

"Where the hell have you been all weekend?"

"At a hotel."

"Fucking?"

"Drinking actually."

"I know, because I can smell it on you. So on Friday when I called you were you having sex? And don't lie because I know your voice when you're fucking."

"No I wasn't."

"Then were you jerking off?"

I laughed.

"No."

"Then tell me."

"I was umm you know."

She folded her arms.

"No, I don't know."

"Getting head."

"From who?"

"Violet and Stacy."

"Both?"

I nodded. She slapped me again.

"Do you know how much I love you?" she asked.

"No."

She turned her back to me.

"Well I love you more than life, and I always will . . . but you're too late."

I could feel the warm tears building in my eyes sockets.

"Now I'm going to walk down that aisle and when I turn around after my vows, I want to see you sitting next to mom and holding Tarina."

I shook my head.

"I'm not too late."

I got down on one knee and took her hand. She turned around and put her finger to my lip.

"Tavon stop right now. You took too long and I don't want to spend the rest of my life waiting for you."

"So you're going to spend it Erin wondering what could've happened."

"I'm not changing my mind."

"Well I refuse to watch you be taken from me. Why did you even call me?"

"Because I love you."

"Do you? Do you really?"

"Yes."

"Then why would you do this to me?"

A knock came to the door.

"Carmen it's time." Melissa said through the door.

"I'm coming now." She responded. She looked at me and dropped her head.

"Time doesn't wait for anyone so you have to be on its side. Today Erin was on time's side, I'm sorry but I'm going to renew my vows with him today."

Why should I even fight against her decision? Her mind is made and I knew what was going to happen, I'd be just the baby daddy. Maybe it was time for me to accept that.

"Carmen, you look beautiful."

She smiled.

"Thank you."

I walked out and went to the sanctuary. I found Renee holding Tarina in the front and sat beside them. Renee looked at me and already knew what happened.

"I don't know what to say."

"It's okay. I'll be okay, you just watch after my girls for me." I say trying my best to hold in my tears like a man.

"Of course, I'm going to miss you."

I nod.

"I'm going to miss you too."

Someone tapped my shoulder and I turned around. It was Derek passing me my keys. I shake my head no.

"I'm too drunk to drive. I'll just take a cab."

He nodded.

"I'm so sorry man."

"I'm okay, at least I think I will be."

The music began to fill the church and everyone stood up. I looked at Erin and he grinned. I wanted to kill him with my bare hands but I knew that wouldn't change the fact that today Carmen chose him and not me. Carmen came down the aisle with her brother Dennis slowly. She was beyond beautiful, she looked like an angel. She got up to the altar and I snuck out the church unseen. When the fresh air hit me my tears slipped from my eyes quietly. I went to the corner and hailed down a taxi.

Carmen

After the pastor spoke Erin began his vows: I could never picture us this far along and still happy. We've been through so much and I'm surprised you can even look at me the same. An I feel so special to have such a unique wife to renew my vows with. Any man would be lucky to have you but luck must be on my side because I have you. And baby when I say I love you there will never be any doubt in them. I would be more than happy to live out the rest of my days on Earth saying I love you Carmen every day. Carmen I love you. Everyone clapped and silence came right after. I smiled and cleared my throat.

"Thank you. Well Erin we have been through a lot and I can sit here and say today my love for you is not the same. It has changed and gave me a new understanding. We became closer and best friends and Erin I must say that you no longer mean as much to me anymore. I love you but not like I use to. Its more of a friend love and I don't want to be with you anymore. But I do hope we can be friends."

The confusion on his face was a true Kodak moment.

"What?" he said. I turn to look for Tavon but he wasn't there. My mother sat there with Tarina and no one else. I scanned the room quickly as I begin to panic.

"Carmen, what are you doing?"

I turned to him.

"Erin we have been too much and I gave you a lot of me, and in between all that I fell in love with Tavon and I love him more than I have ever loved you. And now that I've gotten you back for everything you've done to me I'm going to be with him."

I went to go down the altar steps and he grabbed my arm. I looked at him and he looked crazy. The anger in his eyes was unlike anything I've ever seen. It actually scared me to see him like this.

"You're not leaving me at this altar." He said in between his teeth.

"Get your hands off of me." I yelled as I snatched my arm away from him. I walked back down the aisle. I pulled up my dress and began to run.

"CARMEN!" Erin screamed behind me. I turned around to look at him and he tackled me. Everyone was yelling and getting out of control. As I wrestled with Erin, Dennis was trying to pull him off of me and Larry was pulling Dennis of Erin while Melissa and Karen were fighting. Derek pulled me from under Erin and helped me off the floor. Once Erin stood up Derek punched him directly in the face knocking him out cold. I turned and ran out the church. I dashed down the church stairs on to the street and franticly looked both ways. I pulled up my dress and ran to the corner and looked down the street but Tavon was gone. I turned around and Karen stormed down the street to me.

"You disrespectful little bitch!" She screamed as she approached me. She slapped me and all hell broke loose. I jump on her and she fell straight to the ground. I swung wildly trying to destroy her face. She pulled my hair so I pulled hers and we rolled around on the ground for a moment until someone pulled us apart. I pushed every one off me.

"Fuck this!" I yelled. I took my ring and threw it in the street.

"I'm tired of all this shit!" I continued. I saw my mom rushing down the block to me with Tarina and smiled. I met my mother halfway and took Tarina into my arms.

"I'm going home." I said looking at my mom.

She laughed.

"Good idea." She said.

A LIVING NIGHTMARE

7 Months Later

Tavon

I was almost done packing my bags when Derek called me. I sat laid on my bed and stared at the ceiling.

"Can't believe you're really about to fly a plane to Florida tonight. Are you excited?" he asked.

"Yeah a little, but this what I've been trained to do."

"I know. We should hit a strip club to celebrate."

I laugh.

"No I'm good. Plus ain't you watching your son for the night?"

"Yeah, but I was going to drop him off at my mom's house for the night because I'm really tired of the shitty diapers."

We both laugh in union.

"I can't believe you're leaving."

"Leaving? You acting like I'm never coming back. I'll back in a couple of days."

"That's a long time."

I sit up and laugh. I looked at the presents wrapped in the corner and sigh.

"Hey, while I'm gone will you do me a favor?" I ask.

"Anything."

"Can drop off these gifts I've brought for Tarina?"

"Sure. What are they for?"

"Christmas is tomorrow and I want her to get them."

"What about her birthday?"

"I'll be back by then."

"Okay."

"I'm going to leave my mailbox unlock so you can just hit it and it'll open up and I'll leave my key in there for you so you can get the gifts."

"Alright."

"Good, so I'll speak to you later."

"Alright later." I hung up and continued to pack. I still had a few more hours to spare so after I finished packing I just laid on my bed and relaxed. I hadn't seen or spoken to Carmen or Tarina after she renewed her vows. Renee called but I told her if she wanted to speak to me she had to promise never to bring up Carmen and she agreed. She always sent me pictures of Tarina and caught Tarina on camera walking and sent that to me also. Derek still kept in contact with Carmen but he knew better to speak about her to me. I know something crazy happened after I left but I felt it would be best if Carmen's business stayed just that. Carmen called me so many times but I refused to answer. I deleted her messages without listening to them because my heart wouldn't be able to take any more damage. I needed to heal from the wounds I already had, so I changed my number. I wanted to be happy for her and support her like she wanted me to but I couldn't, so it was for the best that I kept my distance. I got up and grabbed my bags. I hated to think about it because the excruciating pain. I'd rather just be early to work or maybe I'll just drive slowly.

Carmen

I rocked Tarina to sleep and put her in her crib before I headed to bed. It was around the time Derek calls so I sat in the living room waiting on him. I had moved back into my condo and put Tavon's pictures back up. He wouldn't talk or call me back. A few months back I actually went to his door but he never answered. My gut told me he was home but just didn't want to see me. I knew he didn't know me and Erin split and he was stubborn to find out. I asked Derek to ask him but when he tried him and Tavon stop talking for a while. I didn't want to be the reason why they weren't friends so I told Derek to leave it alone. I just hoped one day he would change his mind about everything and come back to me. He just needed time to adjust his life. The phone rang bringing me back to life and I answered.

"Hello?"

"Hey Carmie."

"Hey Derek, how's everything going?"

"It's going good."

"So do you have any news for me?"

"Yeah, he wanted me to drop of Tarina's Christmas gifts tonight."

"Okay that's great. When will you be here?"

"By the next hour or two."

"Okay, anything else?"

"Not really."

"How was he?"

"Same old, same old. He seems fine but he's a weird guy. You never actually know something's wrong until you looking him in the face."

"Well okay then. I guess I'll see you when you get here."

"Okay, later."

"Bye" I hung up and sighed.

Tavon

Finally after getting to Florida I was in my hotel. I was unbelievably tired and stressed. I hit the bed and felt peace. I guess I just needed something soft to lie on. I wasn't flying back until tomorrow night so I knew I could get some good sleep by then. I grabbed the hotel phone and ordered a bottle of vodka and two long island ice teas to help me sleep. I jumped in the shower and by the time I got out room service was at my door. I grabbed a towel and wrapped it around my waist. I answered the door and gorgeous woman stood there with room service. She was Latina with long brown hair and beautiful green eyes. She looked so familiar but I couldn't quite remember from where I knew her. She brought the tray inside and placed it on the table. I reached for my wallet.

"No it's okay, really." She said.

"Okay, well thanks." I said walking her to the door. She turned around to face me and smiled.

"So pilot, will you be needing some company later?" she said. I smiled.

"I'm good, but thanks for the offer."

"Suit yourself." She said as she walked off down the hallway. I closed the door as I shook my head. I down the first ice tea then second and sipped some vodka. I laid down on my bed and waited for it to hit me. The hotel phone rang and I picked it up.

"Hello?" I say wondering who would have this number.

"Tay it's your mother."

"What do you want?" I said sighing.

"Are you going to hate me forever?"

"Yeah, probably."

"What else do I have to do?"

"Mary, you can't fix this."

"Your dad told me she wouldn't take you back."

"Oh, so your talking to dad now?"

"When stop answering my calls I had to stay in contact with you somehow."

"What do you want?"

"To hear your voice, I'm sorry about ruining your relationship."

"You didn't ruin my relationship, you ruined lives."

"Your life is just fine."

"But my daughter won't know me. She just get random gifts from a stranger, so you ruined my daughter's life. And right now your ruining my vacation so goodbye." I hung up before she could respond. I lay back down and dozed off quickly. Soon after I felt the bed move and as I opened my eyes Carmen climbed on top of me. She took my hands rubbed them down her body.

"What are you doing here?" I ask confused. She put her finger to my lips and pulled her shirt over her head. I unsnapped her bra and groped her breast. She kissed me and sucked on my neck. She hiked her skirt up and I felt on her ass. I ripped her thongs and flipped her underneath me. I pulled off my towel and place myself in between her thighs.

"Give it to me papi." She said. I penetrated her deeply and thrusted continuously until I came inside her. I lay beside her afterward and pulled her close.

"I love you." I whispered to her. So many questions were running through my head but they would have to wait for later. She fell asleep in my arms and I fallen asleep right after.

The morning came sooner than I expected and the sun's ray beamed into the room waking me up. I sat up and looked around but Carmen was no longer beside me. I got up walked around and heard the shower running. I exhaled and walked into the bathroom. I watched her through the glass door before I joined her. She had her back to me as she rinsed her hair. Almost immediately I notice how much longer her hair was and how lighter her complexion was. I just brushed it off and pulled her into my chest. She giggled as I kissed her shoulder.

"Good morning beautiful." I said in her ear.

"A good morning it is papi." She said. I let her go swiftly and backed up. One thing I knew for sure was Carmen didn't speak no Spanish and this girl's accent was crazy strong. She turned around and smiled. I noticed she was the same woman that brought me room service last night. I got out the shower and grabbed my towel as my mind raced clearing me of my mistake.

"Papi are you okay" She said.

I walked in to the bedroom area and grab my clothes and started to get dressed. The shower went off and she came out with a towel on.

"Tavon are you okay" she said.

"Have you been here since last night" I said.

"Yes don't you remember?"

"Oh yeah, I remember."

"Is there something wrong?"

"Yes there is something wrong."

She walked up to me and touched my arm and I pulled away from her.

"You didn't have a problem last night when . . .—"

I cut her off.

"About that? How the hell did you get in here?"

"I asked the manager for your key."

I pulled my shirt on

"Where are you going?"

"Getting out of here."

"Don't leave."

I looked at her confused

"Why?"

"Because I wanna get to know you."

"There's no need to."

"What the hell is your problem."

"I didn't know you was . . ."

"Was what? Spanish?"

"No I just thought you were someone else."

"Who Denise?"

"Who's Denise?"

"Don't act like you don't know. The brunette girl with huge tits. The filght attendant you seem so attracted to."

"What."

"When you were talking to her last night in the coach area of the plane."

"How would you know?"

"Because I'm a flight attendant.""I thought you worked at the hotel you brought me room service."

"I was trying to have a reason to come to your room so I gave the guy fifty bucks to let me bring your order up."

I studied her for a moment. That's where I knew her from.

"Oh I forgot."

"No, you just didn't notice me because Denise's big tits but I don't mind."

"Denise isn't half as sexy as you are."

"You didn't think that before we had sex."

"Yes I did when I saw you at my door I thought you were very attractive."

"So why did you turn me down."

"Because I'm not looking for sex."

"Then why did you have sexy with me."

"I was so drunk I thought you were my ex fiancé."

"Oh you still love her."

"Yes I do."

"Well that explains why you told me you loved me last night."

"I sat down on the bed and she walked up to me.

"I don't know what you been through but I been through some crazy shit myself. My name is Jackie, maybe we can help each other."

"Like a relationship."

"For now let's just call it a friendship." She said as she dropped her towel.

Carmen

I had been working as a receptionist at a major magazine company. It wasn't the best job but it paid well and gave me good hours. Tomorrow was New Year's Day and Tarina's first birthday and I was excited to see her open her gifts. I had already recorded her first Christmas so I decided not to record her birthday since it was only week after Christmas. I had left so many messages for Tavon about Tarina's birthday even though I knew he wouldn't call me back. Even so I kept hope alive and believed he would if it consisted on Tarina. As I gather my things to leave for the day my desk phone rang. I answered with my fingers crossed.

"Hello?"

"Yeah, you called."

My heart fell from chest and landed in stomach.

"I had left you a few messages."

"Oh, well I haven't gotten to them yet. I've been busy."

"I called hoping you would come by tomorrow for Tarina's first birthday."

"Well I actually something to do tomorrow."

I sat in my chair slowly.

"Oh, well okay."

"Carmen?"

"Yes."

"Do you really believe I would miss my daughter's first birthday?"

"Well I hoping you wouldn't."

"Good, because I wouldn't miss it for the world."

I smiled knowing Tavon wasn't as cold-hearted as he pretended to be.

"Okay, good. I moved back into my condo I know you know where that is and I'll see you there."

"Okay, thanks."

"Alright."

"Bye." I hung up with the biggest smile on my face. I took a breath and got ready to go home.

After I picked up Tarina from my mom's, got home, fed her, her, put her to sleep, and ate dinner I wrapped her gifts and pil neatly I laid down in my bed. I had a cup of egg nog with cr and rum. I remember when I spent Christmas with Tavon tw and now we both are over worked and beyond tired. Maybe th coming in will be different for sure. My phone and I answer

"Hello?" I said cheerfully.

"Before you hang up just hear me out."

I sighed.

"I'm giving you three minutes Erin."

"I'm over you leaving me at the altar because I deserved it. I'm begging you to come back home now. I promise no more bullshit please just don't finalize our divorce next week."

"It's been months since I left you. Just move on already, this divorce will be good for the both of us."

"Fine, this is the last time I'll ask you to stay. After this you won't hear from me ever again."

"Good because your three minutes are up." I hung up and sighed.

"This type of love is worth risking everything." I whispered then sipped my egg nog.

Tavon

New Year's Day

I sat up in the bed while Jackie brought me breakfast.

"Waking up to a new year, and breakfast with a side order of thongs." I said.

We laughed. She placed the tray of food on my lap and put on her thongs and started shaking her ass. I put the tray on the night stand and pulled her on the bed. We wrestled around the bed kissing and then she put her finger on my lip.

"Wait, wait don't you have to go see your daughter today?" she asked. I exhaled.

"Yeah, actually I'm about to get ready to go."

I lay back on the bed and she got up.

"Well, I wanted to ask you something." She said with her back to me.

"Ask away."

"I wanted to come with you to your daughter's birthday."

I sat up.

"Sorry, but no. I don't want to introduce my daughter to anyone."

She turned around sat beside.

"I understand that but I'm not just anyone. I care about you Tay."

"We just met. I think it's too soon to make big decisions like that."

"Fine Tay."

She stood and got dressed. I sigh and watch her. She looked at me.

"Are you even going to ask me where I'm going?"

"Okay, where are you going?"

"Home. And do you know why?"

"Why?"

"Because you're not open and ready to love. Your shallow and empty and don't give any room for love to grow. I think it's time for a change in your life and when you're ready for that call me."

I sighed.

"Is this your way of trying to change my mind?"

She poked her lip out.

"Is it working?"

"No."

She folded her arms.

"I think that was a very good speech though."

She smiled. I stood up and kissed her softly.

"So after the party you're going to call me?" she asked. I nodded. She kissed me once more.

"Okay, I'll be waiting for you."

We kissed once more before she left and I got ready to go.

It was around two o'clock in the afternoon when I made it to Carmen's. The Christmas music filled the condo most of the time but more surprisingly Tarina warmed right up to me. Her hair was curly and long. She was running and climbing on everything. She let me hold her and she shared her toys with me. She screamed and laughed all day and smiled like her mother and brightening my heart with her little cheeks. I loved her and it brought me so much joy to spend the first day of the year with her. I picked her up and sat her on my lap and opened all her gifts with her. I fed her and we watched movies together. Around eight o'clock she fell asleep in my arms. I put her in her crib and stared at her while she slept before I left her room. I walked in the living room and Carmen was putting the toys away. I got down on the floor and helped.

"Her room looks amazing did you do it yourself?"

"Yeah, Jazz and I got it together before she was born."

I nod as I pick up Tarina's clothes.

"So, how you been?" She asked.

"Pretty good."

"Have you met anybody?"

I sigh.

"Sure you can say that."

"Are you two serious?"

"I don't know." I answered.

"Do you love her?"

I finally look at her and she was staring at me. I stood up and so did she.

"I like her, she makes me happy."

"But do you love her?"

"Why does that even matter?"

"Why wouldn't it matter?"

"What are you getting at with this? Huh Carmen? Just say it already."

"I miss you Tay. And I still want to be with you. I'm sorry about . . . -

"Stop! Carmen just stop."

I stared at her for a moment.

"Not again. Don't confess anything to me, keep it to yourself because I don't want to hear it. I've moved on after months of trying to get over you. Telling myself you no longer wanted me. My mind has been fucked up for months. The more I didn't want to think about you the more I thought about your beautiful heartwarming smile and cute laugh. The way you use to say my name."

She kissed me and wrapped her arms around me. I pushed her back.

"No. you do this to me every time. When I'm finally doing better here you come back into my life. Killing me more and more every time."

"Tay, if you miss me I'm right here. I ain't going anywhere this time. I'm here to stay."

She took my hand and led me to her room. Maybe I should've turned around to leave but I just couldn't turn away, not from Carmen. She sat me on the edge of her bed and took off her shirt. I gripped her by the hips and admired her curves. The same curves I knew Erin was holding on to everynight. I pulled her closer to me and pulled off her jeans. I laid her on the bed and took off my clothes. I got on top of her and lift her leg onto my shoulder. I entered her and all I could imagine was what Erin making love to her like I always was. I hadn't notice how rough I was getting with until I felt her wet cheeks on my chest. I notice then that she was crying quietly. Even though I never intented to hurt I her hoped next time Erin made love to her he'd feel a difference and know I been inside her for the night. I looked away unable to look her in the face knowing what I was doing to her. I just hated her for what she did to me. After I came I lay on top of her for a while and she held my body close to hers. I looked at my watch and remember I had to call Jackie. I got out the bed and started to get dressed.

She pulled her knees into her chest as she laid there and watched me. I looked at her but didn't know what to say, so I didn't say anything.

"So I guess you're going home to your girlfriend now?" she asked sobbing quietly.

"Yeah, I am."

"Are you going to call me?"

"Probably not."

She laid quietly after that, so I left just as quick as I came. I got home and jumped in the shower. After I got out I called Jackie.

"Hello?" she said groggy.

"Hey baby, do you want to hang with me tonight?"

"Well I just fell asleep, but just give me an hour to get ready."

"Okay, see when you get here."

"Later baby."

"Later."

Carmen

Tavon had left a while ago but I just couldn't move. The tears kept flowing and my sobs got heavier. The passion in our sex we had before was gone. He hurt me badly and he knew it. He hated me and I could tell. The phone begin to ring on the night stand and I gathered up enough strength to answer.

"Hello."

"Carmen is that you?" Jazz asked.

"Jazz he hates me."

"Huh? Carmen, are you crying? Did something happen?"

"Tavon hates me."

"No he doesn't."

"Yes he does. We had sex and he hurt me."

"How did he hurt you?"

"He was so rough with me"

"He was rough with you?" she shouted.

"Did you tell him to stop?" she asked.

"No, but he saw me crying. He just didn't care. He hates me Jasmine."

"How could he do that to you, I swear when I see him . . ."

"No Jazz, don't."

"Fuck that shit, he pretty much raped you and you want me to sit back?"

"He has his reasons and I probably deserved it."

"Bitch snap the fuck out of it. There ain't no reason to rape somebody."

"It wasn't rape."

"Then what was it?"

"Not rape."

"Fine, but he doesn't have the right to get rough with you."

"I know."

"Good, because when I see him it's going down."

"Please, Jazz don't get out of hand with things."

"I won't but I am going to slap the shit out of him"

"Jazz!"

"Carmen!"

"You're overreacting."

"And you're underreacting."

"How about you just leave it alone for now? Okay?"

She sighed.

"Whatever. Anyway I'm coming over tomorrow and were going to the mall to do some girl things. You and me, we're going to leave the kids with Jacob and the babysitter. Okay?"

I nod.

"Yeah, that sounds like something I need."

"Good, then I'll see you in the morning."

"Okay, good night."

"Good night."

Jasmine had come over bright and early with Jacob and Hailey, their babysitter, and forced me out of bed. We got our nails done and massage before heading to the mall to shop. Around lunch time we headed to the food court and sat down. Once I looked up I regretted getting out of the bed this morning. I looked down hoping and praying Jazz wouldn't notice Tavon walking past with some girl. I knew she had to be his new girlfriend, because she was unbelievable beautiful. I knew why he didn't want me anymore. He found the next best thing. Jazz caught me looking from the corner of my eye and followed my gaze.

"What are you looking at?" she said turning around. I grabbed her arm.

"Nothing, I was just scanning the area."

"Then why you getting so hype?" she said removing my hand from her arm. I dropped my head on the table and knew there was nothing I could do to avoid this disaster.

"Oh hell no." she said. I bit down on my lip knowing she saw him. She pushed her chair back and I grabbed her hand.

"Please Jazz don't do what you're about to do."

"And he has a girlfriend. Did you know this?"

I look down in lap.

"He's been treating you like shit and you're letting him."

"Please don't make things worst then they already are."

"Carmen what has gotten into you?"

"I love him Jasmine."

She snatched her hand from me and stood up. She stormed over to him and I couldn't move. I could only watch and wait for the worst.

Tavon

Jackie giggled as she held onto my arm. We had been just cruising the mall for fun and cracking jokes.

"Tavon!" I heard someone yell from behind us. I turn around and Jasmine walking towards me and she looked mad as hell.

"Hey Jazz."

"Don't hey Jazz me. I can't fucking believe you Tay. I've been on your side since day one but you've gone too far."

"What are you talking about?"

"I couldn't believe my ears when she told me you got rough with her."

Damn, everything was clear now. Shit, I even knew I was dead wrong to do that to her last night.

"Jasmine I'm sorry."

"Sorry doesn't cut it."

She slapped me and her hand stung the left side of my face. Jackie jumped in front of me.

"Don't put your hands on my man bitch." She yelled. Jasmine got in her face.

"Bust a move and watch me lay you the fuck out."

I pull Jackie away from Jasmine and stepped in between them.

"No Jackie, I deserved that."

I looked past Jasmine and saw Carmen sitting there. She put her head down and I sighed. I should be the one ashamed not her.

"I'm sorry Jasmine."

"I don't want you around her if it has nothing to do with Tarina."

I nodded.

"Okay."

Jazz stormed off. Carmen couldn't even look at me. Jackie took my hand getting my attention and led me away.

"So that's Carmen sitting over there?" she asked. I nodded.

"Yeah it is."

She wrapped her arms around my waist.

"Let's just go home papi."

I nod and head for the exit. We got to the car and I begin to drive us back home.

"So you had sex with her last night?" She asked calmly. I looked at her then back at the road.

"You don't even have to . . . because I already knew. No party for a one year takes that long."

"I didn't want to but . . . -"

"Don't explain, let's just move past it."

"Okay."

When we got home we sat in the living room and watched movies while I massaged her feet. She stared at the screen while I kept my eyes on her.

"I want you to move in with me." I said bluntly. Her eyes shifted to me quickly.

"Really?"

"Yeah, you're always here so you might as well."

"Well when you put like that."

"Pretty much I'm trying to say I want you here with me all the time."

"Good, I like the way you just fix that up."

I chuckled. She swung her feet around climbed on top of me and kissed my lips.

CRASH LANDING

Carmen

This weekend Tarina supposed to stay with me but since Tavon was flying out to Georgia he halfway begged me to take her this weekend. He told me he would take pictures and make sure I had copies so I couldn't refuse. Since I had nothing planned for tonight me, Jasmine and her friend Patricia decided to go out to the club. I was running late so they went without and I told them I'd catch up. I had on my tight pink hip huggers' jeans, pink spaghetti strap shirt, and my pink open toe heels. I looked like Malibu Barbie. I curled my hair, glossed my lips and added eye liner. I parked my car a few blocks down where I could find parking and walked to the club. As I walked down the street a guy walked up behind me. I smiled and continued down the street.

"Hey, what's your name?"

"Don't worry you probably won't ever see me again."

"What makes you so sure Barbie?"

I stopped and stared at him. He kind of handsome with a low cut fade. He had to six feet tall and had deep dimples.

"My name is Carmen and yours?"

"Brian. So where you headed?"

"To the club down the street."

"Let me escort you there."

"Sure."

He took my hand softly and walked me down to the club. Once I turned the corner I beginning to change my mind about going to the club. The line was longer than I expected it to be. Bryan just continued to walk and pass the line. I started to say something it seemed like Bryan knew more than just a few people. Once we got to the entrance the security lifted the rope and let us right without speaking. Once we were inside the music bumping loud. I had almost forgotten what it was like to be at a club. He brought me to the bar and sat down.

"Can I get you anything?"

"Well after getting me in like that I couldn't refuse."

He smiled.

"Let me get two apple martinis." He yelled to the bartender. I searched the club spot Jazz walking across the dance floor to me as she eyed Brian. The bartender brought our drinks and he picked them up.

"Go grabbed up your friends and meet me over there." He said as he pointed towards the back of the club. I nod and meet Jazz halfway.

"Who's that guy you came in the club with?" she asked immediately. I shrug my shoulders.

"I don't know but he got me inside without waiting in line so I guess he's kind of important around here. Anyway follow me." I said taking Jazz hand and leading her to the back of the club with Patricia on our heels. Once we got to the back Brian guided us through the VIP section. Once the door shut behind us the loud music ceased. The music that played now was low key and more relaxing. The VIP was more of a lounge. Bryan grabbed a booth and we scooted down into it. He introduces us to a lot of his friends and we talked and laughed for a while until Brian asked me to dance with him. So we got on the dance floor and he pulled me and close and wrapped his arm around my waist and I took my hand in his as I laid my head on his chest. He smelled all types good.

"Where's your fiancé?" he asked.

"Huh." I said confused.

"Your wedding band is pretty much cutting up my hand."

I laughed.

"No, divorced. My daughter's father proposed but soon after we separated but the ring lets me know one day he'll be back and will get married."

"You do know there are plenty of men who would love to marry a beautiful woman like yourself."

"Yes but there's only one I want."

"How can you be so sure about that if you haven't even tried to look for anything else?"

"He helped me realize how strong I was and I love him for that."

"So won't you let someone else help you stay strong?"

"What are you getting at?"

"Just trying to understand you."

I stopped dancing and took my hand back and stepped away from him.

"I'm not someone most people understand. I think I should be getting home now."

"Wait Carmen, I know this may take you off guard but will you come home with me?"

"What? No, you really thought since you brought me a drink and got me in a club I'd give it up easy."

"I'm not trying to have sex with you."

"Oh really."

"Yes really, I live out here in the Bronx I got a condo uptown we can just talk."

"Sorry but I'm not that naïve."

"I promise I won't even attempt to touch you."

"Why am I supposed to believe you?"

"I'm just asking you to give me the benefit of doubt."

I studied him for a moment.

"Under one condition."

"Okay."

"I'm driving my car just in case I need a quick getaway if you try something funny."

"That's fine." He said as he smiled.

I gave Patricia and Jazz a hug good bye and left with Bryan. He drove his car and I drove mine as I followed him to his place. When I got upstairs I was impressed. He was living in the lap of luxury. His condo was looking more like a five star hotel. He led me to the living room and I took a seat.

"Would you like something to drink?" he asked walking into his wide open kitchen.

"Sure I'll take water."

"Water coming up."

I took my jacket off and slouched back on the sofa.

"How did you get the money for this place?"

"I own a few clubs like the one we were in tonight."

"You own it?"

"Yup." He said walking back into the living room. Passed me a cup of water and sat down. He stared at as I sniffed the cup of water.

"I didn't put anything in it." He said smiling.

"Making sure."

He chuckled. I took a sip.

Tavon

I kissed Jackie on the lips and checked on Tarina that was sitting beside in her car seat strapped up tight. "How's my two favorite girls?" I ask.

Tarina was sleeping great.

"Tarina's been good. Mostly she's been sleeping." Jackie said.

"Okay."

"Is everything going good up there?"

"Not really, the storm is getting bad so were landing at the next station. What's worst is George isn't looking too good. That's why I promised him this will only take a second to come check on Tarina."

"Oh okay."

"So I gotta get back up there."

"Alright."

I kissed her once more and walked back to the captain's room. As I walked back the plane dipped right and jerked forward swiftly. I rushed towards the front while passengers begin to scream. I opened the door and George was pulling the wheel up but the plane wasn't responding. I jumped in my seat cut off auto-pilot. I pulled the wheel but the gauge was broken. The alert system came on and the oxygen bags were released.

"What happened?" I yelled.

"Something in the storm hit the right wingspan and its down."

I grabbed the radio.

"This is flight 270 we are in need of assistance. We have a 483 H45. The storm is bad."

George passed out at the wheel. I dropped the radio and got George out the chair. I picked him and threw him over my shoulder. I opened the door and sat him in the nearest empty seat. I buckled him and dashed for the coach section. I had to get to Tarina. As I ran pass everyone was holding onto their seats and others were falling forward. I pulled back the curtains I and the pressure from the impact pulled me back.

Carmen

I woke up laying beside Brian. He had his arms wrapped around me. The warmth of his body felt wonderful. It had been so long since I've cuddled and I missed it. I look at the clock and it was ten past seven in the morning. I had on his giant's jersey and it swallowed me. It felt good to be held by a man that didn't want sex. I remembered when Tavon was once like that. My cellphone rang and I picked it up off the dresser and sit up. I sat on the edge and answer.

"Hello?"

"Oh my God Carmen, where have you been? I've been calling you all night and all morning." Jazz yelled hysterically.

"Jazz calm down I'm fine."

"Carmen you have to watch the news, right now. Cut it on."

"Why?"

"Just do it, because I can't say it."

I get up and Brian eyes opened.

"Where you going?" he asked smiling.

"I need to see the news."

He nod and gets out of bed. He took my hand lead me to the living room. I sat on the couch and stared the blank television screen. He grabbed the remote and turned it on.

"Which channel Jazz?" I ask.

"Doesn't matter, it's on every news channel."

"Any channel Brian." I said. He sat beside me and switch the channel.

Debra is on the scene. Debra, Thank you Kathy. About 6 hours ago an airplane coming from New York to Georgia crashed in Virginia with over one hundred and fifty passengers. Twenty passengers have been dug from this tragedy untouched, fifteen in a coma, thirty pronounced dead on arrival, thirty-five in Virginia's hospitals in the intensive care unit, and over fifty still lost . . . As she continued I dropped my phone.

"You okay?" Brian asked.

. . . One pilot died and the other in a coma. In last night's storm it had begun to hail knocking the plane's right wing out commission and busting its gas chamber causing the plane to fall from the sky . . .

Tears slipped from my eyes instantly.

"Baby, why are you crying?"

I pointed to the screen lost for words.

"My . . . fam . . . whole . . . family was . . . on . . . that plane."

Everything was cloudly. I could only remember bits and pieces of what happened afterward. I didn't know how I got home but I made it there. Jazz helped me pack some clothes crying hysterically along with me. Ever since we've heard the news the tears wouldn't come to end. Jasmine was going to drive me out to Virginia with hopes that Tavon and Tarina would be the two out of the twenty passengers that made it out untouched. Right after, we hit the road. The first hospital sent us down to the next and so here we were. I rushed in the crowded the hospital pushing past every one. I got to the front desk and tried my best to speak clear.

As I opened my mouth to speak the receptionist shoved a form in my face.

"Fill this out first ma'am." She said. I slapped the paper out my face.

"I didn't come here for that shit."

"Oh the plane accident, sorry miss. Name?"

"Tavon and Tarina Holmes."

She typed for second then looked up at me.

"The pilot was brought to the hospital about two miles down the road. Best hospital in the area and Tarina Holmes is not on my list so she is either still lost or . . . -"

"Dead?" I said bluntly.

"No I was going to say not in the system yet, but I'm pretty sure they wouldn't separate the pilot from his family member so she's probably at the same hospital." I nod.

"Thank you." I turned and rushed back to the car. Jasmine drove further into and soon after we came to the next hospital. It was hardly full but the news reporters stood out front. We both got out fast and ran past them inside the hospital. We rushed to the front desk.

"Yes, how may I help you?" the lady at the front desk asked.

"I'm Carmen Venus I came to Tavon Holmes and Tarina Holmes."

"Oh yes, Tavon Holmes is being set up in a room right now so you'll have to wait in the lobby. Tarina Holmes ma'am, well I'll call the surgeon down immediately."

"Okay, thank you."

She nodded and picked up the phone. Jasmine took my hand and led me to the seats. I sat down and she sat beside me. A few minutes later the doctor walked into the waiting room.

"Tarina Holmes?"

I stood up.

"That's my daughter."

"Well ma'am Tarina passed away 2 hours ago on the emergency table. A picece of the plane was in her liver and such a big operation on a small child, well her body couldn't handle it."

In between him talking my knees went weak and I fell to the floor. Jasmine held me tightly.

"No, not my happiness, not my sunshine, my angel. No! jasmine my baby's gone."

"Ma'am I'm so sorry, I did the best I could."

"You're lying, she can't be gone. She just got here, she just can't. No. God wouldn't do this, why would he do this. You're lying! Let me see her!" I screamed hysterically. Jasmine shoved my face into her chest. I didn't want her to hold me though, I just wanted Tarina. I push her off me and she held me tighter until I held her back.

"Well ma'am I can't stop you from seeing her. I just don't think that you would want to her at this time." He said.

"Just shut the fuck up." Jazz said to him. He stepped back and nodded.

"He's lying. I know he is, Tavon wouldn't let this happen. He would've stopped this."

"I know if he could have he would of." She said in my ear.

"Mr. Holmes have been set up in a room already. He can go to his room if you want." The doctor said.

I sat there rocking in Jasmine's arms.

"Do you want to see him?" she whispered. I shook my head no.

"Okay, you don't have to."

She helped me off the floor and brought me to the car. She drove around until she found a motel. I jumped in the shower then got in the bed. I couldn't deal with seeing Tavon at the time. I felt it was his fault, if he didn't beg me to let him take her this weekend. Jazz got in the bed and pulled me to her chest and held me. But nothing could change the pain in my chest and flow of my tears, nothing.

The next morning me and jazz headed back up to the hospital. The nurse showed us to his room. As I walked in my feelings for him rushed back. He was hooked up to machines. A cast on his right arm and leg, a neck brace, bruises from head to toe, and a breathing tube down his throat. I walked to him and covered my mouth. I closed eyes and rested my hand on his arm.

"He's in a coma. We don't know when he wake up or if he ever will because of the severe brain damage. We're not even sure if he'll recover. I'll send the doctor in for the details but until then that's all I know." The nurse said before walking out. All I could do was cry. I was losing my family all at once. After sitting by his side for an hour the door opened and Jackie walked in. I stood up noticing the bruise on her cheek. Inside I felt she deserved to be the one lying on this bed not Tavon.

"Oh, I didn't know you were here." She said.

"Nor did I know you would stop by."

"Well ever since he was brought here I've been here."

"It's funny how you walk away from a plane crash with nothing but a bruise and my daughter and my man has to suffer and lay up in a hospital bed in a comma with broken bones and brain damage."

"Number one Carmen, Tavon is my man. Second, you have no idea how I've been hurting mentally. Do you think I would rather live to see Tavon like this and Tarina gone? Hell no. I would have done anything to have a different outcome then what this is now."

"But you can't and bitch I blame you for it all."

"Excuse me?"

"You heard me Jackie. I know your God damn ears work just fine. If you wouldn't have asked Tavon to bring Tarina we'd still our baby. So I blame you."

"Carmen I know how you feel."

"No the hell you don't. You don't know how I feel, so don't say that you do."

"Okay, I understand how you must be feeling but directing it towards me ain't going to bring Tarina back."

"Get the fuck out of my man's room now."

"He's not yours anymore Carmen, he's mine. I'm pregnant and my man wants to be with me not you. I'm sorry about what happened to Tarina but my baby will in that gap in his life." She said smiling.

"What?" I said tilting my head.

"Carmen, why are you even here, your just embarrassing yourself. He doesn't care about you anymore so just leave."

"Bitch your about this close to getting your ass handed to you." Jazz said.

"You think if you stick around when he comes out this coma he's going to come back to you. Well he won't so just pack your shit and haul your ass back up to new York and live your life because there aint no reason for you to stick around here any longer."

"Carmen say the word and I'll all over this bitch like a fat boy on cake." Jazz said.

"You ain't gone touch me bitch."

"You wanna bet."

I grab Jasmine's arm.

"She's right."

"What?"

"He ain't coming back to me. He got all he need right here in this neat ghetto package, and he can have it."

I picked up my jacket and purse.

"Let's go Jasmine. I have a funeral to prepare."

BROKEN BUT NOT SHATTERED

Carmen

It's been two weeks and I still wasn't feeling any better. I quit my job once I got back home. They told me that they understood and I could come back if I ever wanted to, but that would just be unnecessary. I made Jasmine go home to her family last week. I had to practically throw her out because she didn't want to leave me alone. She felt I was unstable at the time and didn't want me to do anything stupid, so I had to promise her if I was feeling too down to call her. Instead she was the one calling me every hour. Yesterday was Tarina's funeral. Just thinking about brought tears to my eyes. What made it worst was it was a beautiful day. The sun was shining and the weather was wonderful. Brian told me "It's just God letting you know Tarina's in good hands". He was so sweet and I believed God was taking good care of her. Brian had some things to take care of today so left early promising to be back shortly. My condo was too full to be so empty. I just couldn't stay at home and be surrounded by my memories of my dead family, and I just wasn't ready to get rid of their belongings. An I don't think I'd ever be ready for that so I stayed with Brian because I couldn't face my mother again. She's been quiet ever since she heard about Tarina. I wouldn't speak for no one, I knew this was her way of coping but watching her in pain only hurt me worst. Plus she wouldn't even look at me yesterday. I know she wanted to try to hold on to Tavon but I knew Tavon wasn't going to recover. I accepted that so I could begin healing but I could tell mom knew I was just giving up on him. I knew that if he did I would be the last person his mind so I was just preparing for the worst. My cell phone rang and I answered.

"Hello?"

"Carmen its Robert."

I sat up abruptly as Robert's groggy voice echoed in my ear. I clear my throat.

"Hi." I said.

"I don't know if Tavon ever told you but I got my life together. I turned over a new leaf and umm we patched our relationship."

I listened to his voice and noticed the sadness. If I wasn't mistaken he was sobbing.

"Tavon and I actually talked on a regular basis for the first time ever. I know I wasn't able to meet Tarina but the from the pictures he showed me she looked beautiful. And out of everyone Tavon's every introduce me to, you're the only one that made him change . . . and made him change me. So I'm stuck with the hardest decision in my life and I'm turning to you for your advice. Tavon isn't looking good. The doctors told me there's been no brain activity in two weeks and he may be brain dead . . . there's still a chance he may recover. Should I pull the plug or pray and be patient?" he cried. The pain in his voice brought me to tears. I hated how he felt and how his feelings were rubbing off on me. I wiped my face tried to stay strong from him.

"Robert, as much as I want you to keep hope alive I think we both know the truth. He has too much brain damage and his body has suffered incredibly. Even if he did wake up it would hurt worst to watch him lay in a bed for the rest of his life in misery. Just let him go so at least you can finally begin your healing process, because the longer you hold on . . . the longer you'll have to deal with this agonizing pain."

I knew I wanted to stay strong but I couldn't. This was a huge lost for us both and the pain needed to be released.

"Your right, thank you. And I just wanted you to know that you will always be a part of my family. If you need me just call, I'll be there."

"Thank you Robert."

"Okay, bye."

"Bye." I hung up and dug my face in the pillow behind. It was my fault he was gone, I told him to follow his dreams and this is where it led him. The man that I will always love taken from me in a blink of an eye. Life is too short and I know that now. I heard the front door and I jumped out the bed. I ran to the front of the house jumped into Brian's arms.

"Is there something wrong?" he said franticly. I shook my head as I dug my face into his chest. He held me close to him and kissed my forehead.

"You scared me for a second." He said pulling me back so he could check my face. I smiled lightly and he wiped my cheek with back of his hand. I stared at his handsome face.

"What?" he asked. I stood on my tip toes and kissed his lips. He pulled me into him and picked me up. I wrapped my legs around him and he brought me to the room. He placed me on the bed and took off his jacket and shirt. He went in his night stand pulled out a condom. As he climbed on top of me I took the condom from him and laid back. He looked at me for brief moment.

"Are you sure that's what you want to do?" he asked.

"Yes."

He sighed and sat beside me.

"I understand how your feeling, but you can't replace Tarina." He said looking away from me.

"I know." I said sitting up.

"Then I think you should wait."

"Please Brian, I know it's a lot to ask for but I'm begging you." I said pulling my knees into my chest.

"I just don't think we should do this for the wrong reasons."

I got off the bed and grabbed my jeans. He stood up and took my hand.

"Wait, I'm not saying I wouldn't. I meant I don't want to do this if you're not doing this for us, because this is a huge step . . . that I'm willing to take if that's what you want."

"I want this." I say looking at him.

"Okay, but I don't want to fill in your boyfriend's shoes. I like my own sneakers just fine."

"I'm not asking you to be my ex. I just want a baby."

"Then why so soon? If you want a child now you'll want one later too."

I put my back to him.

"Please don't leave Carmen." He said.

I closed my eyes.

"You don't get it, I know Tarina's gone and she ain't coming back but I built my life around a child. So without one . . . I'm lost. I having nothing to do but lay in my sadness and replaying these horrible memories. I need a family because mine is gone."

He pulled me into him.

"Okay, I would love to start a family with you. It's just I want you to stay with me."

I nod.

"I don't mean just for tonight, I mean as long as our hearts pump our blood through our bodies."

"Yes I'll stay until death do us part"

SHOTGUN FAMILY

8 Months Later

Carmen

Jasmine stood behind me zipping up my wedding dress.

"Damn this dress is tight." I say rubbing my round belly.

"I told you to get a size bigger because your stomach will be really showing. You're seven and a half months, did you really think you weren't going to grow." Mom said fixing my Tiara and veil.

"Momma, you know I'm hard headed."

"Well you only have to wear it for thirty minutes. Then for the reception you can put something else."

I shook my head.

"No, I'll wear it to the reception. It's not too uncomfortable."

"Okay. So are you guys ready." I said as I turned to face every body.

"Okay, let's do this." Jasmine said. She pulled up her light pink bridesmaid dress and push up her breast. I laughed. I looked at mom and she smiled. She pulled my veil over my face then covered her mouth.

"You look so beautiful." She said. I giggled.

"You say that every time you see my in a wedding dress."

She chuckled.

"Well you have been in a few."

I laugh and fan her away. Soon after Brian and I said "I do" and we walking down the aisle hand in hand. Once we got in the limo I exhaled deeply. Brian rubbed my belly and smiled.

"Can't believe we're really married. I thought you wasn't going to show up." He said. I rubbed the side of his face.

"Well I guess I proved you wrong."

"Yeah, you did. I love you so much Carmen."

"I know you do." I say avoiding the "L" word. I kissed his lips leaned on his shoulder.

1 hour later

I sat at one of many tables that was scattered around the room. Brian, Jasmine, and momma sat at the table with me and watched everyone act a fool. I didn't have much family but Brian did and they all were a little Looney. The music stop and Brian's brother Matthew got on stage with a microphone. Everyone grabbed a seat and settled down.

"Well first let me congratulate my brother Brian. When he told me he was getting married I thought the nigga was bullshitting but when he introduce Carmen I knew why he was getting married. Besides the fact that she is insanely sexy she had a big heart and warm personality. So welcome to the family Carmen and I wish you two the best. Now let's celebrate like it's never been done before."

We all clapped and raised our glasses. Jasmine stood up and grab my hand.

"Let's boogie." Jazz said. I looked at Brian and he waved for me to go.

"I got to use the bathroom so I'll meet you on the dance floor." Brian said. I nodded and got up. We squeezed in between the crowd to the middle of the dance floor and got down. Not even a minute into the dance Matthew interrupted.

"Can I get dance with the bride?" he said pushing in between us with his hands in the air and swaying his waist. Jasmine backed up laughing.

"Okay, okay. I'm going to hit the ladies room to freshen up." Jazz said. I nodded as the rhythm slowed. Matthew took my hand and held my waist. We slowly danced in a circle.

"So how you feeling?" he asked.

"I'm feel great, besides my feet hurting."

"Okay, so did you like my toast?"

I chuckle.

"Yes I loved it. I never knew you thought I was sexy but yeah, it was good."

"Well thank you. I hope you guys are really happy together. I'm hoping for the best."

"Thanks Matt."

"Don't mention it."

"Can I get my wife back?" Brian asked walking up behind. Matthew gave him a hug and walked off leaving us on the dance floor. Brian pulled me close and I laid my head on his chest. As we twirled in circles we were silent. I was glad to have Brian in my life. As I looked up across the room Jackie stood at the door smiling as she watched me and Brian. Her belly was big like mine. I stared at her for a moment confused wondering what the hell she was doing here. As I let go Brian she turned swiftly and left. I stared at the door briefly before Brian took my hand.

"What's wrong?" he asked. I shook my head.

"Nothing."

After the reception we headed to the Harbor to catch our cruise to the Bahamas. Our honeymoon suite at the hotel resort was beautiful. They had already laid roses petals on the bed and candles around the tub. It was wonderful, but the elephant in the room was crowding the place. I lay on the bed and Brian sat out on the balcony. I rubbed my belly and sighed. What kind of honeymoon was I on? It was too much distance between us to be so close to one another. I turned and looked at him and he stared into the sky.

"Come lay with me." I say getting his attention. He looked at me and nodded. He stood up and walked over to the bed and sat on the edge. I got up on my knees and began to rub his back.

"I want to ask you something that's been bothering since the reception." I said.

"What's going on?"

"Well, there was a girl there I thought I recognized and I wanted to know if you invited her. She was a pregnant Spanish girl."

He removed my hands and stood up.

"She's not important to me anymore."

I sat down surprised. He did know her, so he must have invited her.

"Is she a part of your family?" I ask.

"No, just an old friend."

"An old friend."

"Just forget about her." He grabbed his shirt and put it on.

"I'm going down to the beach. I'll be back."

He didn't even give me a chance to ask him if he wanted me to join. He left quickly. I grabbed my cell phone and sat out on the balcony. I called Jasmine and waited for her to answer.

"Hey honeymooner, is it going good out there in the islands?" she asked.

"Actually it's horrible."

"Babe what's wrong?"

"Ever since we got here everything has been going wrong. The only time we're next to each other is when we're sleeping. Also at the reception, I saw Jackie. Before I could even approach her she left. Now he's acting weird and he doesn't even want to talk about it. I don't know what's going on."

I sighed.

"Well, actually I have to tell you something that I heard and saw at the reception. When Matthew asked you to dance and I went to the bathroom I saw Brian and Jackie talking. So I stood around the corner and I heard them arguing.

"Like I give a fuck, you ditched me remember." Jackie said.

"That was two fucking years ago, get over it. You know I don't do that shit no more." Brian responded.

"Did you really think it was going to be that easy? Did you really think you were just going to get out and settle down? If you want me to stay quiet you know what you'll have to do."

"Don't threaten me Jackie."

"I helped you and now it's your turn. I'm pregnant and you're going to help me."

"I can't believe you came to my reception with this shit."

"Look, I got somewhere to go but I'll keep in touch. Oh yeah, congrads on the wedding."

"After that I walked off so they wouldn't know I was listening." Jazz explained.

I looked over the balcony and Brian stood on the beach with his feet in the water. I couldn't believe he was hiding something from me. I know we hardly knew each other and we had a gunshot wedding but I told him about my past. Not once has he ever mentioned Jackie. I sighed.

"I wanted to tell you after your honeymoon because I didn't want to ruin your vacation, but babe I think maybe Jackie and Brian use to be something."

I shake my head. That's what I didn't want to hear. I didn't want to believe that Jackie had been a part of Brian's life like she had been with Tavon.

"You're probably right, but umm I'm going to call you back." I say.

"Okay."

"Bye." I hung up and placed my phone on the table. Tavon had passed away and he still managed to settle himself in my life. I already felt weird about the fact that the only thing left behind by Tavon was Jackie's unborn child. I would've given up everything to have his child again before he left. Instead I'm forced to acknowledge that, that was physically impossible. Brian turned around and looked up at me. I stood up and walked inside. I knew marrying Brian couldn't be a mistake once Tavon died, but that was beginning to look shady. Brian was a sweet guy and treated me great but I didn't know Brian. Maybe it's good that I don't know him. I lie back on the bed and sigh. I stared at the ceiling. Is this what God wanted for me, or was this just my karma catching up to me. Once I thought I was finally reaching a happy place, life threw live grenades at me. They were still ticking but when they exploded, hopefully I would be a good distance away from them. Brian walked back in the room and sat down the other side of the bed.

"Are you hiding something from me?" I ask.

"What would give you a thought like that?" he responded.

"There is something you haven't told me about yourself. Maybe I don't need to know what it is but if I'm your wife I should know everything about my husband."

"I love you and that's all you need to know." He said getting up. I sat up and looked at him. He walked to the bathroom and shut the door.

"Brian." I say. He didn't respond. I got up and followed him to the bathroom. I knocked on the door.

"What?" he asked with an attitude.

"We're supposed to be on our honeymoon, or did you forget."

"How could I forget? I'm paying for it." He said through the door.

"I didn't even want to leave New York but you said otherwise and that's why I'm here".

"Is that the same reason why you married me?"

"What the hell is that supposed to mean?"

"You don't even love me. So what other reason would you have to marry me?"

"You knew I didn't love you. I wanted a family and you said you would be give me one. That's why I married you."

The bathroom door swung open and he stood there with an attitude.

"Exactly, this isn't even a marriage. It's a deal. So I don't have to tell my business partner anything about me if it's not pertaining to our business arrangement." He said walking pass me. I stood there for a moment before I turned around.

"If this was just business then why the hell did you even bring me out here? Why did we get married? You could've just given me a child and went on your merry way. You don't have to be with me, because I'll be just fine on my own."

"Oh stop being so damn dramatic. You're acting like I said I don't love you."

I shook my head at him and began to pack my bags.

"Carmen you're not leaving." He said.

I ignored him and continued. He came up behind me and grabbed my arm. I turned around and pushed him off me.

"Don't touch me Brian." I said before I continued to pack.

"Fine, it's not like it even fucking matters. Just pack your shit and leave." He said. I zipped up my bags. He picked up the hotel lamp and slammed it against the wall. I put on my sneakers and tied them.

"Just get the fuck out!" He yelled as he punched a hole in the wall. I looked at him.

"Yeah, just destroy the room and pay for the damage later. That's fucking intelligent."

"Just be lucky it's not you." He whispered.

I put my hands on my hips.

"Is that what you're hiding? You're a woman beater?" I ask. He looked at me.

"No I'm not."

I picked up my jacket and grabbed my duffel bags. Brian jumped in front of me and blocked the door.

"Get out my way." I say sighing.

"I'm sorry okay. I didn't mean to bug out on you."

"Oh, I guess that suppose to make up for everything you just displayed."

"Carmen, I'm just got a lot on my mind."

"So everytime you got a lot on your mind your going to treat me like this?"

"No."

"Then I guess that excuse is useless."

"Jackie and I use to work together a few years ago when I lived in Detroit. After I came to New York I stop communicating with her and started my life over. I don't know how she found me but she showed up to the reception asking for my help. I declined and that was it."

I looked at him and sighed.

"So you two never dated?"

"No, we were only coworkers. Now can you put your bags down?"

"How do I know next time you won't be throwing shit at me? I'm not trying to lose this child this time around."

"I would never hit you. I was angry and I just was talking out my ass."

I stared at him for a moment in silence.

"I'm ready to go home. Maybe we can try this honeymoon thing some other time, because I doubt if I can enjoy the rest of the week like this."

He nodded.

"When you say home, which one do you mean?"

"I meant my own place."

"Carmen please."

"I need some time to myself."

"All couples argue."

"Not on their honeymoon."

"You told me you would stay with me."

"I know, and I meant that. But I'm not going to lose my child stressing out about stupid shit like this. I'm just letting us cool down and try to start fresh after we get some time a part."

"Okay, but let me escort you back home. There's no reason I should stay here if you're not. An I definitely don't want you carrying all these heavy bags."

I nod.

"Okay."

Once we got to the harbor I went straight to my condo. Brian tried to stop and talk me out of going home but I still left. He showed me a part of him that I didn't know he had in him. I didn't want to leave him because he promised he would give me a new family. Though, I was worried that maybe Brian was a closet woman beater or worst. All I knew was the skeleton in his closet from his past was catching up with him. If not, then maybe Jackie was just catching up with me. I didn't tell Brian I knew Jackie, and I had a feeling Jackie was going to enlighten him about it. I took a deep breath once I got in the door. A few months ago I had movers come and remove all of Tavon and Tarina's things and take it to storage. After that I felt more comfortable in my home. I kept the walls bare and colored all the walls white. I liked to keep everything plain. The more simple and to the point the better I could cope with my condo. I walked in and dropped my bags off in the living room and headed straight for the bathroom. I ran my bath water and tied my hair up into a bun. As I undressed my house phone rang. I dashed in back in my room and grabbed it off the night stand.

"Hello?"

"Are you sure you don't want to come over?" Brian asked. I rolled my eyes.

"I'm staying home."

"Okay, then can I come over?"

I sighed.

"I told you I need some to myself."

"I know, I know. Just hoping you would change your mind."

"Well I'm not."

"Okay, I just want you to know I love you and I'll be waiting."

"I know you love me, but I need some time to adjust to this new you."

"Baby I'm still me."

I shake my head.

"If I'm going to take my time and learn to love you, I am going to need time getting to know you better. And this weekend you introduced me to a new side of you that I've never seen. So maybe this time a part will help a change in our marriage, but you're going to need to be patient with me."

"I am being patient, but it feels empty at my house. I just want to be where you are."

I smiled.

"Good night Brian."

"Yes, it will be a good night." I hung up and got in the tub. I soaked my skin for an hour before I got out. The pain in my back was still there but the warm bath helped the swelling in my feet. After I got dressed I made myself dinner then laid in my bed with my favorite book. Halfway into my book my phone rang.

"Hello?"

"Jazz told me you left your trip early dear. What happened?" momma asked worried.

I sigh.

"We got into an argument and Brian changed into whole other man. He started to destroy the room and I just couldn't even believe what was happening. He frightened me a little; I didn't feel safe with him. So I decided to come back home."

"Wow, I would have never expected Brian to be out of control."

"It surprised the hell out of me. He's so kind and gentle but he just snapped."

"Are you planning on staying with him?"

I rubbed my belly.

"He's the father of my child, I couldn't abandon him. Plus we just got married and what type of wife would I be if I ran out on him already. I at least want to try to make this work."

"Okay, well that's wonderful sweetheart."

"Thanks mom."

I knock came to the front door and I sat up almost instantly.

"Well I wish you two the best."

"Okay mom."

"Bye."

"Bye." I hung up and tossed the phone on the bed. I knew Brian would show up after I told him not to. He was persistent. I got to the door and swung it open and expected to see Brian's puppy dog eyes. Instead I stood face to face with the lingering tissues of my past.

No, this can't be. This isn't possible. Maybe I was really losing my mind and I was finally beginning to hallucinate. Yes, that was a reasonable answer. I was in a mental heartbroken stage of my pain. Maybe behind this image God was waiting to tell me I didn't make it to the gates and this was my punishment I had to endure. No, my mind was playing tricks on me . . . that had to be the case.

I stared into the hollow eyes of my past ghost. He smiled and dug his hands in his pockets. My chest felt huge and I realized I was holding my breath. I exhaled and tried to breathe normally but instead I was breathing heavily and uneven.

"Did you miss me?" he said. I opened my mouth but the words didn't come out on time.

". . . Ta . . . Tavon?"

To be continued . . . . . .

"Through the Storm"

Prologue

Robert

I stood in the hallway of the hospital allowing the tears running down my cheeks to drip from my chin. Trina held my hand tightly as we both stared at the room Tavon had been in for the two months. I had been numb for so long but finally I could feel something, but I would trade it in for the numb feeling again. As I heard Mary's heels coming down the hallway in our direction I closed my eyes. Trina grabbed my arm and shoved her face in my chest. Mary stopped in front of us and I opened my eyes to look at her. She was dressed in all black with a black veil falling from her hat that covered her face. I knew she was angry with me for the decision I made without her but I didn't need her permission.

"Well, I'm here." She said coldly.

I tried to clear my throat as best as I could.

"Are you ready?" I asked taking Trina's hand in mine.

"I'm as prepared as a mother can get to watch her son be murdered."

Trina whipped her head around to face her.

"How could you say something like that?" Trina asked staring at her in disgust.

"It's funny how you can stand in my face shedding these fake tears when you're the one who made this decision." She said folding her arms.

"Haven't you made him suffer enough?" I said through my teeth.

"I've made my mistakes, but I'm not the one killing him right now."

"Well you have no authority over this decision. I am his legal guardian not you, and you know why Tavon wanted it that way."

"If he knew you would give up on him so soon I highly doubt if he would have allow you be over him."

"You don't know a damn thing about my son." I said slightly moving Trina aside.

"And you do? You never were around, I raised him while you ran off chasing tail like the dog you are."

"You're right, I wasn't around but I've never took away the one person in his life that made him want to be all the man he could be. Compared to you I'm the best damn parent he could have ever had."

She turned her back to me aburtly. She slowly opened the door to Tavon's room and stared at him as he laid on the hospital bed. I shook my head slowly as I stared at her.

"You killed him a long time ago." I said pulling Trina closer to me. She walked into the room and went to his side. She took his hand and brought it to her face and kissed it.

"I know what I've done. I've apologize a million times and I'd apologize a million more. But he hasn't forgiven me yet." Mary said laying her hand on the ventilator.

"An if he dies now I'll never know if he will." She turned and looked at me.

"I've already taken his heart, the only thing left keeping him here with us is this machine. Why would we take the last thing he depends on from him."

We stepped into the room.

"I spoke to Carmen, and if she feels letting him go is the best way then I can only follow her wishes. She loved him and I know she wouldn't steer me in the wrong direction. So I'm sorry but I've made up my mind. I'm ready to get pass this stage of grief."

She nodded and looked back at Tavon. Trina took Mary's hand and stood beside her. We look down at Tavon and knew it was time to let go. The doctor walked in and cleared his throat. I closed my eyes held onto Trina's hand tighter. I could hear the nurses coming after him preparing the room for him.

"Hello, my name is Dr. Genitch I'm here discontinue Tavon's ventilation machine. Mr. Holmes there some questions I must ask for legal reasons before we remove any equipment."

I look at him nod.

"Okay." he said as he pulled out his clipboard.

"Did you sign Tavon's dismissal forms as his legal guardian?"

"Yes."

"Do you understand that removing the ventalitor may be the cause of Tavon Holmes death and you're under contract that restricts you suing any doctors or the hospital if this occurs?"

"Yes."

"Okay, and are you still allowing I, Steven Genitch, to remove the ventalitor from Tavon Holmes."

"Yes."

"Are you under the influence of acholol, marjuanna, myth, or any other drug that cloud your judgement."

"No."

"Okay. May you sign here." He ask passing his clipboard. I signed on the blank line and passed it back to him. We all took a step back as the nurses began to take the breathing tubes from his nose and mouth and remove his ivy. The doctor pressed a few buttons on the ventalitor and then check his vitals. The heart rate monitor continued to beep for every heart beat. I held my breath as I waited for the flatline. The nurses put the tubes in the diposal and cleared out the way for the doctor. He pulled out his chart and began writing. We all looked at each other confused as the doctor continued to write. He finally stopped moving his pen and looked up at the one of the nurses.

"We're going to need another ivy and someone page Dr. Jenkins, and call in an order for a x-ray downstairs." He said swiftly before he looked at us. I could feel pressure building in my chest and my eyes began to burn forcing me to squint.

"Tavon's breathing on his own. Maybe he's been breathing on his own for a while but we'll have too run some test to make sure. And if we see any brain activity this could be a sign that he's pulling through. Though I'll have to speak with Dr. Jenkins befo . . . ."

I dropped to my knee as my tears flowed out of my eyes. I could feel Trina rubbing my back and I just knew from then on everything was only going to get better.

Here and in the Flesh

Carmen

I took a step back wondering what I should do. Maybe I could scream and hopefully wake up or hold him tightly and tell him to never let me go. He stepped inside and kissed my cheek as he walked around me and entered my house. I closed the door slowly and leaned my forehead against the door trying to believe that this wasn't real, but the feel of his lips left on my cheek proved me wrong. I turned around slowly and watched him as he sat down on my couch. I slowly crept around the sofa and stared at him. He smiled the way he use to bringing back my months of bad dreams and sleepless nights.

"Looks like you've seen a ghost." He said lightly laughing. I sat down across him to keep distance between us just in case he turned into some demonic like creature. He looked around the living room and back at me.

"Looks empty in here. Don't tell me your movng out."

I shook my head.

"I like things plain and simple now."

"Okay, well it's been a while whats new?" he asked sitting closer to the edge of the couch.

"How are you here in my living room right now?" I ask swallowing hard.

"You're pregnant? Wow . . . you only get pregnant after I'm gone. I guess that's no surprise."

"I thought you were dead." I said trying to hold back my tears.

"I heard you got married. So where is this lucky son of bitch?" he said avoiding my question once again.

"I know you heard me."

He sat back and sighed.

"I heard you told my dad to let me die."

I dropped my head in my hands at the thought of that conversation with his dad. I gripped all the hair in my face and pulled it to the back of my head.

"Your bones were broken, you suffer brain damage, and you were cover in bruises from head to toe. What the hell you wanted me to do?"

"You gave up on me."

"You don't know what it was like to see you the way you were. I had to bury Tarina by myself and you wanted me to sit back and watch you lie in a bed unable to even open your eyes."

"Yes, I expected to open my eyes and see you. I lost a child too."

"You're the one that begged me to let you take her that weekend."

"I knew you would blame me for her death."

"I never said that."

"You don't have to. I see it in your eyes, you still hate me."

"Yes, I hated you at a time, but not for the reason you think. I hated you for being everything I wanted you to be because if I never loved you I would've never had Tarina. An if I never had Tarina I would've never lost my entire family. So if my love for you was human I'd probably slaughter the bitch and bury her in my back yard and sleep well for the first time in months."

He nodded slowly.

"If you really loved me, you would've fought for me."

"I did. Just not the way you wanted me to. I wanted a family so bad because I missed the one had."

"So . . . has ya replacement family been working out for you."

"Nobody compares to you and Tarina."

He stood up and headed for the door. I jumped and grabbed his arm.

"Where are you going?" I ask. He turned around and looked at me.

"I'm always too late to be with you. Your always already married."

"You haven't even told me how long you been back?"

"About six months ago I woke up. It felt like I been sleep for a few days but I found out I was in a coma."

"Did you remember what happened on the plane."

"No, I cant remember any of it. I was just released two weeks ago. I've getting use to myself again."

"Hold on, you been out your coma since when and never picked up a phone to call me."

"I was angry. The first person I saw was my mother."

I sat down and sighed. Ugh . . . Mary was the last person on my mind. He sat down beside me and took my hand.

"I thought you hated me for what happened and when I saw the wedding invitation you sent my dad I knew you had moved on. My dad begged me to call you but I was so stubborn. Now I just wish I had."

I didn't know how to feel. The love of my life that I thought died months ago sat in my living holding my hand. While the father of my unborn child wasn't the man he had claimed to be. It didn't take a genius to know what I should do, but how could I break Brian's heart like that? He promised to console me and help fill the gap in my life and give me the family that I had been missing. How could I leave him now? I was eight months pregnant, it was too late. I couldn't be so heartless.

"Tavon you know if I wasn't with Brian I'd run to you with open arms."

"I wasn't going to ask you to leave him. I just needed to see you. You're the mother of my child, I will always love you."

"Aren't you with Jackie anyway?"

He slightly laughed.

"She disappeared on me. I'm not worried though. She wasn't really my type."

"Well months ago when you were in a coma and I went to see you she popped up telling me you and her were starting a family. That was when I was hoping you'll be with me when you wake up but that wouldn't happen. After that I never went to see you anymore. She's one of the main reasons why I moved on because I thought you would've went back to her if you did wake up and I would have wasted my time."

He clenched his jaw and exhaled through his nostrils.

"Trust me, Jackie will never be apart of my life in any way ever again."

I watched him try to calm down.

"Did something happen between you two?"

He rubbed my hand.

"Don't worry about it."

I nodded.

"Okay."

We sat there in silence for a while staring into each others intensly. Before I knew he leaned in to kiss me and I particly jumped his face. I closed my eyes as I put my tongue in his mouth and bit on his lip. I didn't realize I hadn't taken a breath until he pulled back. I grabbed the back of his head and forced his lips back to mine. He tried to stand up and wrapped my arms around his neck and stood up with him refusing to let him go. He pulled my arms from around him and pushed me off him.

"Carmen stop." He said shaking me. I opened my eyes and looked at him. I shook my head.

"I just want to hold you a little longer."

He rubbed the side of my face.

"You know I'd hold you forever, but you got somebody to do that for you already. Plus I'm not the same Tavon you knew . . . and I know I've put you through enough."

"What are you telling me?"

"I shouldn't be here right now, this was a mistake."

He pulled from me and dashed to the front door. I dropped back on the couch.

"Please don't do this to me, not again."I said faintly while staring into space.

"I'm doing this for you." He said before he left. The door shut tearing me apart. I laid back slowly feeling my baby kicking. How could he walk in my life and walk right back out. Atleast before I could cope with the pain, now I was hanging on to life with one hand.